JAGGED
Heart

JAGGED
Heart

Love So Deep You Meet
The Fear Buried In Your Soul

Broken Bottles Series: Book 3

Pamela Taeuffer

OPEN
HEART
PRESS

Published 2016
Printed in the United States of America

ISBN: 978-0-9899529-5-8
Library of Congress Control Number 2015904953

For information, address: pamelataeuffer@gmail.com

To Dad and Denise, I have felt you guys each day through this process.

Claude, Aaron, I love you.

All the mustangs that have come before me—because of your life's twists, turns, bruises, and rewards, you have freed me.

Thank you for your sacrifice.

The Story So Far

*N*icky Young grew up with the broken promises of her father's alcoholic rage and her mother's codependency. Because of the way they abandon she and her sister, Jenise, Nicky learns by example it's up to her to make her way in life—and making her way out of her household is all that is on Nicky's mind.

The Goliaths, a professional baseball team in San Francisco, accepted her entertainment plan for six high school friends to cheer, dance and perform songs in between innings. The first of its kind in professional baseball, her plan helped her get into Stanford, the college she's been dreaming of since a little girl.

Everything goes according to Nicky's plan until one of the Goliaths star pitchers, Ryan Tilton, set his sights on her. At 6'2", with blue eyes, golden brown hair and tattooed biceps that are a beacon to women, he appears to have it all. What no one knows is he hides the grief of losing his father to war at only fourteen. He's practiced keeping his heart well protected every hour of every day. Through hard work and the relentless pursuit of his goals, he has reached a high level of achievement in his sport. Next on his list is to forget the pain that pounds against his heart. Ryan Tilton plays hard on and off the field.

It isn't until the very smart Nicky Young—with the alluring curves of a woman and the innocence of a child—Ryan feels his spirit begin to glow. From the moment he spots her, he knows she is the woman he's been longing for. Determined to win her body and soul, he sets out on a slow and steady plan of seduction.

Dating her is anything but easy.

Dating Ryan is unlike anything Nicky has experienced.

She keeps her "safe" options close. Her childhood friend, Jerry, is someone she's certain she'll need to fall back on. They share family secrets—she, an alcoholic father, and Jerry, a dad who doesn't think twice about physical punishment. Broken promises are the lessons she's learned from her parents. Due to that, she's certain anything good always ends and Ryan will tire of soothing her insecurities.

Although Nicky and Jerry consider dating, even spending a sweet night together at the Pt. Reyes headlands, her sensuous night with Ryan in Half Moon Bay is transformative. The man she fears is too much for her shows her his vulnerable side. She embraces him in every way and he interprets this as a sign that she is ready for more. He plans an evening of full press seduction: an emerald necklace and an expensive dinner at an intimate nightclub.

As *Fire Heart*, Book 2 of Part I, in the Broken Bottles series ends, she is sitting on Ryan's thighs, both of them naked except for their underwear. He urges her to open to him in every way.

Nicky is the daughter of an alcoholic. Trust does not come easily for her. While Ryan makes her feel out of control in a way that both frightens and excites her, Jerry tempts her with the sweet comfort of familiarity. This leaves Nicky deliciously caught between the kisses of a boy and a man. It also leaves her caught between being a girl and a woman as she adjusts to her changing life.

WARNING

Nicky here.
This book is part of an ongoing series with steep cliffs.
Hang in there!
There is a very good reason for them. When coming home to face
my family's battle with alcoholism, I never knew what waited
behind the front door—just turning the doorknob was an exercise
in fear.

I know from living with my family's addiction that:
- Good things will end.
- My opinions don't matter.
- Peace never lasts.
- Those who love me will abandon me.

This is my family's saga and what we endured to break the chains
of dysfunction and my love story: love of friends, parents, siblings,
those relationships that give us life lessons and of lovers. This is
about intimacy in all levels. Despite the lack of trust I have for
others I'm desperate to have it. I'm only eighteen, but my entire
life I've longed for the sweet touch of someone who wasn't afraid,
raging, or drunk. I want joy.

Be patient, please. I formed years of bad habits, fears, and
irrational behavior while trying to survive my dysfunctional
family. This is my story.

When you finish, can you please leave a review for me? I'd
REALLY, REALLY appreciate it if you would:
Amazon: bit.ly/JaggedHeart
Goodreads: bit.ly/GoodreadsJaggedHeart

Table of Contents

Prologue

" *W*hat are you doing standing here by yourself? Get out there, Nick!"

Friends and family are helping my husband and me celebrate thirty-five years of marriage. I've stepped back to have a moment alone, watch my loved ones interact, and witness the raw emotions of an ever-changing life. They have no idea I'm looking at them. Peeking in is what I've always done, ever since I was a little girl.

I guess it's one of the twisted gifts my father gave me. You know what I mean—unintentional blessings we receive despite the ugliness they came from.

Learning to survive in a family battling alcoholism forced me to stay in the shadows until I knew it was safe to come out. Observing while hidden was necessary—my family had to be sure the danger had passed before we dared show ourselves.

Years later, like on this day, I use the same technique—but not because of fear. Now I used it to embrace the sweet, unplanned moments that often fly by unnoticed.

My good friend, Alexandra, finds me. As soon as I smell her perfume, I know she is at my side.

"What are you doing, girlfriend?" she asks. "Come on and join the rest of us."

"I will. I was just thinking back on our early days. Remember when you invited me to LA and I met the lieutenant governor? God, you were a cool customer. What a powerful woman you are."

"That *was* a fun trip. *And* a great connection for you," she smiles as if the memory warms her. "What else is going on? Your face was in a frown just now."

"The awful night in Yountville with my first love," I wrinkle my nose.

"That was a tough one." She reaches for my hand. "But after all, it led you to Ethan."

"Now he is definitely a bonus, right?" I watch Ethan play with grandchildren as we laugh and continue thinking about what happened that night, thirty-five years ago, and how life unfolded.

A LOVE THAT'S MINE

I know I have love, don't I
My parents love me, don't they
I never hear them say the words
They have problems with emotion
So that's why they stay quiet, isn't it

My friends love me, don't they
We don't say it enough to each other
Brushing away the seriousness of love
Telling jokes instead
But we say it more than my family says it to each other

We're numb
I'm numb
I have a heart that beats
Still, I know it's frozen
It has had to shut itself down
So it wouldn't die

Sometimes I think its death might be a better option
Instead of watching the rage
The insults, the sarcasm that we wear
The dark secrets we keep
The false faces and smiles
We paint on our faces
To cover
The love that
I'm sure I have in my life
Don't I

Chapter 1

Jagged Pieces

"Say you're ready for me, Nicky." Ryan's masculine voice seemed to hum. I was certain he had plucked a string and made it vibrate in my body. "Please say it. Tell me you want all of me like I want you. Make tonight your declaration. Tell me you're mine."

Earlier in the evening, Ryan had taken me to Gary Danko's, a restaurant in North Beach that catered to couples looking for exquisite food, quiet music and romance. I was only eighteen, but Ryan's local fame kept the staff from questioning my age.

While on the dance floor together, he held me in his big arms; they caressed my body. His masculine cheek rested against mine. The smooth music serenaded us while his head dipped and lay on my shoulder.

We were only dancing, but to me, those gentle movements were how I'd imagined sex might be: slow, every feeling heightened and exaggerated, my body succumbing to a new

1

rhythm.

After dinner, he took me to the Irish Cultural Center to watch his brother, Chris, perform with his band. I sat next to Frances, Ryan's sister-in-law, who filled me in on their extensive travel schedule and had also warned me not to wait too long to tell Ryan I loved him.

Capping off the evening at the Yountville Inn, we chose to be close to the Veterans' Hospital where we'd planned to volunteer in the morning. After settling in with a snack and several games of cards, suddenly the atmosphere changed.

Our date had been fantastic.

Ryan had asked me to trust him. Reassured me he wouldn't push my boundaries.

Perhaps not realizing how aggressive he'd become as he encouraged me to be his lover, he moved on top of me, igniting my passion, pressing my body into the soft mattress of the room's four-poster bed. It was as if this would cause me to give in—even though *give in* was what I'd fought against.

The moving, sensual parts of his body—his hips, thighs, belly, and chest—drew me closer to my edge. The point of my letting go had blurred. I felt like his muscles were preparing to take me inside them.

The fire in his eyes seemed to wait for my surrender. A shiver of heat rippled through my body. He moved on, above, behind, and underneath me. Was he was encouraging me to reconsider the agreement I'd made with myself to stay a virgin until marriage?

Our lips met. Luscious, passion-filled kisses followed. The tingling that teased every part of me made me tighten and then loosen my legs around him. I gasped for air as our mouths rubbed and pressed side to side for more. Ryan's soft touch guided my lips to his as we repeatedly enjoyed the greed we found in each other.

I squeezed his arms. Hands. Thighs. My belly ached as it pushed out, wanting a connection and anxious for more.

I didn't know when I was excited, a man could feel it the way I felt it. I thought Ryan needed my verbal confirmation to move ahead with sex. Without knowing it, I had telegraphed a message to the man touching me: my light is green.

My trembling limbs clung to his sides as he changed positions. Forcefully, suddenly, I found myself on top of him, stretched open around his hips. He readied me to receive a man inside of me for the first time.

Everything about him seemed ready to love me.

"Say you're ready for me, Nicky." His masculine voice turned up my thermostat to its hottest setting. "Please say it. Tell me you want all of me like I want you. Commit to me. Tell me you're mine."

Although I'd been enchanted throughout our glorious evening and I was beyond excited, my mind wouldn't let go. As if on repeat, I heard, *give in and he'll leave you.*

I sat on top of him. Only my panties were in the way of being filled with a man's physical love and pleasure.

Sensations came hurling at me—hands that inched slowly down my body, thighs moving like an orchestrated symphony, my thighs joining his rhythm, the chest I loved bare and in front of me—heaving, prominent, and taunting. Our bodies' undeniable yearning brought memories of the waves swelling, cresting, and pounding down as they had during our remarkable evening at Half Moon Bay. He'd bared his soul while we sat on the beach there, revealing his passion, desire, and vulnerability—all to strengthen our relationship.

Although I'd fallen under Ryan's spell at the Yountville Inn, his

3

words flurrying around me and sprinkled with the gold dust I loved, I covered myself with the thick armor of my childhood.

I retreated.

A glass-like ice inched around my heart.

My fear of intimacy and letting someone get too close immobilized me.

The heat I'd just felt was now frozen in the cold paranoia of abandonment.

This was too much too soon.

I wasn't ready to let go completely.

Giving in would allow him inside me in every way, exposing every insecurity and vulnerability. The thought of opening and letting him see deeply into my dark soul scared me to death. As I pulled from his embrace, I felt my heart crack under the pressure of my emotions. Layer upon layer had piled up, until I was covered in the thick barrier of mistrust.

"I want to be with you in every way except intercourse," I forced the words. Struggled to break free from my dripping desire. "I'm sorry, I'm just not ready for sex."

I stared at a corner of the room.

Time fractured.

Once again, I was a little girl.

My long hair covered my face.

I couldn't look at him.

A failure—I knew that's what I was with relationships. Because I couldn't let anyone get physically or emotionally close, I pushed everyone away.

That night, it was as if a face of the clock I'd watched all my life had split in two. The minutes crumbled to the floor. Shards had splintered everywhere; I heard the pieces break all around us.

The scene I'd imagined so many times before—loving a boy and giving my body to him— shattered.

As I waited for the mood to shift and Ryan to turn away, I imagined him pulling the blankets with him, leaving me uncovered and exposed.

I let my shadows cover us with the finality of evening.

Because I didn't surrender to Ryan, he'd taken it hard. Making things worse, I didn't know how to explain myself so his feelings might be soothed.

The chill of finality settled on me.

All that was left was the act itself.

"I respect that you're not ready. You need more time." Ryan's voice held no emotion. "It's all right." The passion that had filled him a moment ago . . . gone. His erection went soft beneath me.

I held my breath waiting for him to get up, dress, and drive me home. The only word left? Goodbye.

But he's still here, Nicky—he's still here.

"Ryan, I didn't—"

"Don't worry." His hand cupped the back of my head. He reached up to turn off the light with one of his tattooed arms. I knew it might be the last time I'd see or feel his embrace.

We lay together that way—me on top of him, my breasts against his magnificent chest—for the rest of the night.

Just that quickly our magic had disappeared. The language of his body, his tender kisses and the way he held me—all the things that once told me I could trust him—vanished. I knew I'd lost him.

And yet he stayed, Nicky. He's here.

I was wide-awake most of the night. Afraid to move, certain I'd broken our fragile bond of a couple—had I lost our friendship, too? Could that part of us survive, even if the romance died?

5

Chapter 2

A Cold Wind Blew In

*L*ight overtook the sky.

I felt Ryan move.

The entire night I lay awake rehearsing our goodbye.

There was no tangling of bodies, luscious stretching against his belly, or rubbing my foot on his hairy, masculine legs.

He dismissed me quickly. Kissed my forehead and patting my back. Lifting me off him, he rolled out of bed with the finality of our failed evening.

That's the friendly pat on the back that says goodbye.

I had more than six hours to contemplate the oncoming loss and prepare myself and I still wasn't ready. There was no lingering or hugging that morning. Ryan seemed far away and never looked back at me as he headed for the bathroom. I tried to gather my thoughts while Ryan showered. I knew everything would completely break apart if even one finger twitched.

Wasn't he already moving on with his life?

"Don't wait too long," his sister-in-law, Frances, had said.

"You'll regret it forever," my sister, Jenise had warned.

"Bathroom's ready if you want to shower." Ryan stood with a towel wrapped around his waist. His hair wasn't even dry.

"Okay, I won't be long." I fought hard to hold in my emotions. Showering with water and tears, I grieved over my failed relationship. I shouldn't have taken the risk.

Would I ever find the person who could endure my need for constant reassurances? Was I so much work that I might never find love? Perhaps I already had the answer: Ryan was ready to give up on me after he'd tried to *fix me and make me all better.*

When would I be able to make the jump into a secure woman who knew she was worthy of being loved? I was young, I knew I needed to mature, but how long would it take?

I had believed Ryan's gentle promises—a man who'd taken me in his arms and told me he loved me. If I couldn't trust him with all we'd shared, was it possible to believe anyone? Was there a man who would be my friend without judging and rejecting me because of the things I *wasn't* able to give?

Even though I didn't want to have sex before marriage—at least that was the belief I kept returning to—I was aggravated Ryan couldn't respect that part of me.

Could any relationship last if I didn't give in with sex?

Was Ryan's promise to wait for me only guaranteed for three dates? After that, I expected to go all the way? Was this typical of the way men and of women got together?

Just as my heart felt open and ready, the possibility of love ended. The ugly face of betrayal from another person—and also myself—had been revealed.

It hurt like hell.

My fear of another bad thing coming had arrived right on time.

Ryan obviously expected me to open my body, even though he agreed not to push and I had repeatedly told him I wasn't ready for sex. Maybe in his mind, whatever signals he'd interpreted overrode my actual words.

I just needed time. Why couldn't he understand that? I never tried to hide that part of me. Didn't he hear me?

Feeling like a hypocrite, I quickly pulled on the pink sports outfit Ryan had given me. My hair was back in a ponytail. I didn't take the time to dry it—time had run out.

When I came out of the bathroom, he was dressed in sweats and a T-shirt. He stood in the doorway with his back turned to me.

Why won't you look at me? Have I done something so terrible?

"I'm ready," I offered timidly.

When he turned, it was as if he'd given a forced smile to some invisible woman standing in the shadows behind me. Once outside, I stood at the passenger door to his car, waiting for him to open it as he had each time we'd been together. Instead, he used his remote to unlock it. Perhaps to avoid even more rejection, he walked to his side of the car and got in.

There was no opening of *any* door for us that day.

They had slammed closed and locked.

Everything sweet had vanished right before my eyes. Our relationship. Intimacy. Friendship . . . they were suddenly broken into pieces.

When we pulled up to Veterans' Hospital, I didn't wait for Ryan to open my door. In fact, I almost jumped out before he came to a stop. Quickly walking through the entrance, I put as much distance as I could between us. As soon as I got my first smile from Queenie, a divorced woman with two children and diagnosed with breast cancer, I worked hard to stay in the moment, concentrating on the veterans who needed our attention.

Because I was able to focus, my day there was wonderful. The joy of being around the men and women of our military were experiences unlike any I'd ever had.

Vincent was a man in his thirties who had three tours of duty and was now in a wheelchair. Although he could have dwelled in the dark parts of his life, his stories were positive and uplifting. He was focused on moving forward.

It was a reminder I needed that day.

Brandon was newly admitted and only nineteen. I gripped his remaining hand and listened to his story of how he'd lost the other to a roadside bomb. He never said so, but I knew by the Medal of Honor that hung around his neck, he had probably saved other lives because of his action.

The bright eyes, honest smiles and sometimes tears that accompanied their stories, almost made me forget about the twisting and writhing sickness that possessed my body.

Come on, Nick. Look at the challenges you see all around you. What these men and women wouldn't give to be in the turmoil you are. Keep your mind with them!

Even as I walked around in the cute, pink sports outfit Ryan had bought for me, I felt him pulling away.

We entered the room of my favorite vet, Johnny Mantle. He and his mother embraced us. Our conversation quickly focused on the call from Lieutenant Governor Del Sol and the invitation they'd received to attend the upcoming charity event in Los Angeles.

I had gone to LA with Alex a few weeks earlier. Alexandra Flowers was the fiancé of Darrell Sweet, a pitcher on the Goliaths and teammate of Ryan's. Along with her friend, Tara Summers, wife of Matt Summers, also a pitcher on team, the three of us had gotten close. She'd invited me—actually demanded—I go with her on a modeling shoot. Unbeknownst to me, her agency had arranged an interview with Mr. Del Sol. It highlighted Traumatic Brain Injury, aka TBI.

We were invited to a dinner with executives and some of the head designers in the fashion world after the photo shoot. Mr. Del Sol had discussed openly to those at the table how I'd inserted several important questions into the already formatted interview I'd gone over with him over iced teas. Partially because I'd taken such a bold action, he'd reached out to Paul at the Veteran's Hospital asking him if there were any vets I knew who might benefit from the planned winter charity gala. As a result, he extended an invitation to Johnny and his mom.

"It all happened because of the things I've learned from coming here and visiting with you, Johnny." I turned to Samantha, his mother. "Were you surprised when the Lieutenant Governor called you?"

"Shocked!" she almost shouted. Both of them sped up as they talked about their reaction.

Suddenly, I wondered . . . was I was taking something precious away from Ryan? On this visit, *my* successes were acknowledged instead of his fame.

He'd carefully shared this rewarding place with me. It was the first part of his private life that he'd shared. Was I stealing it, making it my own? It was the first time since I'd been dating him that no mention was made about the Goliaths or Ryan's pitching.

The expression on his face seemed woven in worry.

I feel so sorry for him. Even though we were only volunteering together last year, visiting here was like our first date. It's his passion. Oh, God. I feel sick taking away the attention that should be his. What a mess we've made.

We wore the smiles of clowns: false in almost every way.

Avoiding each other as if we had a contagious disease, I wondered if there was anything left between us. Were we dead to each other now?

We were careful in the hallways and hospital rooms, making sure not to touch hands and arms, brush a thigh together or accidentally bump hips. We made big, wide circles whenever we maneuvered in the rooms. Even though we spent several hours there, I looked away from his face and he from mine.

He finally turned to address me.

Looked directly in my eyes.

My heart jumped in excitement.

I thought our morning of silence might be over and we could go back to how we were before the cold night fell on us.

"I need to leave." It was four words and the only thing he said. Our day at the Veterans' Hospital ended. After his announcement, he immediately looked off into the distance.

My stomach churned in acid.

I thought I might throw up on the spot.

We got into his car the same way that we did when we left the motel—in complete and deafening silence.

Before I had agreed to stay the night with Ryan, when he had reassured me that I could trust him, when our promises and love meant something, he held nothing back.

Hands that previously made sure I was settled were nowhere to be found. The remote control to open both car doors was enough. He had made a decision that he didn't have to take care of me any longer.

Maybe he felt relief.

Maybe I was more of a burden than he had realized.

Maybe he was thankful a weight had been lifted off him.

This time on our drive home, we didn't stop for lunch.

We did not talk.

The only thing I had to keep me company was my terrible thoughts and his stony expression.

It was as if we were back to our beginning; people who weren't sure if they had anything in common, hunting and pecking with small bits of conversation, quickly answering the meaningless questions that hung in the air.

"I'll talk to you later," he threw out after pulling up to my house.

"Please don't be angry, Ryan. I thought I was ready for a physical relationship with you. I'm sorry. No one feels worse than I do."

First Jerry, now Ryan . . . what's wrong with me? Am I so weird because I want to wait? Do I want to wait?

"I'm not angry." He kissed me on the cheek. "I'm just rethinking things. I'll see you tomorrow at the game."

What kind of statement is that? Rethinking what? Everything you promised? All the sweet things you said? How do my feelings fit into your thoughts? I'm left out of the decision process and if you decide we're still okay, I'm supposed to gladly go along with you? I drop everything because you choose me? Is that fair?

Ryan once told me, *I won't leave you or let you go.* Those were words I'd longed to hear all my life. I wanted to believe wholehearted they were true. I believed they *were* true when he said them.

"Bye," I whispered, hoping he'd hear, hoping he'd respond and tell me we were okay. I closed the door.

Silent.

Standing at the curb.

Holding my dress. Coat. Shoes.

I took a deep breath and dared to watch him turn the corner, hoping he'd wave goodbye. No muscular arm that I loved showed itself to reassure me I'd see him again.

A child raised in a family battling alcoholism knows these fears well: something bad is coming—it always does; I'm too ashamed to ask for help; I can't talk about our secrets—no one understands; I can't trust anyone—they always leave.

The last fear—of being abandoned—was the one I was most afraid of and now it had happened to me with my first love.

Once upon a time, I saw my relationship with Ryan as the glowing, red heat from the burning embers of a fire. It seemed to simmer inside our hearts, waiting to explode into joy.

After his car disappeared from sight, I watched those same ashes scatter into the air, searching for another moment in time, another friend, and almost certainly another love.

I knew something sweet was gone forever.

Chapter 3

The Next Step

*M*y head was down when I walked inside my house.

The only things holding me together were imaginary staples and paper clips.

My mother passed me as she was coming down the stairs. She started to say something but stopped when I turned away from her.

I locked my bedroom door. Spent the next few hours crying into my royal blue, Adrianna Papell lacy sheath dress. Cast off. Impossible. Untouchable. I knew those were among the descriptions that defined me when it came to an intimate relationship. The man who I thought was so special made me feel castoff and never a serious consideration. Good enough for him? I wasn't even fit to spend an evening with him unless I *put out*.

Ryan said he'd wait for me to get comfortable with sex and not push my boundaries. As he caressed my body, he reassured me that everything was possible and we were meant to be together.

What I found out at the Yountville Inn?

I was disposable.

A sudden shiver covered me and I wondered if I was a part of a cruel joke after all.

What happened made me realize how physical, fast, and intolerant his world was. It was obvious now: If I didn't go along with his plans, I was no longer welcome in his life.

I knew he didn't expect to date me forever without having sex, but how soon was normal? Was intimacy in a relationship impossible without sex? Even though we'd known each other for over a year, was there was no other way to move into deeper levels of intimacy without intercourse?

I guessed I was to blame for our disaster because I hadn't given in. If I had, wouldn't we still have ended in this broken place for some other reason?

Did my words mean *anything* at Half Moon Bay when I'd said we could be there for each other no matter what happened romantically?

Maybe I was naive to think he had been speaking from his heart when he said he wouldn't push or pressure me. Even if he was out of patience and changed his mind, didn't I deserve more than a pat on the back? Did the gesture mean I wasn't worth the effort? And what did, *"I'm rethinking things,"* mean?

On the other hand, what did he know about my feelings? I never told him anything more than I liked him a lot. Maybe he'd decided I wasn't ready for *anything* he had to offer and, in his heart, knew he should leave me alone. If that were true, I wished he'd have said so. I might have understood, instead of feeling so empty and gutted. I felt devastated and hopeless.

"But it doesn't matter now," I said out aloud.

The shadows fell as I repeated my mantra, the one I knew to be true, even when I was five-years-old: *Don't let people get close, they'll hurt and then abandon you.*

I'd only just begun to build my foundation of trust.

Before I could even raise the frame of my house, it had crumbled to the ground.

"Nicky?" Mom knocked on my door.

"Yeah?" Shit. She'd obviously noticed the look of turmoil on my face when I passed her on the stairway.

"You all right?"

"Mm-hmm," I whimpered.

Even on the rare occasion when one of my parents reached out to help me, I found it difficult to accept. I didn't dare depend on them. It would only be a matter of time before I was left waiting on another promise and believing in changes, when nothing had.

In grade school I waited for parents who were so embroiled in their alcoholic battle they didn't remember I was waiting for them to take me home. No more. I didn't want to stand alone to face another failure because of empty words—from anyone.

Everything could fall apart if I didn't take care of what I needed. It was only a matter of time.

"You don't sound okay." Mom's worried tone rattled me. "Let me in." She kept knocking on my door.

"Just," I sniffed. "Just a minute." I put a cold washcloth on my eyes. Blew my nose. Opened my door and then faced my mother.

"Why have you been crying?" Her face turned red. "What did *he* do to you?"

"Nothing," I grieved. "We had an argument."

"Over sex?" she demanded an answer.

"No." *I'm not telling you anything.* "Stupid stuff. It's just, I'm not used to any of this and my emotions are all over the place."

"I told you it wouldn't be easy with him," she chastised.

"I know you did." I wasn't in any mood to argue. "I'm okay. It's only . . . I'm all stirred up. I was just getting ready to take a walk."

"Why don't you stay home for a change?" Mom looked at the crumpled dress on my bed. "Is that the dress Jenise helped you pick out?"

"Yes." I started sobbing. "Isn't it pretty?"

"*What* did he do?" she repeated. "I have half a mind to go to the ballpark and . . ." She took one step closer and put her hand on my shoulder. It was the first time she'd made an affectionate move in months. Sure, there was the cursory hug for a special event like graduation, a birthday, and Christmas.

This was different.

I saw the changed look on her face.

Perhaps her protective instincts had risen to the surface. Maybe the mama bear in front of me was barely able to contain her anger. The wash of hurt that crossed her face immediately softened as if she understood I was suffering.

I wasn't ready for that.

I didn't know how to reach back to her—the distance had been so wide for so long.

"It's both of us. We're not ready and . . ." I wiped the tears from my cheeks. "I told him he needed someone more experienced. When I reacted in a way he hadn't expected, he didn't understand. I probably should stay home, but I'm restless. I can't sit still, Mom. I need to . . . I don't know what—do *something*. Maybe if I walk this off I'll calm down."

"*Why* won't you tell me what happened?" she insisted. I knew underlying her inquiry was the hope that I'd share more with her.

"Can you understand that it's hard to be with someone who has already done so much? I don't know why I do, but . . ." I grabbed for her hand. "I feel secondary. I'm not ready to date, that's all. Or maybe I'm just not right—for anyone."

"It's not you, it's him. He's too old for—"

"It's not his age," I interrupted. "Not like you mean. It's . . . his world is . . . I'm not ready for that."

"I can't tell you what to do." She took her hand away. Perhaps the intensity of my sadness was too much for her. "Take some time and write in your journal. I think you understand the battle you're facing. Being with boys your age is definitely easier. In any case, I'm sure the answer will present itself to you."

"You're not suggesting I break it off with him?" I could hardly believe she wasn't pushing me to end it.

Maybe she knows it's already over.

"That's not my call." She tugged on her sleeve as if she was still trying to get over the same hurt feelings. "You just went through an experience that should be talking to you—actually screaming at you. In your gut, you should discover your own answer."

"What *are* you suggesting?" My neck stiffened.

"Take the time you need to make the right decision." She got up from my bed. "I think you know what that is. Let me know if you need anything or want to talk." She closed my bedroom door.

After she left my room, I let out the full onslaught of my emotions. There was more to it than an evening of mistakes with Ryan. Feelings I'd held back were making themselves known.

You have to deal with your fears and sadness. The time is here.

I screamed and slammed my pillow into the wall, pounded my bed and ripped off the covers.

I wrote depressive, hellish poetry.

I listened to the saddest songs I could find.

Finally, as they inevitably do, my tears stopped.

I began taking full breaths.

When I thought about how matter-of-factly Mom handled herself and the courage it took to knock on my door, I actually admired her boldness.

Using the time I needed to heal, I moved slowly. I took a bath, gave myself a facial, super-conditioned my hair, and then styled it.

Was our relationship changing?

Three sniffles turned into two, and two into one.

The eye of the storm settled on me.

My mind began to clear.

I tried to stay home.

I did my best to relax.

Continuing to spin, the mist of anger crept into my body along with a sinister and dark sensation that took the place of my hurt.

Revenge.

Starting as a simmer, almost immediately it pushed outward and demanded release.

Soon, I boiled with fury.

My vast emotions, usually shoved far underneath my surface, were ready to explode.

Symbolically, I closed the new, white leather journal I'd purchased and titled, "My memories of Ryan Tilton." Although angry, I was sad that our story was shorter than I'd ever imagined.

I hesitated.

Ran my hands over the cover.

Lifted it to my nose and smelled it.

Flipped through its pages, reading about the days we'd spent together, when the promise of love was still ahead of us.

Finally, I threw it in my hope chest, forever merged with all the journals from my past.

Ryan Tilton was now my past.

I hated even the way it sounded and couldn't consider the concept for too long.

"He's a wild boy, Nicky," Tara had warned. *"Stay away from him."*

"He's not the right man for your first experience," Alex had confided. *"He's been with too many women."*

"Go with a boy your age and experience things together," Dad had cautioned.

My mind focused on Jerry. I knew he'd never abandon me the way Ryan had. In addition to experiencing everything new with my childhood friend, I could safely walk through my life in control. I'd lost my vision and allowed myself to become hypnotized. I wouldn't make that mistake again.

Jerry already knew the darkness of my family and I knew his. There would be no surprises. Each of us would have a say in decisions we made. We'd never turn our backs on each other because we were friends and offered each other the security we needed.

From now on, one hundred percent of my efforts would be on my future and college. After all, what did love do for my parents and *their* happy endings?

My Evil Twin slowly wrapped her arms around me.

Within her dark embrace, I realized anger was necessary for recovery.

It's the baby steps, Nicky. They begin with the rush of confusion, tears, sadness, and harrowing feeling of emptiness. But soon, your head and heart will fill up again.

Lessons of how these little steps could transform me into a

fearless woman had begun their reveal. Taking a little risk towards being open and vulnerable to love, daring to expose myself for a chance to have intimacy—could these dreams actually be a part of my future? Could I ever embrace them?

Even as my insides swirled, I was gaining strength.

I'd taken my first step into a minefield.

I knew if I didn't march ahead, my fears would permanently rip me apart without the chance of healing until many years into my future.

For now, I'd made the decision to walk quietly and gather my courage. So when the next cycle of grief came over me, I knew that being alone wouldn't soothe my raw and aching soul. My sister wasn't home and I couldn't reach my friends. Plus, there was no way I could talk to Tara and Alex about Ryan. They'd done nothing but discourage me from seeing him. I didn't need to hear *I told you so,* when I'd already said those words to myself dozens of times.

Surrounded by hundreds of people was what I needed—people I didn't know, to be exact.

It was time to leave the house and do what was comfortable— have coffee at Java House on the Embarcadero.

I put on a nice pair of jeans, a form-fitting white blouse, and a navy blue, down-style vest that was thick, quilted, and warm. I grabbed a new journal and tucked it into my backpack.

On my way out, I saw Dad sitting in his recliner.

What if it's too late and he's already been terminated? Now that we've crossed each other off of our invisible checklists, would Ryan tell Sid Freeman to stop helping my family?

The night on my front porch—after I sung the National Anthem, at Sammy's, and in the Embarcadero Hotel Lounge— he'd asked me to give him a chance.

22

I did.

Someone that was kind enough to give his time to veterans wouldn't be so cruel as to punish my entire family because I didn't give in to sex—would he?

Should I talk with my guidance counselor at Stanford and admit I may need financial help? Will they take me if my tuition isn't fully funded by my parents? Maybe I should look for a job so I can put away some money. That way, I'll have at least half of the first semester's fees and can hopefully negotiate for a loan.

Dark emotions crested as I tried to erase the sweet memories of my night on the beach with Ryan. Before they could take hold and drag me under, I quickly swept everything that had been lovely out to sea.

I need a battleship to ride these giant waves.

Dad wasn't drunk yet, but judging by his facial expression he was in the first stages. Before I could hear his slurred voice, I nodded to him and then headed out.

People chatted around me, carrying on with their lives as I waited at the streetcar stop. Couldn't they feel my pain? How was it the world hadn't stopped for any of them like it had for me? In only minutes, I boarded and rode through the Twin Peaks Tunnel, into another world.

When I stepped off?

I was on the waterfront.

People passed me.

I didn't notice their faces.

My thoughts followed the rhythm of my steps—purposeful and head-on. This time, no one would tie me down or share myself so carelessly and openly. My heart was my own.

I walked to the Java House and didn't stop.

Something more powerful, something I didn't fully

23

understand, was driving me forward that day.

I continued walking—to the Goliaths' stadium.

Committed to face my fears of abandonment head on, I had to witness the way Ryan bounced back from my rejection. I had to know. I wanted to see anything but him focusing on a woman to soothe his hurt, but it was a step toward being healthy—I had to see how he handled himself—and understand what we were when I saw the inevitability of him moving on.

I'd see it all unfold at the railings where the gorgeous women stood waiting to hook up with an athlete. It would happen in a matter of moments. He'd pick from the lineup—fun loving, easy to be with, always present, and waiting to be told when and where. There was no doubt in my mind Ryan would run to his peers— peers like Tabitha Sable, the exotic dancer who'd come to our table at the Embarcadero Lounge and reminded Ryan to come see her. She could play the games he was used to. She would help him shake off his disappointment.

Or perhaps it would be in the players' lot after the game where the lovely blonde I saw from before would be at his side, waiting to take his hand.

I needed to be validated and freed from the guilt I still felt from our last evening together. Shifting into automatic as I sped headfirst into my darkness, I arrived at the Bay Gate.

The twists and turns of getting there must have been erased from my memory. It seemed I was magically transported and I'd awakened from a daydream.

When I *snapped to,* I found James, the head of gate security.

"How ya'll doin', baby?" he asked in his charming Southern accent.

"Shitty, James. Real shitty." The edge in my voice was undeniable.

24

"What's wrong, honey?" He looked at me as if I was a stranger. Maybe that wasn't exactly right—it was more that I wasn't a child but not quite a woman—a stranger I needed to get to know. She was new and edgy, no longer passive, hesitant, or *soft*.

That girl had vanished . . . at least for now.

"A friend betrayed me, James. At least, someone I *thought* was a friend. I don't know what to do with myself." I took a breath. "None of my friends are around, so here I am."

"What can I do, baby?" He pulled me close for a hug.

I was always uneasy when asking for help. To me, it was a sign of weakness, manipulation, and a way to use people. Just as I was about to dismiss his kindness with my patented answer, *I'm okay*, the story my sister shared with me rushed into my mind. She told me she couldn't have recovered from being raped without the help of others. She opened up because a variety of people helped her to trust and take chances again.

Maybe asking James to help me wasn't weakness at all.

Maybe, there was an immense strength in being vulnerable.

Even in my anger, the door creaked open.

"Do you think there might be a free ticket floating around?" I held my breath waiting for him to say no. "Maybe one by the visitors' dugout or . . . anywhere, really?"

"Let me see what I can do. I think we have a single for an occasion just like this one." He winked and then radioed an usher somewhere in the ballpark.

Taking that simple chance, asking for help and then receiving it, I knew then I was walking into the pain—and light—of risk.

My heart beat with the power of thunder.

Chapter 4

A New Friend

$\mathcal{M}$anagement could have dismissed the entire cheer team and withdrawn their letters of reference to our colleges if they'd known about the free ticket I'd asked James to get for me. That was nothing compared to the consequences I could face if they found out I had been dating Ryan.

Both actions were completely against policy—and I knew the policy.

Before our first game, my teammates and I were called into the Goliaths Entertainment Department. We met with management and signed a document that made it clear we were not to fraternize with the players, receive freebies, or enter any contests sponsored by the team.

"Come on through, baby." James waved a pass in the air.

"Thanks, James." I already felt better.

You took a risk and got what you wanted! My evil twin spoke softly and pushed me forward.

"Sure, baby. Just ask and I'll take care of you." His broad smile was welcoming. I followed him through the gate. We walked toward a corner away from the incoming fans. Once again, he radioed ahead. This time it was to an usher in the area where I'd be sitting. "You're all set. Check in with Mark in 108. He'll show you to your seat."

"Thanks, James. Don't worry, I won't ask you for a favor like this again." I tucked the ticket in my vest pocket.

Well, maybe I will . . . this was pretty easy.

"No prob," he smiled. "Ya haven't asked me for diddlysquat in over a year. Enjoy the game, honey."

As I stood in line to buy a crab sandwich, I considered how lucky those of us who lived in the Bay Area were to have such a wide variety of fresh fish available. I'd taken for granted how abundant it was—so much that it was sold in a San Francisco baseball stadium. In addition to seafood, one of the unique things about the Goliaths' ballpark was the great cuisine from the city's pocket neighborhoods. There were stands that offered fresh pastas and cioppino from North Beach, Thai and Mandarin Cuisine from Chinatown, Pub Fair representative of the small pockets in the Irish Sunset and old Mission District, Mexican Food from the new Mission District and wonderful Soul Food from the Fillmore.

In many ways I'd grown up having the stadium as a part of my life. Now, instead of taking joy in all the things happening there, I focused on one man on the team I'd rooted for all my life.

Although I was alone this time, it felt similar to when I'd brought Jerry so I could spy on Ryan. *Am I repeating negative patterns? I need to make sure I don't go down the rabbit hole like my father did.* While waiting for my sandwich I took several deep breaths. Prepared myself for disappointment. Face that I'd soon witness the proof I needed to show I was never a serious consideration in Ryan's life.

You're repeating a pattern, Nicky. Break down that damn door! My Evil Twin was shouting this time.

When I arrived at Section 108, the usher James had radioed let me through. Although my purpose in being there was divisive, I was torn about it. I hadn't formally committed to him. I got that. He told me he loved me and my response had been I loved him as a friend. All in all, he had the right to see other people.

Honesty, if he'd been up front about what he wanted, I might not have been so upset. Initially, I'd been prepared for it and told him as much the first night on the beach. When he promised he'd given up seeing other women, I had different expectations. I let myself sink deeply into what appeared to be love. Admittedly, it would be difficult to watch him join his bachelor teammates as they leaned on the railings to survey women. Because of the things he said, I'd built up my hopes, dreaming I might be his person and he mine—at least for a little while.

It would have been lovely to be the only one to hold his hand.

The choice wasn't mine.

He'd cut me off.

I had to face our end.

And I knew the exact moment it would happen.

The thing was, I didn't believe Ryan intentionally played me for sex. I was convinced he'd discovered a side of himself he hadn't been aware of—until his first attempt at having a serious relationship. He had to be with someone who wanted to travel, attend lots of social events and enjoy sex.

I knew that all too soon I'd see Ryan look into the crowd and wink or smile at his choice of lady, beckon them with a finger to come to the railing, and that would be that.

The pattern generally went like this: a ballplayer casually identified two or three women he considered attractive. If she responded, he made his move by tossing a baseball to her. If the game was on, there was a note attached. She'd read: *Sweetheart, I can't keep my eyes off you. Meet me in the tunnel behind section 123 after the game? Be sure to write down your number and give it to the usher for me. You are so beautiful!*

Little did she know that unless he flashed his wry smile or gave her a wink or two during the game, he'd spotted another woman and she would be left standing alone. The new woman was invited to meet him at a different place.

The jocks that were well-known would simply ask a security guard to hand a woman his note that asked for her phone number. If receptive, she'd write it down and it would be returned to the player. He'd go into the clubhouse and call her from there, using a phone with a blocked number.

Easy.

That's all it took to line up after-the-game entertainment—if he wasn't going to a club.

There were long lines of feminine prospects that hoped for a baseball or a wave. Women positioned themselves to be noticed near the railings at every game.

If he'd already had sex with her and they were reconnecting she only had to meet him in the tunnel. An understanding had already been made with his nod, wink, or other signal.

Of course, he didn't want any lingering possibilities by taking her to *his* apartment. Only when he was certain she wasn't interested in a commitment was she allowed inside his world—well, unless the sex was so exceptional that he stored her number for the inevitable booty call when he came back to town.

Acid churned in my stomach.

My legs were restless.

I didn't know what to do with myself.

I felt as if my skeleton was trying to crawl out of my body and run away.

Off-center and shaken with more than forty-five minutes to go before the start of the game, I couldn't sit still. I hadn't been able to shake the spinning in my body.

"Excuse me, miss?" A ballplayer from the opposing team approached me just as I'd gotten up to walk around the stadium.

Oh, damn, not another one. Just leave me alone.

"Yeah?" I asked dully.

"Are you with anyone?" Thick lashes framed his big brown eyes and freckles dotted his face. Dark brown hair peeked from underneath his cap and fell to the nape of his neck.

"Yes, I am."

Just act disgusted and he'll go away. Damn it, another jock searching the railings. And yet . . . here you are sitting at them.

"Sorry," he shuffled his feet. "It didn't look like—"

Not understanding why, I felt compelled to tell him the truth. His nervousness was unlike Ryan's confidence and was refreshing.

"No, you're right. I'm here by myself. Honestly, I um, I came here to be by myself. I was just getting up to walk around." I grabbed my backpack. "So, I guess . . . have a good game."

"Wait, w-w-would . . ." He put his head down. "I know this is forward. Actually, this is *really* forward. You'll think I'm lulu."

Lulu! Ha! I'm going to challenge him on that.

"May I ask what a lulu is?" I stood with my arms folded.

"Oh, ya know . . . dingbat. Dumbo. Backward."

"You don't strike me as any of those," I responded.

"Off to a good start, then," he smiled. "In that case, would ya consider having coffee with me sometime?"

"*Sometime?*" I repeated sarcastically.

"After the game?" He flirted. Seemed innocent enough. Even so, I got the feeling he knew what he was doing.

"Tonight?" I repeated.

That's damn bold of you. On the other hand, you're not tossing me a baseball or asking me to meet you in the tunnel.

"I know." His laugh was friendly and not sexy like Ryan's. It stirred my curiosity and not the sensual feelings in my belly. "You probably don't want to. You won't believe me . . ."

"Try me." I encouraged, enjoying our back and forth.

"I've never done this before. Asking a woman for her phone number, I mean. Shoops, I sound ridiculous."

"*Shoops?*" I cracked up. "What does *that* mean? You seem to have your own unique language."

"My family's polite word for shit," he grinned. "I'm from the Midwest. We never swear in the presence of a woman."

"I see." *He seems nice . . . maybe too nice?*

"I'm new. Do you think, well, would you? Just ta talk. Maybe get some coffee or hot chocolate? You have a kind face. I'm a good guy who's dying to be with someone my own age. Will you?"

"I don't know." I noticed a small plane overhead with a sign in tow that read, *The Dare Foundation.* I took it as a sign. "Well—"

"It's only for coffee, miss." His eyes sparkled.

"Um . . ." *He does seem sincere and he's rather adorable.*

"We can meet wherever ya want. Even somewhere busy with tons of people. Would that sway you? Everyone's asleep in my family by the time the game is over. I'm plain goin' nuts! I feel like I've got mad cow disease or somethin'!"

I tried not to laugh. Maybe he was just what I needed to perk up—a boy who looked to be my age. I liked that.

"Ethan Mathers." He extended his hand. "I was called up from the Avengers' farm system a few days ago. I need someone I can relate to for friendship—just friendship. Promise."

"How old are you?" I asked.

"Twenty," he replied quickly. "Do you live here?"

"I was born here."

"Can I be honest?" he tossed a ball in the air.

"Sure."

"My teammates are giving me crap because I'm a rookie. They're older than me and most of them have families and friends here." He tossed the ball from one hand to the other.

Don't toss that thing to me.

"Everyone's made me feel welcome. It's not that they're rude or anything. I've got too much ta say. I'm tryin' to fit in, figure things out . . . I'm not like this normally," he continued. "Somethin' about you says . . . maybe you could use a friend, too?"

"Maybe," I answered slowly as if I had trouble getting the word from my mouth.

"If we're havin' coffee and you say to yourself, *this guy's a jerk,* or you say it out loud, although I hope you won't, you can just leave. No hard feelins." He tried reassuring me.

He's funny! What a sucker I am. He seems so innocent. Probably not. Maybe. Hmm. He seems honest. Maybe we have a lot in common. Maybe he's someone like me.

"Are you twenty-one yet?" he poked.

"Nope." I wasn't ready to reveal my age.

"Good," he wiped his forehead in a mock gesture of relief. "I can't go in the bars so . . . hot chocolate?" His expression seemed optimistic. "If you're not a coffee person, that is."

Oh . . . I miss Ryan and the hot chocolate he made for us when he stayed the night in my room. Why can't I stop thinking about him . . . his confession on the beach, the night in Half Moon Bay lying naked together . . . I'll never get over it. Shit. I've got to quit thinking about him. Come on, Nick. Stay in the moment. This boy seems open and honest.

"Either would be great. I am most definitely a coffee person. I also love hot chocolate." I extended my hand. "Nicky Young." He shook it a second time. "There's a coffee shop on the other side of the big lawn area to the left of the player's lot. It's by the harbor and called Java House. There's nothing fancy about it, just basic diner food, but it's good and open all night."

"Awesome. Meet you there." He nodded his head and closed his eyes for a second as if in relief.

"Okay, Ethan. Oh, by the way, I can't wish you too much luck in your game tonight. I know I'm sitting on your team's side of the field but I'm a huge Goliaths fan. In fact, tomorrow and Saturday, I'll be cheering on the field."

"You're one of the cheer team? Cool!" We high-fived. "I've heard the Avengers might do something similar. Guess that means you're a big hit?"

"You heard all that from being in the professional leagues only a few days?" I asked with genuine surprise.

"Yeah, well I had to be briefed, ya know. One of the things the guys told me comin' here was to be careful practicing when you guys were on the field and then they told me how good you are."

"I'm so surprised." I buttoned my vest. I loved that he said *you guys* instead of *you girls*. It was generic and friendly. Something about him made me feel good—really good.

"Kudos for you guys, right?" One of the coaches yelled Ethan's name. He straightened his cap. "Well, I should get back to practice before I get in trouble. See ya after the game?" He jogged backward as he waited for my answer.

"Yes!" I shouted. "And if you change your mind, don't worry, no hard feelings. I was going there anyway."

"I'll be there." He yelled his response and waved.

I felt as if a little flash blinded me when he smiled. When I thought about where I was sitting, I laughed.

Then I realized I had just befriended another athlete.

Nicky, what are you doing—another baseball player?

Was I setting myself up for failure? The alpha-male in them always surfaced, exposing what they truly wanted: to compete, win, be on top of their game—every game—have lots of sex, and control their woman—or women.

I'd read somewhere that eighty-five percent of baseball marriages ended in divorce. After dating Ryan, I understood why that might be true. They were in the public eye, desired by men and women, heroes to children, sought after by the press, and faced with every temptation imaginable. If they were talented and near the top at their position, had a marketable face and personality, their lives were filled with baskets of treats—theirs for the taking.

Owners of bars, clubs, luxury car sales, restaurants, clothing designers and gyms—all of them wanted an athlete's patronage. When they got it? The upscale, hip, and good-looking crowds followed. If you were a club owner, you made sure the drinks flowed like water to the VIPs.

Money, sex, alcohol, hookers and sometimes drugs, were available for years—as long as the athlete was young or had drawing power. More often than not, their agent made sure to see to their every desire. Ushered inside immediately, he could party all night long at the popular clubs, was given the best seats, and had the choice from a harem of women in low cut or tight dresses.

Fans adored these handsome and well-built men with million dollar smiles. The positive publicity resulting from their attendance at charitable functions and team events gave them the press they needed to be seen as a giving member of the community.

In the cover of darkness, another story often revealed itself.

After getting so much attention, many believed they *were* special—and invincible. It was easy, especially when in their twenties, to lose their foothold on reality.

What chance did I *really* have with Ryan?

The women he saw every day were mature, gorgeous, extremely fit and not only welcomed and enjoyed sex, but were ready to be with him in any way he wanted.

When I refused to engage in the physical part of our relationship, he understandably shut down. He admitted he'd never had a girlfriend and I'd never had a boyfriend. Neither of us knew about committing to another person.

After thinking it through, that night at the ballpark, I crossed *both* Ryan and Jerry off my list. I could be safe from the hurt that inevitably came—at least I'd be old enough to handle it when I decided to once again try a relationship.

I was broken in one world, while trying to be whole in another.

Chapter 5

Coffee

*I*t was odd, but after talking with Ethan I was able to relax. My stomach settled down immediately.

As I put my feet up and ate my sandwich, I saw Ryan's brother and sister-in-law sitting a few rows behind the Goliaths' dugout.

They look so excited. I wish I were with them, talking about Chris performing at the Irish Cultural Center and discovering more about their lives. Oh, damn it. Why couldn't we have talked about what happened?

My thoughts drifted back to Ryan's desperate reveal near the elevator at the Embarcadero Hotel. He was hurt. Vulnerable. Sorting through the pain from his father's death. The little boy of that evening rushed back into my heart. I couldn't shake him.

He seemed sincere, but when all was said and done, wasn't it only an act?

Just then, Ryan stepped out of the dugout to wave at his family.

A dozen women gathered to get his attention.

I could barely stand to watch.

My hands were ready to cover my eyes.

Me and my bright ideas.

Even though he was free to have sex with other women because he'd let me go, I didn't want to see him throw the baseball into the stands or make a pass at another lady.

But I had to.

That's the reason I came.

Wasn't it?

I don't want to admit anything. I sure miss him.

Preparing myself for Ryan to take the hand of another woman, I spoke silent words of encouragement to myself—I'd used them all my life. *No matter what he does, I'm worth loving. I'll be okay, regardless of his actions. I'm a good person.*

After a few minutes, he turned away from the crowd.

He didn't curl his finger to any of the ladies dressed up for him. Dare I hope? Should *I hope? Isn't it better if it's over?*

The fans next to me were excited after Ethan walked away. They asked me how I knew the rookie baseball player. When I told them we'd just met, they teased me about possibilities.

This feels good. It's exactly how I felt in LA with Alex, enjoying my freedom and the variety of people around me—especially those my own age. I need to pay attention to this.

The Avengers were victorious that night, 9-5. Because there was a four run lead and no save possibility for Ryan, he didn't come in to pitch the ninth.

The usual celebration by baseball men ensued: jumping in the air together, raising their hands to high-five each other and bumping their butts, chests, and stomachs together.

When I stood up to leave, I considered how odd it was that only a few months earlier I had enjoyed baseball for its pure sport and competition. I had rooted for the players and their achievements on the field the same way as my father, before Ryan came into my life.

Longing to once again move through my favorite sport as a fan and nothing more, I wondered if I'd ever again wear my rose-colored glasses and ignore the murmurs of my body.

Even as I yearned for my childhood, it was the sensual bumping together of men and women that occupied my mind dozens of times during the day.

Chris and Frances walked down to the railing. Fans surrounded them as they leaned in to have a word with Ryan. After a few moments of checking in with his family, he went into the dugout. His brother and sister-in-law left the area quickly. I presumed they were headed to a room in the tunnel where approved guests often waited.

Had I thought it through instead of letting my anger get the best of me, I would've realized that because his family was at the game, the chance he'd flirt with anyone was slim to none. Add to that how Chris had already called his brother a Romeo in front of me; I should have known Ryan wouldn't do anything to encourage more of that sarcasm.

As I waited for Ethan at Java House, I nervously bounced from one activity to another while trying to kill time.

I know he won't show up, but I'll be okay.

I read the newspaper, played mini-golf on my cell phone, checked the doorway several times, looked at the clock, talked to a few of the customers and repeated the routine.

Shortly before eleven, Ethan arrived dressed in dark blue jeans and a loose, black T-shirt. There was no beautiful chest, tattooed arms, or lovely blue eyes in my face. No one knew that Ethan was a ballplayer or asked for his autograph.

"Hey," he nodded.

"Hey! Congratulations on your win."

"Thanks." He sat down and scooted his seat closer to the table. "Did you order?"

"Just water so far." I put down my phone. "Did you get enough to eat in the clubhouse?"

"Yeah, I have to get my fill there." He picked up my menu. "Rookies aren't paid much, so I take advantage of all the freebies."

"That makes good sense." *Right now sensible appeals to me.*

"So . . . cappuccino or hot chocolate?" Ethan waited for my response.

"Cappuccino, please." *I can't bear to have hot chocolate yet.*

Once we ordered, we began a conversation that felt natural and flowed easily. He told me about his life growing up on a farm in Missouri and admitted he was naive and overwhelmed by big-city life, the hangers-on, and—no surprise—all the women.

"And the press!" His hands moved expressively. "I have ta be so careful about everythin'. The other day I tweeted 'bout a congresswoman I admire back home. A few minutes later management calls to schedule me with public relations."

"Wow! That's pretty serious!" I tore a napkin in half. "Guess the Avengers thought you might take the team down!"

"I guess so." He started laughing. "The new kid from Missouri rocks a professional baseball team—ha! Cool headlines!"

"Do you have any social media accounts?" I tried to stop smiling.

"Facebook and Instagram. I made 'em private." He took a sip of water. "I started on Twitter but that's how I got in trouble in the first place. Hiring a publicist seems so phony. Can't afford one anyway."

"You're smart not to." I reconsidered my response might have been too bold and I backtracked. "Well, at least, in my opinion. It's just . . ." I frowned as I thought about a twenty-year-old rookie already jaded. "People like honesty, not the canned crap. Of course, I'm talking about something of which I know diddlysquat, as James would say."

"Who's James?" he sipped from his coffee mug as soon as it was set in front of him. "Thanks," he told our waiter.

"He handles security at the Bay Gate. Don't tell anybody, but he let me in tonight with an extra ticket." I felt as if we were schoolmates sneaking a note underneath the teacher's nose.

"My lips are sealed. I can get you a ticket if you wanna see one of my games in Oakland." He dipped his spoon in the creamy head of foam on the cappuccino.

"Cool. I've never been there. Can you believe it? Right in my own backyard and I've never been. Anyway, on your posting, don't get a publicist unless the team insists." I put my hands up to my face and started laughing. "I know that's bossy. Sorry. But I think people will see through those posts and you won't attract the following you want. There's a marketing strategy based on the law of attraction."

"That answers one question for me," he smiled.

"What's that?"

"You're at least a sophomore in college, right?"

"I'll tell you my age later. Back to marketing yourself, be genuine. They need to see the real you. You know, your interests and passions. On the other hand, if people pay that much attention to what you're posting that you got in trouble? Guess that means you're climbing the ladder pretty damn fast, Ethan."

"Climbin' is right. So many people, fans, and friends I didn't know I had—they're all comin' out of some hole in ground. I had a woman ask if she could start my fan club. I says to myself, *Fan Club?* What have I done?"

"Yeah, she probably wanted to *be* your fan club." I laughed as I watched him turn red.

"No she didn't," he said bashfully.

"Oh, yes she did," I insisted. "Seriously, fans do like to hear from you guys. What about blogging or a podcast? You could pick a hobby, a charity, well, that's if you do charity work. I don't mean you have to or anything. I volunteer all the time. I just love it. Or you could talk about a rookie's impression of the big leagues, what it felt like coming into your first game, or how it is growing up on a farm. Oh, I know! What about writing about the Bay Area? Mention your favorite hangouts, the things you've done here so far . . . stuff like that."

It felt good to give him advice and even better to have someone listen to my ideas. I didn't want the conversation to end.

"Good idea, Nicky. Damn. It's like you're a marketing guru. Just a second." He pulled out his cell phone, sat next to me, and put his chin on my shoulder.

"What are you doing?" *This is too close, but it feels good.*

"I'm gonna take our photo and post it. Then I can talk about the new friend I made. Cheese." He snapped the picture.

"Hold that shot." I grabbed my cell phone and also took one of us. "I'll post one, too." We settled in and talked a few hours longer.

I miss my long conversations with Ryan. There is something about Ethan that's different—even from Jerry. It's the way he listens to my ideas and seems to appreciate them.

"I guess I should let you get to bed," he announced. It was going on 1:00 a.m.

"I'm not sleepy." I shook my head. I'm enjoying our

conversation too much." *I won't let you in completely though—just know that.* When he asked me about my career plans, it was all I needed to roll on about Stanford. Another hour passed quickly.

"Well, I'll see ya tomorrow night at the game?" he asked.

"Be there with bells on." I gathered my backpack. "By the way, a few of my friends don't have boyfriends, so if you want to go on a date, let me know. You've probably got plenty of women vying for your attention, but . . ."

"You never did tell me how old you are," he grinned.

"I wasn't going to before we talked."

"Why not?" he asked, tilting his head.

"Because when someone older finds out I'm eighteen their face shows the obvious—nothing I say matters anymore. I'm suddenly too young. It's my hang-up, but it makes me feel insignificant."

"I'd never classify anyone as insignificant, especially *you*," he emphasized. "Anyone can see yer someone to reckon with as soon as ya start talkin'."

"You just earned yourself a gold star," I praised. "That's good news, because when I start talking, I can really speed along."

"Do you have a boyfriend?"

"I did." The waiter filled my cup with regular coffee. "Well, kind of." I poured in some cream. "I'm not looking for a boyfriend, only a friend who happens to be a boy. I've always enjoyed having male friends."

"Me, too. Ya know, friends who are girls. Um, I mean ladies." He cleared his throat. "Well, I really mean women. Sorry, I don't mean to be offensive."

"No offense taken," I reassured. "Being politically correct is a challenge. If the mistake comes from someone with a good heart or someone I've known a while, I don't care. Like um . . .

James at the Bay Gate. He's a southern man and it's part of his culture and charm. He calls everyone baby or honey—even the fans. It's just his thing and it doesn't take long to realize that about him. What irks me is when *girls* is used condescendingly—like we're only cute little things and property to be played with. You know what I mean?"

"Explain."

"The Victoria Secret syndrome," I stated simply. "Here I am for your pleasure, come and play with me."

"Another example, please," he requested.

"Let's say I'm with my friends. You walk by and ask *how's it goin' girls*? That's condescending. Or let's say my teammates and I are cheering and one of the guys says, *lookin' good girls*. That's not okay—unless we were still in our junior year of high school."

"What's the right way?"

"*Nice job* or *hello ladies*. You see? If you don't know a woman, don't call her girl."

"I see."

"Now here's the rub, Ethan. If we were at a party together with people our own age, girls or boys would be okay. But if you're with another guy, older than you? It would be rude. So now that you're totally confused, do I make any sense at all?" I laughed at my detailed explanation and hoped his head wasn't spinning.

"I think I've got it." He finished his coffee.

"Well, friend, I'm glad you asked me to coffee, but I'm spent for sure now. You can talk longer than I can. *That's* a feat!" I put my hand out to shake his. "Really nice to meet you."

"You, too." He pushed out his chair and then stood. "Did you think I was a weirdo coming up to you at the railing?"

"At first. It's just, the railings, you know. Well, do you know? Sitting there, the people, women actually . . . I'm sorry; I'm difficult to get to know. It's just . . . well, I'm difficult, that's all."

"I don't agree with that. Hey, Nicky?" He looked bashfully at the ground.

Ooh, how cute!

"Ethan?" I teased.

"Would ya have breakfast with me tomorrow? You choose the place. I can pick you up or you can meet me if that makes you more comfortable. I don't have a morning game, well, you're cheerin', so ya know. I think we have a lot in common and I'd love ta hear more about your plans."

"You don't know what you're saying." I started to laugh. "I could bore you to tears. You'll be sorry."

"I have a car. I can pick you up."

"You said that." I teased him even more.

"Yeah," he blushed.

"Give me your cell phone." I held out my hand. "I'll enter my address and phone number. What time do you have to be at the ballpark today?"

"Between two and three," he said.

"So let's do . . . 9:30?" I handed his phone back to him. "There's a great breakfast place close to my house."

"Sounds perfect." Ethan looked at his phone as if studying my address. "You'd better let me drop you home tonight. It's too late to be out walking alone."

"Thanks, I was going to ask if you wouldn't mind." I got up.

Each of us left the money for our coffees and started our walk back to the players' lot.

Just as we reached the gate, Ryan, Chris and Frances were coming from the other direction.

My Evil Twin licked her lips.

My mind raced in the many wicked ways I could lash out at the man who had just abandoned me.

I know my eyes must have narrowed and turned demon-red.

The dark deliciousness of revenge consumed my entire body.

Chapter 6

I'll Leave Your Jacket At
The Door

The smiles from Chris and Frances were growing with each
step that brought us closer. As we all slowed to a stop, I looked
straight at Ryan. It was obvious he was nervous. For the first time
since I'd known him, he couldn't look at me. His eyes alternated
from my face to the ground. For me, it was the opposite. I had no
trouble staring directly into his eyes. They were no longer on fire
for me.

Ethan talked rapidly, looking at the harbor, the lights, the
streets, me and everywhere else. He didn't know how badly his
new friend had been hurt and she couldn't yet process unfamiliar
feelings rising up from her darkness.

"Nicky!" Frances called to me sweetly. "Why didn't you come

out with us tonight?"

"Ask your brother-in-law." My anger simmered. I wanted to verbally attack Ryan so he could feel a little of the pain I was also feeling.

Is this how my father feels when he begins to rage?

"Why?" She looked at Ryan and back to me with obvious confusion.

Something surfaced from a tender place in my heart. For reasons I didn't yet understand, I couldn't watch Ryan suffer. Instead of my emotional dodging and hiding, I answered her question calmly; defending the man I still loved. We were both at fault. I needed to share in the responsibility.

"Oh, I, you know . . . wasn't invited." I fumbled with my response and watched the anxiety cross Ryan's face.

"Why *didn't* you invite her, brother?" Chris's question was woven with tones of dare and sarcasm. I was aware of how awful the sarcastic comment sounded. Hearing someone I didn't know well throw out a comment like that to his own brother made me wince.

Ryan seemed caught, unsure of what to say, how to move, and where to look. He chose to remain silent.

"He was caught. He wanted to be with his loved ones." I felt compelled to say something. I couldn't leave him so defenseless and watch him shift uncomfortably. At the same time, he tried to hide our disaster from Chris and Frances. I wasn't about to let them put him on trial.

"We wouldn't have minded you coming with us," Frances scolded. "Ryan, what were you thinking?"

"*I'm* the one who encouraged it," I countered. "I know if you were my family I'd want to spend at least a night alone with you."

"How sweet," Frances placed her hand on my arm. "Thank

you, Nicky."

"Sure." I cleared my throat. "By the way, this is my new friend, Ethan. You probably know he's on the Avengers, Ryan, but Chris and Frances, he played right field tonight in the eighth inning."

"Wow!" Chris said. "Cool." He and Frances took turns shaking Ethan's hand.

"Good game, Ethan," Ryan did the soul shake with him and then let go quickly.

"Thanks, Mr. Tilton," Ethan answered timidly. "Congratulations on awesome year so far. I hope to give ya some competition at the plate someday."

"Look forward to it," Ryan challenged.

"It'll be a highlight of my career," Ethan smiled and then patted me on the back. "Speaking of highlights, meeting my new friend was sure a nice surprise."

I smiled nervously.

Ryan's blue eyes scanned my new acquaintance more closely now that I had stepped nearer to him.

"Well, glad you had a nice time out," I pushed out a response. I wanted nothing more than to move away from the awkward gathering. My voice cracked. Ryan stepped close as if ready to offer some gesture of kindness. I couldn't allow him to drag me back into his web. "I'll leave your jacket and the necklace you bought outside my front door," I whispered. "I won't ruin them." The harder I tried to hold back, the more my tears threatened to fall.

"Nicky—" Ryan positioned himself between Ethan and me and started to raise his arms to gather me inside of them.

I grabbed his wrists to stop him.

Letting Ryan embrace my body would warm my heart again. Although he still had it, I couldn't let that happen outwardly.

After all, wasn't my recovery synonymous with resisting his touch? Didn't I need to protect myself that way?

He'd been right to break it off.

I knew, even when I came back from LA I'd felt it in my gut— we weren't right for each other.

We were at two different places in our lives. The timing wasn't right for either of us.

"Wait!" Frances seemed worried. Perhaps she'd picked up on the tension. "Why don't you join—"

"Ethan and I have to go," I announced. I fought hard to stay strong, hiding the upset and sadness inside of me. "Have a nice evening. Chris, Frances, if I don't see you before you leave, it was great meeting you both."

I turned away.

Tears began their descent.

As I walked to Ethan's car, the only sounds I heard were our feet as they hit the ground. I could feel the three of them— Chris, Frances, and Ryan—standing in silence behind us. I didn't turn around to look at their faces.

"Were you seeing Ryan Tilton?" Ethan finally broke the silence when we settled in his car.

Oh God. Well, there goes my new friend.

"We were um . . . friends," I admitted. "Well, more than friends. I thought we were headed for something special."

"I don't want to be in the middle of anything," he gripped the steering wheel. "That was, uh . . . what did he do?"

"He broke a promise," I mourned.

"What was it if you don't mind me asking?"

"He told me he wouldn't overstep the boundaries we had agreed on and did anyway," I fumbled. "When I didn't give in, he went cold. I think it's . . . well, you guys have so much coming at you.

50

I guess sex is assumed when there are so many opportunities. Um . . . it was about sex. The cat is out of the bag. I didn't mean to say that, but too late now. You know, the thing is, I told him. Right from the beginning I said that we should only be friends. He really hurt me." Without hesitation, I added, "Actually, we hurt each other."

I shocked myself as I said the words. I hadn't considered how it would feel to say them. I hadn't planned them. They were spoken from my heart.

That's being vulnerable, Nick.

We pulled away from the players' lot. I thought more about what had happened. Like me, Ryan was abandoned. Instead of living with a parent battling addiction, his pain came from his father's early death and not being able to say goodbye. At fourteen, he cursed his dad for leaving on another tour of duty to the Middle East. Those words served as Ryan's final farewell to his father; he could never take them back.

Why couldn't Ryan talk about it when I refused his advances? Was it because no one had turned him down—probably since high school? Did sex mean acceptance and approval for him?

Maybe what I'd done meant complete rejection and he didn't know how to put his feelings into words.

Maybe, because of the ending with his father, he was afraid to say anything.

"Yeah," Ethan broke the silence. "But uh . . . wow! That seemed way deeper than just *heading somewhere*." He shook his head. "The gentle way you took his wrists in your hands seemed like love back there."

Run while you still can, Ethan! I'm a mess!

"Let's not talk about it." My voice was almost inaudible.

"Let's do, okay?" he insisted. "I need to know you're all

right. You seem shaken."

"I am." *I'm miserable.*

"I'd be happy to come in and keep talkin' with ya." We arrived at my house. He didn't hesitate to follow me to my front door. "Or we can continue in my car if you're uncomfortable havin' me in your house. I have plenty of time before I need to get to sleep."

"I'd love that." I unlocked the door. "Come in."

He followed me in the house and into the kitchen. After I put my backpack on one of the chairs, I got each of us a glass of water and we sat down.

"Well, where do I begin?" I circled marks from hot pans, red wine stains, and the beads of water from the bottom of a glass that sat too long that marked the wooden tabletop.

"I say dive in." Ethan's warm smile was so friendly I didn't hesitate. His hands rested on mine; patting them as if quietly telling me, *it's all right.*

"We volunteered together last year at the Veterans' Hospital. He was warm, funny . . . I thought he was a real gentleman. He even made sure to introduce himself to my family after only our first visit together. I still don't understand everything—not completely. Anyway, the Goliaths threw an appreciation party for their employees and volunteers last November and some of the players came. He sat down with me when I was by myself and told me he'd like to ask me out when I turned eighteen."

Ethan's face flushed.

"What's wrong?" I probed.

"Not likin' that," he confessed. "It's like, no offense but . . ." He shook his head. "Never mind."

"Like I'm fresh meat?"

He nodded.

"I understand why you'd think that but he's a good man."

"You sure about that?" Ethan challenged.

"I'm sure. He literally blew me away when he held my hands and revealed his feelings." A beat of sadness thumped in my chest. "Then after I sang the National Anthem this year, he did it again. He caught me in the tunnel on my way back to my teammates. You know, we wait in the outfield, behind the fence where that big double gate is? Well, that's where we sit and I had to walk back there. The Goliaths actually got us chairs this year. Before, we had to stand up. You didn't need to know that, but anyway, he really got me. Truthfully?"

"Yeah?" Ethan seemed anxious to hear the end of my story.

"I liked him last year when he kissed my hand. He introduced himself that way. Can you imagine?" I stopped for a moment to relish the sweet memory.

"And?" He nudged my arm.

"Yeah." Although I was in turmoil, I caught myself smiling. "So a few nights ago, Ryan and I were in Half Moon Bay. We sat on the beach together. He poured out his soul to me. What he revealed, they aren't the things you talk about unless you feel a close connection with the other person. Why go to all that trouble? It's crazy, right? Am I crazy? Maybe it's me. Just tell me."

"Sounds like he had, or *has* feelings for you." He spun his phone in his hands.

"Maybe. In the end I guess it meant nothing without sex." I resigned myself to the inevitable. "I *knew* this would happen, but he kept asking me to give us a try. There was something so unusual about him. We just clicked. You know what I mean?" A tear left its trail down to my chin. "It's that we don't mesh. No, that's not it," I reconsidered. "We did mesh. I guess—"

"You're both at two different places in your lives," Ethan

interjected.

"Yes, *that's* it exactly," I wiped another tear.

"I can understand how you'd feel that way," he counseled. "He's almost eight years older than you and been through things you haven't experienced. I'm sure he's charming. I'd also bet he's a lot to handle."

Remember hearing that from your parents, Nick?

"How do you know how old he is?" My voice sounded unsteady.

"Nicky, all the players know each other's age; especially the prominent ones. Even in the semi-pro leagues, we know."

"You think he's a prominent player?"

"Duh," he smiled.

"Hmm. I never thought of him like that."

"Why not? You follow baseball."

"Yeah, I know. I guess . . . he's humble and doesn't seem to get caught up in the star syndrome. Anyway, on his age . . ."

"We keep track because we can't wait to replace them," he chuckled. "At least that's our hope."

"That makes sense." I blew my nose in a napkin and threw it in the trashcan.

"I can see you're in pain." Ethan squeezed my hand. "Sorry for whatever happened. You sure you don't want to be alone?"

"I'm sick of being alone," I stated. "In fact, that's why I went to the game tonight—to be around people. Stay a while, okay?"

"You're alone?" He leaned forward, resting his elbows on the table. "You don't have many friends?"

"It's not that. Well, in some ways that's true. My friends from school—we're drifting away from each other. I know it's natural. We've all graduated and we're going onto other things, but . . ." I sighed in appreciation of my friends. "I'll sure miss my girls. At least I've got my sister, Tara, and Alex."

"Who are Tara and Alex?"

"Tara Summers and Alexandra Flowers," I informed. "Tara is Matt Summers' wife and Alex is Darrell Sweet's fiancé."

"Damn, woman! You sure have powerful friends."

"Well, I never thought about it that way. But yeah, I guess so." I grabbed my glass of water.

"Count your blessings that you have even one friend," he held up his index finger as if to demonstrate. "Until I get back home all I have are acquaintances. I haven't made any friends after high school since I didn't go to college. Not really. So . . ."

"You're a jock," I kidded. "You'll be fine."

"Maybe," he wore a shit ass grin. "That's not the way it feels right now, though. I wish I had at least two years of college under my belt."

Yes! That's exactly what I tried to tell Ryan.

"Yeah, but like I said before, you have to be good to be drafted right out of high school. In professional baseball only two years after you graduated? That's really rare."

"That's what happens when you're driven—like you." He shrugged his shoulders. "We leave friends along the way."

"Will you stay over tonight?" I blurted.

He choked on a sip of water.

"Are you okay?"

"You want me to spend the night?" He wiped his mouth.

Chapter 7

A Little Sarcasm With Breakfast

"*W*e should go to sleep. You probably want to go, but . . . the sofa in the living room opens into a bed. You can sleep there when we get tired of talking. Well, if you want. Do you? It's probably not the luxury of your place, but . . . ."

After I announced my invitation, I laughed aloud. Although it was bold, I felt good I had offered it. He was obviously shocked, which suited me fine. I was in the mood to stir the pot. Just when I thought I might have scared him off, his smile bloomed.

"Talk about ballsy, Ethan. You only invited me for coffee. Here I am inviting you to stay over and we've only known each other a few hours! What do you think of me *now*?"

"My opinion hasn't changed," he said confidently. "I'll stay over. And by the way, I'm in an Extended Stay Hotel, so . . . hardly luxury."

"I'll get you a blanket and pillow. Be right back. Grab the waters and I'll meet you in the living room." I ran upstairs and got two blankets and two pillows and then set them on the sofa. "One for each of us." I wrapped myself in the blanket, stretched my legs, and rested my feet on the coffee table. "Have you ever been hurt by a woman?"

"Nothing too terrible." He kicked off his shoes. Tucked his feet underneath his body and sat on the opposite end of the sofa. "Even though I'm only twenty, I've had disappointments. I know the empty feeling you have right now; it's rough." He hesitated, and then shared, "Do you think he's too old for you?"

You're not the first to suggest it. I still don't know.

My ramblings grew loose and comfortable the longer I was with Ethan. It was easy to respond to the sweet innocence of a twenty-year-old boy who was open and seemed authentic. His innocence was much different even than Jerry's; there was nothing sexual in our conversations.

"Better get some rest if we're gonna make breakfast tomorrow. Actually," he looked down at his watch. "I mean, today."

I didn't realize another hour passed.

"You're not sick of me yet?" I was afraid to ask the question, fearing an answer I didn't want to hear.

"Not even close."

Phew.

"Do you want me to help you set up the sofa bed?" I offered.

"That's okay, I'll just stretch out." His long body settled in.

You look cute all tucked in that blanket.

"Okay, then. Thanks for talking with me." I suddenly had an urge to kiss him goodnight on the cheek. Instead, I surprised him with a hug. "I'm so glad you asked me to coffee. You really helped me tonight."

"I'm glad, too. Night," he winked and then closed his eyes.

I ran upstairs to my bedroom. Although I still ached for Ryan, now that a little time had passed, I saw how letting go was the right decision and the best thing for both of us.

"Sorry we didn't work out." I kissed the sterling silver charm he'd given me on my birthday. It was the number eighteen and I kept it by my bedside. "I'll always remember you."

I crashed hard; getting a few hours of much needed sleep. It seemed only a few minutes had passed when my phone rang at 8:00 a.m.

The sun was out.

For a change, there was no fog.

"Morning."

"Morning," Ethan replied tentatively. "Sorry, the team called an early meeting and I need to be there at eleven. I know we were up late so it's okay if you don't—"

"I want to go." I wiped the sleep from my eyes. "Where are you?"

"Downstairs," he almost whispered.

"You're calling me from downstairs?"

"I'm not coming up to your room. Your dad already looked at me weird when he left the house. I faked being asleep but I saw his face. He freaked me out."

"He looks at every boy that way." I reconsidered what I'd just said. I was worried it may have come out the wrong way. "Not that I've had anyone sleep over. Anyway, I'll get ready now; it won't take me long. Sorry, I should have set the alarm so I woke up before my father and saved you some embarrassment. Do you want a toothbrush, mouthwash, socks, or anything?"

"No, I'm okay," he laughed. "A pair of socks? Ya think my socks are dirty?"

"I don't know what to offer you."

"I'm fine," he went on quickly. "Hurry up. I wanna spend a few hours together."

"I'll be down in a bit." I ended the call and scrambled to get ready. Now that I was awake and facing a new day, I had time to think about Ryan and what we'd done. We'd handled each other so poorly I didn't think our friendship was salvageable. I wanted to call him and apologize so badly. Instead, I did nothing. I was afraid to say hello. I put on a pair of black jeans and a gray sweater and gathered my hair back with a headband. It was 8:15 and quiet throughout the house.

"Morning." Ethan gave me a big hug.

I hugged him back.

"I'm going to start a pot of coffee for my family. It'll only take me a minute."

"You okay?" He pulled back and looked me in the eyes. When I nodded and smiled, he announced, "I'll go warm up ol' Betsy."

I could see the happiness in his eyes. There was something great about meeting a new friend. It was as if my heart had filled with joy. I imagined he felt the same way. In fact, it looked as if he might skip down the sidewalk to his car. I wondered what it might be like to skip after him. I turned on the coffeemaker, grabbed my backpack and keys, and headed out to Ethan's VW Beetle.

"The sun's out! Can you believe it?" I was bubbling over.

"Gorgeous," Ethan agreed.

"Just a warning, when the day begins so calm, it could mean a lot of wind at the ball park." I wanted to educate him about the stadium conditions, in case he was put into the game. "Be ready for some crazy fly balls."

"Okay, I'll watch out for them." He opened the door for me. "You live in a nice neighborhood."

Is it really so nice? To a stranger's eye, maybe, but now I'm not so sure.

"Thanks. It was um . . . interesting growing up here." It wasn't my usual cover up.

Fun? There was definitely a lot of it, but that word wasn't right.

What was the best way to put it? Perhaps that it was a mix of everything light and dark. I knew as soon as I returned home I'd need to write about my new friend's observation.

"Which way?" Ethan climbed in, took the brake off and shifted out of neutral.

"Make a U-turn and we'll go down West Portal. If you weren't so limited on time we could walk; maybe next time. Um . . . you know, if you want to do a next time."

"Well, it's not even 8:30. Let's do it." He turned off the car. "How is it you look so awake? If I didn't know better, I'd have thought you went to sleep early. You look great."

"Thanks, so do you," I admitted. "I guess we both have the adrenaline of meeting a new friend rushing through us."

"Guess so," he agreed. "About that next time you offered?"

"Yeah?"

"Definitely."

We talked the entire eight blocks to the café. Over pancakes, I found out about his friends and family and shared how my mother was raised in Arizona and Dad in San Francisco. Of course I bragged about Jenise as well, and found out he had two brothers and one sister. We didn't stop until we got back to my house.

"Would you mind if I called you again?" he shoved his hands in his jacket pockets.

"You still want to after all my drama?" I pretended to tease him, but in reality *was* serious.

"Oh yeah," he affirmed. "After this series we fly out to Texas. How 'bout we get together when I get back in town?"

"I'd love to! Here, let me give you my email. That way if you want to talk more and it's too long for a text, we're all set. Am I being too pushy? Suddenly I feel like, well, you might as well know that when I'm comfortable, which I admit doesn't happen too often, I want to know everything. It's funny, but when I feel a connection, it's like my heart wants to soar so high I can't imagine coming back to earth."

"What a sweet thing to say." The way he looked over my face suddenly made me feel bashful. It was an expression of warmth, and seemed intimate. I looked to the sky so I could have a few seconds to gather myself.

"Yeah, and I might as well tell you now, I have a tendency to talk fast and a lot. So raise your hand if you want me to stop," I cautioned. "Otherwise, I'll keep going forever."

"Okay, I'll raise my hand." I gathered from his laugh he appreciated my candor. "Thanks for having breakfast with me. See you tonight and have a good cheer!" He got in his car and rolled down the window. "Let your heart soar, Nicky."

I will! I want to!

While waving goodbye, I watched him round the corner. For one of the first times ever, it didn't bother me to see him disappear from my view like it had with just about everyone else. This time, with this boy, I wasn't afraid.

As I closed the front door, I could hear my family talking at the kitchen table.

Jubilant sensations of roses and new places filled me.

Instead of running up to my room and ignoring a chance to talk with parents, I walked in to say hello.

"Thanks for the coffee this morning," Mom acknowledged.

"Just getting in?" Jenise asked. Her slippers flopped on the linoleum floor as she walked from the counter to the table, a cup of coffee in her hand.

"No, I was here last night," I answered. "I met a new friend yesterday. We went out for breakfast, that's all."

"*Someone* was sleeping on the sofa." Sarcasm lined Dad's words.

By the way, still working, Dad?

"Yeah and that someone said you went out early, but here you are," I goaded. "And it's Friday. Why aren't you working?"

"Day off," he said defensively.

Jenise and I looked at each other.

I'll bet. Your bottle was empty. Wasn't that why you left?

"No invitation to your room this time?" He continued trying to get a reaction from me.

"No, not *this* time," I responded with my own jab.

"Going well with Ryan?" Jenise asked, making kissy lips.

My mother looked up. She knew I'd been crying about him the day before. I was up one day and down the next. She probably thought I was crazy. I wasn't ready to share anything—even with Jenise—until I spent more time analyzing what happened.

I wonder if I'll ever understand it.

"Yep," I answered as if I had everything together. "Everything's going great."

"That didn't look like Ryan on the sofa," Dad said smugly.

Jenise looked at me with concern. She knew something was wrong. For once, she didn't press me.

"It wasn't." I shot them all a fake smile and then escaped to my sanctuary upstairs.

Chapter 8

A Circle Begins To Close

𝒯he Dark Room was what I called my inner self after intense trauma. The door always opened after an episode from my father and conversely a great day with friends. It was filled with both the sun and the moon and each of them rose and set accordingly.

It was my creative place.

I wrote a new poem.

Jotted down some ideas for short stories.

Considered writing my aunt's memoir.

The words almost materialized in the air they flowed so easily.

When I finished plucking my thoughts and voices from my mind and body and put them on paper, I took the time to write about Ethan's comment: *"You live in a nice neighborhood."*

How was it to grow up here?

Hidden things.

Secrets.

Hopping fences.
Friends.
Rage.
Hiding.
Staying busy.
Relatives.
Holidays.

I thought back to the early days when my aunts and uncles came over to play Ping-Pong on a Saturday afternoon and the transitioned to a poker game in the evening. Bowls of crackers and cheese, deli meats, salads, bottles of beer and soda on ice, jars of nuts and chocolate-covered raisins were on plates all day.

Dad was sober.

Mom was present and smiling.

The sky opened in magic and Jenise and I were welcomed to participate in the day however we wanted. We dug in to the food, the fun, and even played a few hands of poker. On those days the arms of my father surrounded the daughter that was often his nemesis—my sister. Auntie Barbara and I had pretend tea with one of the play sets she'd bought for me. I was even invited to join in some of their table tennis tournaments.

Our home became a kind of *"Neverland"* in those days, albeit short-lived and not for long.

I wrote about the nights us neighborhood kids played dodge ball, hopscotch, high jump with rubber band ropes, hide and go seek, and of course, baseball.

We didn't worry about getting beat up, kidnapped or robbed—we were safe in our cocoon—a square of four blocks where backyards were shared by hopping a fence or two. It was so easy to connect . . . if one friend couldn't play, we'd hop into another backyard in search of another.

And then . . . there was the other side of living there—like hiding on a neighbor's front steps with Jerry to avoid the black and blue violence of his house; Dad's rage, which we knew could explode at any moment; Jenise's rape, which happened right outside of our safety zone; and Mom's permanent detachment.

Just as I finished writing, my cell phone rang.

"You see the article in SF Gate?" I could hear the irritation in Colleen's voice.

"What's it about?"

"*Well,*" her voice dipped in anger and then rose higher in sarcasm. "Let me read it to you." She read it word for word.

A few weeks earlier a local writer had invited high school graduates to submit an essay describing unique ways they'd gained admission to college. Her blog catered to young and new adults and the title of her article was *Out-of-the-Box-Thinking for Your College Application.* My high school advisor had called me, strongly suggesting I submit my story about how I created and presented my business plan to the Goliaths for the cheer team.

We'd already gained a small amount of notoriety from interviews on local radio, mentions in traditional print and online newspapers, and a nice write-up on the PLB (Professional League Baseball) website. I submitted the essay, focusing on the things that inspired me to create the team and how I put together my research. To bring an element of human interest, I included my love of baseball and a small background story of how Dad took me to the Goliaths games when I was six-years-old.

I didn't intend to dismiss or discount any of my teammates— I knew what that felt like. The anger in Colleen's voice made me wonder if our friendship was starting to fracture.

"What a *joke*," she chided. "Of course, *you're* featured."

"Oh, come on, Coll. The writer just wanted to know how I

came up with the plan. I'd been thinking about it for a few years before I approached you to see if you were interested. Besides, I've given everyone on the team credit numerous times."

"Why didn't you let me know?" she drawled. "I could've written about my design ideas."

"Mrs. Gale found out about it and phoned me because she knew I created the proposal," I reminded. "The focus was about *creating* the plan. Don't get your undies in a bunch. It wasn't to exclude you."

"My undies?" she shouted. "My *undies!*"

Oh, damn, I've flipped her button.

"You wouldn't have your fucking cheer team if it wasn't for the work I do on all the routines, Nicky. Your idea would *so* flop if I quit, *wouldn't* it?"

"Well, *yeah* it would. You *know* it would. What's all this really about? It's just an E-zine article. You've done a great job. I've told you that dozens of times. That's why you're in charge of everything this year. When you submitted some of your costume ideas to Sony pictures, you didn't mention me or the team, right?"

Stay humble, remain calm and deflect.

"It makes me so mad when you take all the attention. *Stanford, Stanford, Stanford*—it's all we hear about. You're always so busy . . . we never see you except on cheer days. And what the fuck is going on with your Facebook?"

"My *Facebook*?" I clarified. "What?" I pulled up the app on my cell phone. *I've got to see what she means.*

"Your selfie with Ethan Mathers. What the hell is *that?* When did you meet *him*? I thought you and Jerry were together?"

"No, we're not—"

"Your page is blowing up, Nick. Suddenly you're Facebook friends with an Avengers player? His family and followers are commenting by the hundreds."

"Oh come on," I kidded.

"Well it fuckin' seems like it. Shit, even his fans mentioned you on their pages—what the hell? And you have a picture of him being cozy on your shoulder on *your* Facebook?"

How do I keep her engaged?

"That was just a joke. I haven't even looked at it; let me—" I quickly opened the app and saw a few hundred new friend requests. "Oh, shit! All from a picture!"

"*Yeah*, oh shit," she repeated. "What did you expect?"

Oh damn! What do I do with all this?

"I don't uh . . . I didn't expect *anything*," I answered honestly. "He's only been in the pros a few days and he wanted to talk with someone his own age. We went or hot chocolate but then had coffee, and well, cappuccinos, but—"

"Shut up! God! Of course you meet him and he likes you." She sounded disgusted. "You're a fuckin' witch."

I felt as if I couldn't say anything without her coming unglued.

"No, it was—"

"Did you tell him you don't put out? *That* ought to make him run for the hills," she hissed. "What will Jerry think?"

"Why should I care what he thinks?" I could almost feel her finger reaching through the phone, pointed at me in judgment. She'd thrown me a sharp insult because I'd made a decision with sex and my spiritual values. I wanted to tell her off, then pour my heart out and tell her what had happened because of my hang-ups. I had to stay calm. I knew this could be a point of no return for us.

"Well . . ." she sounded confused and a little lost.

"I'll touch base more often. Jerry and I . . . we're not going anywhere with a relationship."

"What?" she almost screamed.

"That's okay," I comforted. "I've settled with it. Please don't be mad. You know, you're going to a pretty phenomenal college yourself—*UCLA*! I'm sorry if I haven't listened enough."

"I know, but . . ." her voice trailed off. "You don't like Jerry anymore?"

"It's not that." Although I didn't want to, I stayed with her on the topic a little longer. "I like him."

"You two sure looked cozy at our beach party. You were tucked close in his sleeping bag before the rangers broke up our party. In fact, Jerry told Mark that you guys had another hot date last week."

"God those guys," I laughed. "What gossips they are."

"I know!" she giggled.

Phew, back to normal.

"We did have a great time." I told her all the juicy details girlfriends love to hear. When it came to boys, she could let down her guard.

Apparently, you can, too.

"Anyway," she exhaled. I knew her anger had subsided. "I was hoping to get to the ballpark a little early so we can practice some routines. Can you make it?"

"Sure, what time?"

"How about four?"

"Okay, four," I agreed. "See you there."

After we hung up, I looked through my Facebook page in more detail. I immediately accepted the friend requests from Ethan's family and decided to wait on his friends until I spoke with him.

A nervous energy suddenly grabbed me.

I got restless.

Whenever I had those feelings, I straightened my room, organized my paperwork, took a walk or a book ride, or edited some short stories I'd written.

I might as well mix up my closet again. No need to divide it any longer. I sure don't need fancy stuff for social events—yet.

I put away some of my clothes, threw other pieces in the laundry hamper, and mixed together the outfits I'd previously set aside for outings with Ryan.

I was sure his brown suede jacket was talking to me. Previously, it had marked the division of my two wardrobes: formal and casual. Now, it seemed to scream, *do something. Get this jacket back to its owner and talk to him.*

It was awful that I'd be returning his jacket because of our failed relationship. His original gesture of leaving it with me was thoughtful and came from sweet intentions.

My arm rose slowly. Purposefully. Resisting what I knew I had to do. I took his jacket off the hanger. Squeezed the furry collar and ran my hands up and down the part that covered his chest. I put it on. Reached for the emerald necklace he'd bought for me during our last evening together—the night everything fell apart.

"I've been thinking about something since last year to show you how much I appreciate you," Ryan had said.

Bet he doesn't appreciate me so much now.

Fastening the necklace around my neck one last time, I held the emerald that hung off the gold omega chain between my thumb and index fingers and also stroked the soft suede material of his jacket.

I looked at myself in the mirror.

I told him I'd leave both items at the front door.

As I felt them and enjoyed his scent, I relished our memory at Sammy's and the first night we were together in my room. I decided it would be careless and disrespectful leave them outside.

Although he'd thrown me away, I didn't want to do the same with the things that were once sweet to me. His intentions were innocent at the time—at least that's what I chose to believe—and I needed to hold those in my heart. So until I knew when he wanted to pick them up, I kept both items on my desk.

I lost myself in my daydreams and was the last of my teammates to arrive at the ballpark for our early practice. Colleen was flirting with Sy, the assistant manager in the entertainment department, Marilyn chatted with Lorraine about a recent date, and Kathie and Patty discussed their upcoming family vacations.

Manny, the security guard, opened the gate and let us in.

"Ladies, before you begin your practice, the team has something for you. I'm supposed to escort you inside."

"Come on, Nicky!" Colleen's waved at me to follow her.

"You guys go on ahead. I've already been through those tunnels. Once is enough." I shuddered as I remembered meeting Ryan in them after I'd sung the national anthem.

"Are you sure?" Colleen asked.

"I'm sure." I made a quick decision not to go. Getting an invitation to the clubhouse meant we'd impressed management and the players. The possibility of facing Ryan in the clubhouse caused me to decline. Although I wasn't ready to see or talk to him, it only took a few minutes to realize I'd been shortsighted.

As my teammates started in, I stood at the gate and waited for James. Instead, Manny returned.

"Where's James?"

"On his way. The players have a certificate of appreciation for your team. Hard to believe you'd pass up that kind of opportunity. Don't you want to be a part of it?"

"I don't know."

"I can wait a minute while you decide," he offered.

"No, I'll wait here." I felt dejected.

"Okay Ms. Young, your choice. You might as well come in the

stadium at least. No sense standing outside." He held the gate open until I walked through and then disappeared into the tunnels.

I climbed the steps to the bleachers.

Ryan was already on the field.

Why didn't I go into the clubhouse? I should have known he wouldn't wait knowing I'd be there. Dumbass! I declined a reward for nothing. That's what happens when I lose my focus. Once again I let my anxiety take over.

Focused on his warm up routines, Ryan never turned to look my way—until he saw Ethan jogging into the outfield.

Chapter 9

Observations

The man with blue-diamond eyes continued to hold my thumping heart in his hands. As I watched him observe Ethan, I wondered why he cared what Ethan's intentions were? Was he stunned to find out the woman he'd withdrawn from had made a new friend or wasn't pining for him, locked away in her bedroom?

"How ya doin'?" Ethan tucked his batting glove into his back pocket and stuffed a wad of bubble gum in his mouth.

"Just fine. Did you get to nap before your practice?" I giggled.

"No, but my workout woke me up," he wiped the sweat off of his forehead. "Course all the yellin' from the coaches didn't hurt. Believe me, I'm not sleepy anymore."

"Just in time." I twirled a strand of my hair.

"Yep, just in time," he repeated. "I had to tell ya again how great breakfast was. Your company is mighty fine."

"I feel the same," I adjusted my jersey. "And now you know

where to eat on this side of the bay."

"Plus a new friend to pal around with," he winked. "You look different in your cheer uniform."

"Um . . . thanks?"

"Sorry, that sounded . . . I didn't mean bad," he laughed. "It's just, ya know, you meet someone and they're forever in your head the way you first saw them?"

"Yeah," I agreed. "Like cousins you don't see for a long time."

"Exactly." He looked around the bleacher area. "Where's the rest of your team?"

"They're getting an award." A hint of disgust sprinkled through my response.

"What about *your* award?" He folded his arms.

"I'm fine."

"Oh, okay," he chided. "So you don't wanna be recognized, even though you created somethin' that put you in front of thousands of people?"

"Not today." *I should've gone in the clubhouse. I blew it.*

"You're kind of hard not to recognize," he grinned.

What?

"What do you mean?" I needed clarification.

"Your radiance. It's just . . ." He pointed to his eyes. "The natural glow you have is what gave me the nerve ta ask you for coffee in the first place. That look tells a person you're open."

I look open? I don't feel that way. Does he see something I can't, or . . . won't?

"Thanks, Ethan. Sometimes I wonder if I'm too intense. That can be a turn off for people, not to mention I don't know when to stop talking. Even though I can talk, I'm a good listener. You wouldn't know it, well, yeah, you might since you did a lot of the talking last night, but . . ."

"I appreciate you carryin' a conversation," he smiled adorably. "Most of the time I sit and fidget. I don't know what to say."

"Well, maybe you drew something out of me," I noted.

"Hope so," he grinned. "See ya later and catch ya next time we're in town!"

"Adios!" I blew him a kiss and put on my headphones.

Ryan, who seemed to notice Ethan talking to me, watched as my new friend jogged back toward his team's dugout.

"What do you care?" I said aloud but meant it only for myself.

What did you expect me to do? Swoon for you all day and night? I'm not going to curl up and die. Oh, but I'd love to say hello. I'm so damn confused.

I was aware of my conflicted feelings and wondered if Ryan had the same struggle.

We'd pushed each other away, but was that what we wanted?

Was our connection really over?

As I thought back to Half Moon Bay and the warmth I'd felt being with him, I reflected on how similar we were. It was as if we were children drawn together to find our way, wanting to be loved but not sure how to get there.

Jenise had told me I needed to guide Ryan. How was that possible when I didn't know what direction I wanted for myself?

Each of us floundered as we tried to understand how to bring someone special into our lives.

We needed to throw away our clichés and fears.

Could we?

The day his father was killed fighting in the Middle East, Ryan's life changed forever. His heart—a little boy's heart—was injured. He'd confessed to me that not only was he in pain, he'd also lost the remainder of his childhood. He was thrust into an adult world and become abandoned and lost. His heart had closed, protecting and helping him to survive.

Just as I wanted out from my family's shadows, was Ryan trying to break through the walls he'd built around himself after his father died? I'd done the same things. Rather than burying myself in meaningless physical relationships, I stayed busy volunteering and working on school committees. We'd both avoided confronting our feelings, sweeping them away in denial.

The thing about abandonment issues—the impending sense someone or everyone will leave us—is that it lingers.

Being left behind seems to happen at the worse possible times in our lives.

Fear gives in to every insecure moment.

Self-doubting births our fears—it's a vicious circle.

Even though we know we have valid reasons for some of our insecurities, we have trouble sorting through them.

Our logical minds fall victim to the other side, which creates stories of doom.

Our bodies still suffer from the numbness and shock of too many traumas and broken promises.

It can take us years to learn how to open to life.

It takes us years to trust another person.

It takes us years to believe that we're worthy of being loved.

I ran away from Ryan, who'd promised love, friendship, and the possibility of something different and wonderful. The promises he'd made to keep me safe and not leave me—these were the very promises made to me by my father and mother.

Year after year I heard them.

Those promises broke apart—especially during a bad stretch of Dad's drinking.

Neither of my parents heard me.

When Mom went to work, she really didn't regret leaving her

children. There was nothing wrong with her working; I had set my sights on a career as well. It was that she enjoyed her escape from her alcoholic husband at the expense of her kids. She was getting much time needed away from Dad while she gambled with her daughters' well being, leaving Jenise and I to handle the things she should have.

We were left alone with our father, a man who took us to the bar and drank until he was incapable of driving. Even so, without blinking an eye, he'd head home, Jenise and I in his truck. It wasn't only Mom that gambled with us, but she was the one who was sober. She should have understood differently.

Sometimes, Dad couldn't even get out of his truck after we got home; he'd pass out behind the wheel right after turning off the engine or parking in the driveway.

Eventually, Mom had no choice.

She was faced with quitting her job or changing her shift so her daughters weren't home alone with her husband—a man who couldn't be trusted.

It took too many years for her to make that change.

In the meantime the same pattern continued.

My parents were so intent on escaping each other; they willingly abandoned their children. We were desperate to be held and loved. We simply were not *seen*. The magnitude of this was too much for me to fully grasp, even now at eighteen.

I let that knowledge steam. Boil. Churn. For too many years I let my mother and father's choices affect me.

Could I *really* change my future and live differently from the generations of men and women in my family who had come before me?

Was I destined to become just another distant relative talked about with regret over the holiday table? A woman who seemed to have everything going for her and had been too afraid to step away from her own shadows?

My parents made choices that were subtle and perhaps unintentional. They didn't understand the consequences—how discarded and unloved Jenise and I felt over the years.

Ultimately those choices taught me I'd be abandoned for multiple reasons: because of someone's work, their addiction, their denial, and their inability to cope with life.

Every time I thought I was whole, something triggered my shattering self-doubt.

Would anyone ever care enough to love me?

How could I believe anyone's assurances when my own parents didn't keep us safe?

Did they ever *really* love us?

Did Ryan ever love me?

I frightened Ryan.

Ryan frightened me.

Had my love for him been real or was I clinging to a man I saw as a distraction from my home life and a way out of it?

We were searching to break free of our abandonment issues, grasping blindly and stumbling along in our maze.

We didn't know how to let go of the fear.

Desperate to find security, love, togetherness and what it meant to be someone's woman or man . . . to finally learn how to gain the trust of another—these were the things we wanted in our lives.

Nothing comes without trust.

I knew as long as I held onto my fears, I'd never learn how to trust anyone—most importantly, myself.

I couldn't shake the feeling the next bad thing was ready to strike me.

Children of alcoholics know and believe this truth with every shred of our being.

The only time we feel safe is when we're alone and in control—at least, our perception of control.

Now *that* concept?

I trusted.

Chapter 10

A Shake-up

*N*ot long after Ethan headed across the field, my teammates returned.

"Can you believe it?" Colleen shouted. "Nicky, you should've been there!"

"Let me see!" I feigned happiness. "Where's the plaque?"

"With James." She turned her back on me.

It was as if I wasn't standing among them. They had immersed themselves in some new club and their enthusiasm was meant for members only. I regretted my decision not to go with them more than ever. Because of my choice, I'd separated and isolated myself from their joy.

An invisible line had been drawn between us.

A circle of five, closed without me.

Wearing my *mask of pretend,* I played the part of being strong. I stood just outside the conversation. Acted as if I was included.

Knew I was not.

As my teammates talked to each other, Matt and Darrell walked out of the tunnel and stood by my side. Matt told me that Tara wasn't feeling well and had gone to the doctor for some tests.

"What kind of tests?" A pang of worry beat from my heart.

"Pain in her abdomen," he said quietly. "I'd appreciate it if you could stay with her while I'm gone. Her mom's coming but she won't be here until next week."

"You don't have to ask twice." I put my hand on his arm. "I'd do anything for your sweet wife."

"Thanks, Nick. You've been a good friend to her—to us."

"Kevin said you didn't come in the clubhouse with the rest of the team," Darrell remarked. "How come?"

"You guys weren't there?" I questioned.

"The pitchers were in a meeting," Matt answered.

"I didn't go because I get claustrophobic in those tunnels." Again, I found myself in the world of half-and-half, some of it the truth and some of it a stretch of that same truth, bordering on a lie. "When I went through the tunnel after I sang the National Anthem, I freaked out. I don't want to go in there again."

"I didn't know that," Darrell said and then threw a ball to a little girl. "We gave you guys a plaque of appreciation and we all signed it. When you leave today, remember to pick it up from James."

"Thanks, Darrell. That means a lot."

"Such a great idea you had." Matt leaned in and gave me a hug. "Jose was one smart cookie to pass your business plan on to upper management. You know . . ." he whispered, "Tara's not the only one in love with you."

"I love you guys, too," I whispered back.

Colleen glared at me as she witnessed what she hadn't known

or paid attention to—like her, my friendships were also changing. The two men near my side were a part of my new circle and I cared less and less about her jealousies.

The life in which we were about to enter wasn't like high school.

It wasn't a zero-sum game for attention and love.

Another transition knocked.

It had only been a few weeks earlier I was enjoying school activities, sports, and volunteering wherever I could. Now? I felt as if some other woman had lived that life.

Alex and Tara had become better friends to me than Colleen and my other friends and teammates. I couldn't deny it—sadness had settled over me about the subtle changes.

I enjoyed knowing and loving women who were so accomplished, yet playful. They were inspirations, mentors, sisters, and sometimes parents—mostly they were my sweet, precious girlfriends.

"Congratulations, ladies," James held out the plaque as we exited the gate when the game finished. I reached for it. Held air.

Colleen had grabbed it just ahead of me and held it close to her chest. She was obviously proud. I didn't blame her. If she'd only asked, I'd have given it to her. I suppose there was some inner satisfaction in doing it the way she had.

Perhaps she was taking the first steps of reaching for her own independence and individuality.

"Can you get a ride home?" Colleen asked smugly. "We're going to Mel's so . . ."

"I'm not invited?" I double-checked.

"Aren't you busy with Ethan? I thought—"

"I'm not busy," I interrupted. *We just had this conversation. Have you checked out?*

The crossroad I was standing at made me crazy.

In one moment, I wanted to react like a child and throw a tantrum because I wasn't included. Then in another, I was an adult who wanted to rocket into her future and didn't give a damn about cliques.

That night I learned that I couldn't look back.

My childhood was officially over.

One of the clocks I'd watched all my life—the one of sweet moments with childhood friends—had stopped.

"Come with us, Nicky." Lorraine reached for my hand.

I was about to accept until Colleen shot her a nasty look.

The message was loud and clear.

I wasn't welcome as a part of their group that night.

"That's okay." I squeezed Lorraine's hand. "You should celebrate with each other. This night is yours and it's well-deserved."

My friends turned away.

I walked toward the streetcar platform.

"Nicky, do you need a ride home?" James shouted.

"Thanks, James, I'm all right," I yelled back.

"You shouldn't be out here alone. These streets empty pretty fast. And that wind . . . feels like a blade tonight," he observed.

"It *is* windy, I—" I tripped over a crack in the sidewalk and stumbled to my knees. Several people stopped to offer help. James came running at full speed.

"You okay, baby?" He helped me to my feet.

"Other than horrified at the grace I've just shown to the people of San Francisco? I'm fine." Once I brushed myself off, I thanked the others who had checked on me.

"Klutz," several teenagers kidded as they walked by. "Good thing the Goliaths don't play like you cheer," one of them added.

"I know." I tried laughing off my embarrassment.

Always count on teenagers for their blatant comments.

"You sure you're okay by yourself?" James held my arm.

"It's only ten and we're in tourist season. Thanks for asking. I'll be all right."

"You let me know," he pushed. "My baby doll will be here in a bit and I'd love y'all to meet. That girl's the love of my life, ya know. Hang around?"

"I do want to meet her, it's just . . . I'm not in the mood to be sociable tonight. Plus, now I've got a tear in the knee of my pants. No disrespect, but I think I'll head home and get some rest. Let's plan another time."

"You got my number, right?" He walked backwards, heading toward the gate so he could close up for the night. "Maybe next week the three of us can get together?"

"Sounds good. Goodnight, James baby!" I left him laughing and waited at the streetcar stop for transportation home. Then I changed my mind. The last thing I wanted to do was to walk into the house and explain why Ethan had stayed over—or answer questions about Ryan.

Instead, I went to my old friend, Java House, where an uplifting crowd could be counted on after the game. As soon as I walked in, the chatter helped to relax me. Wearing my cheer uniform meant that I'd have no trouble getting into friendly conversations with fans, helping me forget my awkward display outside.

The black and white linoleum squares, bright red leather booths, wrought iron chairs and bistro tables, were a throwback to my grandparents' era of old soda fountains and malt shops.

All I wanted was to fade into the background and enjoy the laughs and happiness of the fans. Like children, the customers talked about their baseball team with excited voices.

I wished I were one of them, still thirteen, sitting with Jerry.

After saying hello to a few of the fans I recognized, I spotted an empty seat in the back corner. When the waiter came to my table, I ordered a cup of coffee and a slice of berry pie à la mode. I reached for the comfort foods of my youth without giving it a second thought. They were the "friends" I'd had as a little girl. They never let me down and soothed my jagged edges.

Fragmented, irrational thoughts churned in my mind about the people in my life: Mom, Ethan, Jenise, Ryan, Tara, Matt, Alex, Dad, Jerry . . . distorted, circling, gray, blurred, swooping in, coming close and then flying away.

Would I need to take my meager savings and perhaps answer an ad on Craig's list for a roommate, work somewhere for a few years and save money, and then reapply to Stanford? Maybe it was easier to move away and go to a junior college.

Everyone would be gone soon, spreading like the white fluff of a dandelion in the wind.

Maybe if I did something drastic like . . . move to Hawaii? Would that be enough of a change or would I repeat the same fearful patterns there? Perhaps then I could make lasting relationships. No one would know about my twisted past and I wouldn't know theirs.

In a few minutes my dessert and coffee arrived. I poured a little cream in the mug and blended it with a well-used, dull spoon. Its round edges were grooved and scratched.

After a couple of bites of pie, I heard a commotion at the door.
What now?
I leaned out from my table.
I stretched to see around the people in front of me.
Customers had gotten up to surround the person who had just walked in the front door.

When his head lifted, I saw him.
My heart pounded.
His fans encircled him.
He looked directly at me.
Ryan.

Chapter 11

Is The Ground Shaking?

$\mathcal{R}$yan's body seemed to take up the entire front of the diner.

The scene reminded me of the first night we'd spent together. I'd wondered how he had fit through my bedroom doorway because he seemed so big.

His intense eyes focused on me.

I didn't want to look at him, let alone talk to him.

Where's the other exit? Maybe I can slip out while his fans swarm around him. Crap, the other door is alarmed. I don't want to make another scene. Guess I have to sit here and wait for him to make his move. Maybe he just wants to pick up his jacket.

I kept my head down and sipped my coffee while he took his time signing autographs and posing for pictures with his fans. He knew he had me cornered and could bide his time until he finally excused himself.

Is the restaurant shaking with his every step?

"Hi." Ryan slid in across from me.

"Hi," I looked down at the table. "What do you—" Before I could finish, I knocked over my cup, spilling coffee across the table. "Shit." I put my napkin down to soak up the spill, but it wasn't enough to get all the liquid. "Watch your clothes."

"I'll get a towel," he offered. He went to the counter and returned with a damp cloth. "Do you want another cup?" He dabbed the coffee from the table.

"Please," I requested timidly.

He exchanged the coffee-soaked cloth for another mug of java, shaking hands with people along the way. When he sat down, I knew I was about to experience his relentless questioning.

"What happened?" he asked bluntly.

I blended the cream into my coffee. Stirring. Stirring. Stirring it into the hot liquid as if trying to create a vortex into which I could escape. I didn't want to look at his eyes—those eyes that always captivated and stayed me, waiting to draw me in.

"I don't know, Ryan. You were there, so . . ."

"How come you're here by yourself?" He pushed forward as always.

"I felt like being alone."

"You're not meeting Jerry? Oh wait. It's Ethan this time, right? He crossed his arms. "How long until you slice *them* from your life?"

"Excuse me?" The dark clouds gathered. "Do I owe you an explanation? Weren't you the one who went cold?" *Force yourself to say what you need. End this now.* "You've got some nerve coming in here and pressuring me. This is *my* domain, not yours. And I can meet anyone I please. What's it to you? I got your message loud and clear back in Yountville. Believe me, I got it."

"Why aren't you with your friends?" His expression and voice remained neutral. "James told me they left without you tonight."

"They," I stammered fresh from the pain. "They left me alone. It's okay, though," I fibbed. "I felt like being alone, but . . . just . . . can you please leave."

"What's going on? You didn't go into the clubhouse, either. That's not like you to pass up an opportunity to add to your college resume."

"I don't know." I looked up from my coffee. "How did you find out I was here?"

"I asked Manny follow you and make sure you were all right. He let me know you wouldn't come to the clubhouse and you seemed . . . off. I'm worried about you."

I'm off? No kidding, I'm off. What kind of statement is that?

"Don't be concerned," I outlined the handle of my coffee cup with a finger. "I always land on my feet."

"Regardless," he sighed. "I'm going to stay with you and make sure you get home safely."

"What do you care?" I lashed out. "Isn't your only focus to get laid?"

Ryan picked up his chair and moved to my side of the table.

Oh, no. Stay away from me.

"Please leave me alone." I was rapidly losing steam. "You wound me up and made me believe you cared. I don't want to go through all that again." I looked away. The silence made me even more nervous. "I don't blame you. This is *my* fault. I led you on. Not on purpose. I didn't mean for you believe I was ready for sex. I thought I was clear about where I stood on a physical relationship. I'm sorry I—we. Actually *we* let each other down. I tried so hard not to do that, but the people I lo—I . . . care about . . ."

"Go on," he encouraged.

"Obviously we both . . . I'm no good at having relationships,

Ryan. I understand you need sex. I don't want any more seduction. We're smart to end this. All I want is for us to be friends that volunteer together—if we even can do that. We're both hurt so let's give each other space, okay?"

Don't cry, Nicky. Fight to stay in control and show him you're a strong, rational woman.

Even as I tried talking to myself, the tears flowed. I wasn't over him—not even close.

Ryan's big hands were gentle as they brought me to his body. The longer he held me against his chest, the more I relaxed.

Why am I so emotional with him?

I almost sighed in relief, resting on his magnificent mountain. I couldn't let on that he made me melt so easily, however and jerked away from his body. I was afraid we might be destined to repeat the pattern if I didn't do something. Falling in love and then pulling back again would mean the next time our heartbreak would be so much worse.

We needed to be over.

"You think you can take advantage of me because you know I'm weak; it's the way you've made yourself feel good. I know because I've done it with food. You're scared. I'm scared. We can't give in to our weaknesses. I confess that I'll always be attracted to you, but you know by now you need a woman who can play the same games you like to play. I'll never be open to you the way they are."

I just can't risk it, even though I want to . . . I want to . . . I want . . . you.

His arm slid over my shoulder. My muscles automatically loosened underneath the gentle massage of the back of my neck. Once again he pulled me into his chest. This time it was closer. His embrace tighter.

My will faded fast.

Mmm, what a nice bear hug.

His bulging forearms and beautiful biceps were firm, masculine and strong against my body. Sweetness covered me like buttery caramel—hot, bubbling, and smooth.

"You hurt me." His voice carried the sounds of quiet confusion. "You stabbed my heart. What did I do to deserve your withdrawal? And in front of my family."

"Because I didn't reach for you when you put your hand on my shoulder? I tried to cover you so your brother wouldn't make any of his sarcastic comments or get pleasure out of our turmoil." I tried to lift my head. He held me to his chest. *I don't want your hugs anymore, I don't want them, I don't want them, I . . . want them.* "You threw me away because I wasn't ready to have sex."

"No." His heart started to pound.

"*You're* the one who withdrew when I didn't give in. You pushed your way into my life, making me question everything . . . and for what? Why do that? How could you possibly be hurt?" I struggled to free myself but he kept his grip firm. "You turned your back on *me*, remember?" *Oh shit, here come the tears again.* "I believed all the wonderful things you said and you just—you promised you wouldn't let go of me. You said you'd wait for me! After only a few dates, *that's* supposed to be enough? You're no better than a high school kid." My sobs and tears spilled into his chest. I felt as if I were being sucked into his body.

"In fact, you're worse. What happened to all your so-called patience?" He continued to hold me within our distorted wreckage, perhaps fearing if he let go, we'd fall apart and the Band-Aids that held our fragile hearts together wouldn't be enough. "You drew me in with your golden words—and I fell for it. I knew better! What an idiot I was to trust you."

He finally let me lift my head. When he looked at me, I could see he was searching for the right thing to say and do.

"*Idiot*?" he shot back with sarcasm. I recognized it immediately. "You? Aren't *you* the woman who's on the fast track to Stanford? *Everything* is under your control and no one is getting in *your* way, are they?"

"Let me go," I wriggled from side to side to free myself from his hold. "I get enough sarcasm bullshit at home. I came here to be myself. Please leave me alone."

When I saw his tears, my heart began aching. Part of me wanted to continue attacking him with all the force I had. The other wanted to hug him. I couldn't help it. I looked into his eyes and saw the hurt. I frantically analyzed what was happening. Were the same fears seething within Ryan, rekindling the feelings of helplessness from his childhood?

Were they closing in on him?

Or closing in on me?

Had he lashed out at me the same way as he'd done to his father, who he never saw again? Was he afraid that like his dad, I might disappear?

I'd told him many times I *was* going to leave when I went to college. Did he finally hear the way sarcasm sounded, when spoken face to face and he didn't run away?

Maybe the lesson was for *me* to finally hear it's vicious tone when the man I loved used sarcasm on *me*. It cut into me differently hearing Ryan use it than when my family did. I found the pain unbearable that night.

"I'm sorry." He lowered his voice and rested his head on my shoulder. "I'm sorry I teased you about Stanford. And I'm sorry I made you feel bad."

"Too late for apologies," I warned. "I'm sick of taking everything in stride. I've played it safe for years, nurturing everyone's needs instead of my own—all so I wouldn't be abandoned or could escape. I suppose Dad will lose his job now, even though you promised to help him. Still, I'd never stay with someone who won't have a relationship with me unless I have sex. I might as well get used to junior college and start earning a living, huh?"

My airplane had sped down the runway, and my emotions took off.

"Maybe I'll work in some little diner where no one knows me. I've been thinking about moving away. Yeah. I'll go to college far away from here," I declared recklessly. "I tried us and we didn't work, so—"

"Are you finished?" he interrupted.

"No." Ryan searched my eyes. The longer he looked, the more I felt the strength of his stare. "For now," I relented, giving in a little.

"Can you look at me?" he asked softly.

"I don't want to." *Please don't explain or go into a long conversation. I don't want to be another woman dazzled by your glittery words.* "I don't want to see your looks and smiles. Feel free to leave me like you did the other day. Now I understand your expectations . . . and your disappointments."

"Nicky." He put his hand under my chin. "Look at me."

"Don't touch me," I said stubbornly. "Damn it, what?" I gave in. With tears in my eyes, I looked up at him. I tried to keep my anger red-hot. When I saw the sadness that had saturated his face, I couldn't help but soften.

"Please don't pull away from me," he pleaded. "I didn't leave you in Yountville. I don't ever want to leave you. You tear me apart when you accuse me of abandoning you. I wouldn't do that."

"You already did," I returned coldly.

Chapter 12

Fighting

" *Y*our anger hurts." He blinked. "Just for a moment, can you please stop hurling it at me? Please."

"Wait." I swallowed. "Let me get clear about this moment. In Yountville, weren't you the one who completely shut down and patted me on the back the next morning? I mean, *a pat on my freaking back*. What the hell was that?"

"It was . . . I'm trying to explain . . ." For a change his speech was scattered. He seemed frightened. "Can you allow for the possibility that there's more to me than some jerk who's only after your body? I'm asking you to search your heart. All I've been doing the last few days is searching mine. Will you?"

"Why should I?" I challenged. "After all, you said you're *rethinking* things, right? Let's see, how did you say it? Something like . . . if you decided we were okay, then I should leap back into your arms? Shouldn't we just admit we're not right for each other? Aren't we done?"

"What else?" he asked.

"What do you mean?" I countered.

"How else do you want to attack and slice me from your life?" He held my shoulders.

"Give me time to—"

"What other words do you have to pull out of your arsenal so you can shoot me down?"

"I . . . I don't know." It was almost like I was thrown in reverse. "Let's um, just . . . get this over with."

"Get this *over* with?" he retorted. "*Those* are the words you use to encourage the man who is reaching out to you?"

I looked away, unsure of how to respond.

"Will you listen to me?" His hand covered mine.

"Hmm." I pretended to be disinterested.

"I'll wait until I get a firm yes or no," he insisted. "I'm a friend asking you to listen. Can you?"

"Yes." I answered in earnest.

"Can I get you anything?" The waiter came to our table with a pot of coffee and a second mug. He looked at Ryan. "Coffee?"

"Sure."

"Anything to eat?" he asked after filling both of our cups.

"No thanks." Ryan shook his head and then took a sip of the black gold. He stared into the mug. I waited for him to begin again, knowing how difficult it was to put our feelings into words. When he looked up at me, his eyes seemed more focused and clear. "You say your friends have abandoned you—you say *I* abandoned you—but I only wanted time to rethink my options."

"Then you should have said that," I explained. "You barely spoke to me. We avoided each other all morning and you knew I felt bad."

"I know I should have," he admitted. "I was shaken. Confused. What happened . . . I blew it and I'm sorry."

"Everything seems to be shutting down," I said mournfully. "I don't know what to do."

"Nothing is shutting down for you. It's only that you've begun to leap into a new part of your life. Sometimes transition feels like a funeral. It's hard to believe it as they're happening, but those endings force us to grow." Suddenly Ryan's face flushed shades of red. He looked away from me. I had been so engrossed in our conversation I hadn't noticed a female fan had stopped to talk. "When we're done talking, my girlfriend and I will see if you're still here. For now, we need privacy."

She walked away.

The way he'd taken control and kept the focus on us made my heart beat with pride.

"Growth feels like death," I admitted cautiously.

"You've had a lot to deal with." He dipped a napkin into my glass of water and dabbed my eyes with it. "I can't imagine all the terrible things you've had to face at home with your father's alcoholism. In my opinion, the trouble you've gone through with your family has made you an amazing woman."

"Thanks, but—"

"Have you ever paused to think about why Tara and Alex got so close to you?" he interrupted. "They've witnessed the way you hope for the best. You want to embrace people. We feel it. Even though you're afraid, you try so hard to let them in. You take a chance and your eyes shine with such innocence and joy that it makes us feel good, too.

"I love that look," he searched my face. "I know you're afraid, but that look—the way you give—it's what made me fall in love with you. And by the way, do you really understand what you've done? To have the *first* business proposal you designed accepted by a franchise the size of the Goliaths? How much more do you have to accomplish before you realize you're a force?"

"It never feels like enough," I confessed.

"You've done it. You're on the way, Nick. The people at Stanford have seen everything before, and yet . . . you were accepted." He paused, and then in a thick and steady voice, said, "*I've* seen everything before. You're different."

"Being different hurts." His comment shook me. "All I've ever wanted was to fit in. I never could."

"As you become a more confident woman, you'll be thankful for your uniqueness." His eyes softened. "Tara, Matt, Alex and Darrell are all attracted to the maturity and wisdom in your heart. Those are people who are careful about inviting someone new into their lives. They listen to you. You can trust them and they trust you. Do you understand what I'm saying?"

"Yes."

"They see the generous, smart, loving woman you are. I see her, too. And I hope . . ." He let the words hang between us.

"What? You hope what?" I straightened, leaning and desperate to hear his words.

"I hope I'm the only one who can have all of you." He seemed exhausted and let out a long sigh. "I want to have you the way a man and a woman have each other. I need your intelligence, your loveliness, your magic—that essence from inside of you that made me notice you immediately."

What's wrong with me? I can't resist him. I've never heard anyone explain things the way he does. I feel hypnotized.

"Walter called me after you left his office." He raised his hand to get the attention of our waiter. He came to the table immediately. "I'd like a bowl of soup. Split pea."

102

The young man hurried to the counter, ladled the soup into a bowl and brought it to our table with two packets of crackers and a pat of butter wrapped in foil.

Ryan took several spoonfuls, leaving me hanging with the anticipation of what Walter had said to him.

"What did Walter say?" Finally unable to wait any longer, I asked what the comments were from his friend, high school coach and mentor. He was the man who'd helped him turn the corner and soften his rebellion after his father died.

"He spoke with the head of the business department at Stanford. Turns out they were hoping you'd begin in the fall. You already have their attention; they know you're going to be special. And even though Walter knows I'm desperate to have you in my life . . ." He trailed off and looked away.

"What?" I pressed again for the answer.

"He told me I should let you go."

I don't like the way that feels, but Walter is right. It's what we should do for each other. Oh damn, I don't know what to do.

"You need to experience all the things at college waiting for a single woman." He raked his hands through his hair. "The thought of not being with you makes me feel like screaming. I know we're right for each other. Why would you believe me now, I guess. I'm convinced whatever connection brought us here, we're meant to be. You'll be all right and I will, too. If we move on, I feel certain we'll never have what this is."

He lifted my hand and placed it on his cheek.

Ropes that had been wrapped so firmly, tightening around me every year, seemed to unravel.

"Don't you think if we're meant to be, we can start seeing each other again when I finish college?" I dared myself to say the words I'd been afraid of.

"If you turn the corner, I'll never see you again." His entire body seemed to shake. "You told me you can't watch me or anyone else pull away in their car or walk away from you? For me it's the opposite. I need to watch you for as long as I can."

Oh damn, I'm giving in.

"I know you're scared." His cell phone buzzed. "Sorry, I need to . . ." He took it from his pocket and looked at the screen. He smiled and put it away. "It's Chris. They're on the plane."

"I ruined your goodbye," I regretted.

"No. We're bleeding and need to find a way to forgive each other. This is important. Believe it or not, I'm scared the same way you are. If you shut me out we might never conquer our fears."

"I said before I want to be—"

"Friends," he acknowledged. "I don't want to be friends. I want you to be my best friend, my lover and my woman. Truthfully, I'm not sure I can look at you again if we don't make it together. I don't think I'll ever overcome it. You're intense. I feel drawn inside you and you in me, and—"

"You're not an easy person to be with, either. I don't—"

"I don't take for granted you have an entire vault of fears." He moved closer. "Can't you see me differently? Everything I've planned and done since we met has been for you."

"How can that be?" I whispered.

"I love you." He held my hands in his.

My thoughts circled, trying to form new conclusions. I was caught in the middle. Didn't know what to do.

You were so cold in Yountville—why didn't you text or call me that day?

"Don't leave me behind." He caressed my hair. "I promise I only mistook your signals. I didn't know what to do. You threw me like I never have been."

104

He kissed my cheek.

Rested his forehead on mine.

We quietly absorbed each other.

Continued to hold hands.

Wove our fingers together.

"I tried to let you in." I had calmed and was more rational. "You rushed me and then backed away when I didn't respond the way you thought I should. I'm not ready to open up physically—at least the way you're open."

"You don't understand how you rattle me. I thought . . . your signals in Half Moon Bay . . . you were naked with me . . . I thought you were ready."

"I never considered that," I admitted.

"We're both learning." He sipped a spoonful of soup.

"Your lifestyle won't let allow you to be patient. You come and go all the time on your road trips and everything is so big and fast. How can I trust you enough to even argue with you? You're gone for ten to fourteen days in a stretch and if you're mad there's always someone waiting. That's torture for me."

"*Us*," he corrected. "It's not easy for me to leave you either."

"Yes, us."

"Let your heart open to the possibility of love—my love. We can do it." He painted such a positive picture. I wanted to believe him. My whole body seemed to strain, yearning to move closer.

"We'll have to take risks if we want to be together."

"I have, though. I don't know how much further I can stretch myself. You've had the experience and practice that I haven't." I offered honestly. "That's the thing I'm most afraid of. If I don't give in . . . if I don't keep the peace—"

"Won't you jump in with me? When it comes down to it, aren't we both taking a risk?" He took my hands in his. "Yes, I have to go on the road and you'll be in school. I'll also be home all winter and half of the rest of the year. In summer, you'll be home. Give me a chance. If we don't work out, you're not stuck with me."

"I've never felt stuck with you." My senses were suddenly alive. I was trembling and tingling. I felt Ryan—and myself—in a new way.

"I don't want to lose you. When you fly away, I want it to be with *me,* Nicky." He let go of my hands. His thumb moved affectionately on my cheek. "Don't you understand why I backed off in Yountville? I needed to reassess *everything* I was doing. I thought because of the way we were together in Half Moon Bay a few days earlier you were ready to make love.

"When you retreated, you shocked me to my core," he continued. "What you don't know is, I was awake all night as you lay on top of me. Your sweet body was just like a soft kitten on my chest and hips, your bare breasts rubbing on me . . . I was trying to answer the question that kept returning—how could I get the trust of the sweet lady with me and have her in every way."

I didn't even think he was awake. Now he tells me he was thinking the whole night?

"Even in Yountville, as I watched you move, my mind wasn't on the vets. I was punishing myself for what I'd done wrong, trying to find a way to make the woman I'd held so closely, look my way forever." He paused. Searched my face. "Please accept my apology. I promise that I didn't intend to make you feel bad. I'm not going to look for someone else just because you hesitate with sex or disagree with me." He lifted my hand to his lips. Kissed it. My skin seemed to absorb the warmth. "The last thing I wanted to do was to make you feel abandoned. Do you believe me?"

I nodded.

"Will you talk to me instead of holding back and shutting me out going forward? This is the second time you've cut me off. The coldness is so final. You don't realize how it hurts."

"I do know the hurt," I replied. "You stood waiting for me with your back turned. The doubts . . . I was spiraling. I apologized to you and all you could say is you were rethinking everything. You wouldn't talk so . . ."

"I was trying not to let you see how sad I was. I felt broken." He brushed his cheek as if there were still tears on it. "I'm putting everything I have right in front of you. I'm not playing games and I wouldn't discard someone so precious."

We talked well into the early-morning hours.

I finally began to breathe normally.

Ryan's hands moved alternately from my cheek, hair, and my shoulders.

Slowly my fingertips walked to his.

I traced them lightly. Carefully.

Between the words, the fears, and reassurances, we dared take a small step into our unspoken dreams. We whispered it silently and out aloud, *I'm afraid and very fragile.*

We talked like adults. Friends. Peers. Not as a boy wanting sex from a girl or a girl afraid to have sex with a boy. That night, I felt like a woman who had an opportunity to become a part of a good man's life and bring that good man into mine.

Although I was tired of fighting, I started to understand—part of life, of love, of joy, of trauma, of dysfunction, and of striving forward—was the *fight.*

Fighting for what we want is normal.

Fighting for what we want is necessary.

Transitioning didn't mean I had to isolate myself from others or sever Ryan from my life. Our friendship solidified in that early morning. I knew he'd be someone who was in my life, forever.

Chapter 13

An Invitation

$\mathcal{S}$itting with Ryan at the Java House in those tender hours
of morning seemed to transform our connection from fragile and
broken, to woven and tight.

The night was unforgettable.

If I had never opened my journal to write it down, I would have
remembered every word of our conversation.

"You know, the deep feelings I've revealed aren't because of my
desire to have sex with you," Ryan lifted my chin.

"I know that," I managed a weak smile.

"Sex with you is something I want for more than one night,
one week, or one month. I want all of you all the time." He
tucked a strand of my hair behind my ear. "I want to take you
deep into a love affair. You're not a quick fantasy to me."

I felt as if we'd just finished telling each other all of our
secrets.

In some ways, that was exactly what had happened.

"I value who you are, Nicky. The things I see for us are too important to throw them away for a quick sensation of pleasure. I want to *add* to your life, not take from it. Do you believe me?"

"Yes." I responded immediately. "I always do."

"Are you sure I've answered your questions and addressed your doubts?" He kissed my cheek. "Let's get them out while our hearts are wide open. I'll stay here as long as you need."

"You've answered everything." I wiped my eyes. "I'm exhausted and I can't talk anymore." *My brain is on overload.*

"If you're ready, then." He held out his hand for me.

"We'd better look for that woman who stopped at our table," I reminded. "You don't want some bullshit online about what a jerk you are."

"I don't really care this morning." Like me, he was obviously spent. "But . . ." He strained his neck.

We spotted her sitting by herself on the other side of the diner. Now that I had some time to look at her, I saw she was an attractive lady with blond hair, somewhere in her mid-twenties. She had a good figure, was dressed in jeans and a loose T-shirt. She wore a ring on her finger.

"There she is," I pointed. "We'd better go over."

He left money for my coffee and berry pie—both unfinished.

"Sorry about being so abrupt earlier," he shook her hand. "Did you want—"

"My husband was a patient at the Veteran's Hospital in Yountville a few years back." Her eyes were brown and thickly lashed.

"What's his name?" Ryan's face softened.

Thank God we stopped to visit with her.

"Trevor Loughton," she said.

"How's he doing now?"

"Really good," she said. "He's on graveyard shift. I'm killing time waiting for him."

"Where does he work?"

"Across the street at The Towers. He handles security. I just wanted to get your autograph for him. He follows you and always brags about the visits he had with you."

"I'll do more than that." He reached into his pocket and pulled out his wallet, removed a card, and wrote something on the back. "Here's the number to my agent. Call her and give her the code I've written on the back. She'll get you tickets and let me know what game you're coming to so we can visit."

The tears welled up on her eyes.

"Thank you," she said weakly. "You're just as nice as he said you were. I'm sorry to have bothered you. I debated a while; I could see you were having a serious conversation, it's just . . . thank you."

"I'm Nicky," I shook her hand. "Ryan made me a big fan of the Veteran's Hospital. I volunteer there, too. You were no bother."

When we left it was a little after four in the morning. As we walked to the players' lot together, Ryan brought my right hand around his waist. His arm circled my shoulder.

Oh, whenever he does this I feel so safe; so breathless.

"Gentle woman," he sighed. "That's you. Your bark is fearless, but your bite . . . you're a sweet kiss waiting to happen, you know."

"Thank you." I was embarrassed he'd showered me with praise.

"And thanks for reminding me about her. I was ready to—"

"Dismiss her as another woman waiting for your attention?"

"Yeah."

"Ryan, you know I love when you do the hug thing."

"Hug thing?" He pulled me closer to his body.

"When you put your arm around my shoulder and take my hand to put it around your waist," I took a breath. "It's like everything's okay."

"It's a way we can be close until . . ."

"Until what?" I had to know everything.

Ryan stopped walking.

Faced me.

Placed both of my arms around his waist.

"Until you're confident that you're safe and ready for another level of intimacy." His body seemed to get bigger. "Until you trust me." His hands caressed my back. Before I could think of a response, he took me into his embrace, making me feel the power and want in his body. He kissed me deeply. His hands squeezed and then released parts of my body as if reviving me.

I didn't fully understand that at the time, that's exactly what our conversation had done—it had brought me back to life and helped me understand having relationships differently.

Leisurely walking his fingers through my hair, his beautiful, masculine voice seemed to sing to me. I knew it was only my ears that heard his deep-throated sounds, but they brought to mind those visions of intimacy he'd just mentioned.

His mouth covered my lips and his kiss took me into another dream. I knew that being his love was all that I wanted. Our kisses released the hurt.

We rejoiced in being together.

I wanted more.

We'd found each other again.

"I missed you." He opened the car door for me.

"Me, too." I looked at the ground. "I have a confession."

"What is it?" His fingers drew circles on my shoulder.

"Although I keep suggesting you're better off with someone

older, I don't want you to go with anyone else, it's just—"

"Just what?"

"I'm trying to communicate rationally and without so much emotion . . . you have to know someone older wouldn't put you through the things I have." I took a breath. "I could be all over the place for a while. To be honest, I don't know if I'll ever settle with it. My feet want to take off before I open my mouth because I can't see how we'll work together."

"All I ask is we keep talking. If we make a promise to talk through our fears, we'll become more comfortable as something challenges us." When he smiled, the twinkle in his eyes seemed to light up the entire area.

We were silent on the drive home. He pulled to the curb and left the engine running when we reached my house.

"Good night, sweet Nicky. See you tonight."

"Tonight?"

"Our double date with your sister and her boyfriend."

"Oh, God. You still want to?" I was only half-kidding.

"You know I do."

"What about Chris and Frances? Weren't they leaving for Seattle after the game? Where are they?"

"They already took off," he reminded. "Chris—"

"That's right, he texted you. I'm sorry. I know I'm the reason you didn't see go to the airport. I left them with a terrible impression. I embarrassed myself and you . . ."

"No," he shook his head. "I explained how I made a mistake. They understood and haven't judged you."

"I'm sorry I let you down," I added.

"I let *you* down." He turned off the car. "You didn't attack me in front of my brother. It took courage and maturity it took to do that." He took a deep breath. "You could have let me have it and I fully expected it. Even in anger you stuck up for me."

I put both of my hands on his heart.

"I hope I can grow my own heart to match yours, Ryan."

All the anger I felt during the past few days spiraled up and faded away. The embers that had previously scattered into dead ashes swirled back into my heart as glowing certainty.

Lifting my hands from his chest, running my fingers through his golden brown hair, I was overcome with the desire to taste his kisses once more and placed my hands on his cheeks to coax his lips to mine.

We gave ourselves over to each other.

Our souls entwined once again, sharing a light that had temporarily left us. Our mouths created the connection I longed for and I kissed him until I felt the urge become full in my belly.

"Do you want to spend the night?" I pulled away, almost gasping within the heaviness of my breath. "We can lie together just like the first time you stayed in my bedroom."

I dreaded having people come to my house spontaneously, earing my father would show up drunk. With Ryan and oddly enough with Ethan, I didn't worry about either of them being exposed to my family's dysfunction—and just as important—they wouldn't judge me. Each man seemed to be on a different level of maturity than my friends had been over the years. When I was with them, I felt courageous and bold. I was ready to shout out to my family, *"This is my life, too! I'm not hiding anymore!"*

"It's almost morning anyway. We could sit on the sofa or lie on my bed and just talk. We can go get breakfast, I . . . I want to be with you, and I—"

"I know, Nicky, but—"

"Now that we've talked everything through, I don't want to let go of this—or us," I interrupted. "I was so devastated before."

114

"Why?" he caressed my hair.

"Because."

"*You're* seeing other people. Why did it make you feel bad when you thought I'd given up on us? Why shouldn't I see other women?" Ryan asked pointedly. "You see Jerry, you've made friends with Ethan—aren't you holding me to a double standard?"

"I guess it looks that way. I'm not seeing other boys the way you just inferred, though."

"How long should I stay away from other women before you say, *Ryan, you're the one.*" He rolled on. "How long are you asking me to believe and wait for you? You torture me with kisses. Your body pushes out to me. Tell me why I should trust you. Tell me. I need to hear you say it. Why should I wait for you?"

His voice was calm. Loving. He urged me to dig deep. Claim my love and say aloud and without hesitation, *I love you, Ryan. I only want to be with you. I choose you.*

"Because, well, I know I sound like a hypocrite, and um . . . I guess I am in a way, but . . . because . . . I'm not having sex with anyone and you're . . . um, more than just a friend. I have strong feelings for you. Very strong."

I can't say the words. I want to scream them, tell you that I love you, but I can't.

"That's what you say," Ryan's eyes were steady. "I can hear you're trying. The thing is, friends have strong feelings." He breathed deeply. Called my name several times. His lips touched my ear as he spoke. "Nicky," he whispered.

"Nicky." The way his breath caressed my face was as if a light breeze had brushed by me. "Why were you devastated? What are you trying to say?"

"I care deeply about you." The words caught in my throat.

"That's not enough," he persisted. "Tell me. Rip your heart

from your body and show it to me. Why, Nicky?"

"Come up to my room and we can kiss again." My body screamed. I yearned for him. "When we were on my front porch, you asked me to call Jerry and cancel my evening. Stay with me now. Cancel everything for me."

"You can't understand how tough it is for me to say no." He continued to caress my hair. "We're both vulnerable right now. If I step foot in your bedroom—I don't want to take a chance we'll give in sexually because of where we've just been. We're both weak. You may think you only want me to lie with you, but the look in your eyes says more. If you open to me that way, I won't be able to stop."

"I'm ready," I insisted. "Forget all that and come with me." I tugged on his arm. *What are you saying, Nick? You're ready to give in to him sexually? Are you thinking this through?*

"This isn't the right time . . . especially under your parents' roof. During the light of a new day you'll feel like I took advantage of you. And you'd be right."

"No, I won't, Ryan, I—"

"This isn't the right time," he repeated. "I'd like nothing more than to make love to you. This isn't the morning."

Our foreheads touched.

My mind was finally settling. It seemed as if Ryan's did as well. We knew we needed to break from our embrace. Neither of us wanted to separate. As I lay my head against him, his heart beat steady, strong, and fast. It sounded like an echo moving through a tunnel from deep inside his body, then his chest, becoming shallow as it traveled up to his throat and escaping softly across his tongue in a warm wish.

"You'd better go." He brushed my bangs aside. "If you don't leave pretty soon, I *will* spend the night, and the way we're giving into each other . . . I'm barely holding on."

"I don't want to go inside. Let's sleep in your car," I giggled half-heartedly.

"I have to be up in a few hours. We should say good night." He turned his head and yawned. "Sorry."

"I'm a bad girlfriend, keeping her boyfriend up too late."

"You're the sweetest girlfriend this boy could ever hope for."

I scooted off the seat and was ready to close the door.

"Nicky!"

I knelt on the passenger seat.

"I didn't buy you the emerald necklace to bribe you for sex; it's to honor our friendship. It's yours to keep."

"Roll your window down." I shut the door and walked around to the driver's side. "Now keep your hands on the wheel and don't take them off." I instructed and then kissed him. "Good night. I care a lot for you, Ryan. I know I've said it a million times and you're tired of hearing it, but I'm so afraid of new relationships. Especially with boys—well, men."

"What you didn't understand before tonight is that I'm afraid, too. Being without you the past few days . . . my arms were lonely and my hands empty. I longed for the sound of your voice. My eyes search for your sweet face wherever I go. Baby, I need to see or talk to you every day; I can't go without some part of you."

"I want that, too." I pressed his hands to the wheel when he started to reach for me. "No, no," I teased. "We'll never be done with goodbye if we keep this up. Good night." We kissed again. Forcing myself to turn from him, I walked toward my house.

Fearing he'd never return, I didn't look back.

When I closed the front door, I heard him pull away.

I walked silently upstairs and dropped my cheer uniform on my bedroom floor. When I climbed into bed, I thought about Ryan and how he'd made sure I felt safe. The time he'd taken to talk things through was courageous. He'd taken a chance. I was angry and yet he took a risk I'd listen to him.

I knew it was time to take the same risks he had.

As the night faded, I felt the internal chains in my body release.

It was as if I had been holding onto a cliff all my life, digging in with fingertips, afraid I'd fall, while the pebbles, rocks and boulders dropped around me into the abyss below.

Suddenly, I felt a weight lift off of me.

I stood on the edge.

Looked down on the debris.

My thoughts and views were changing.

All of my life's trials, bruises, and errors happened so the deep crevice could fill up and allow me to step down. I hadn't understood until that night, those boulders had to fall. By taking a risk, each pebble that plummeted filled up the darkness.

My fears of abandonment, of being vulnerable and intimate, made me believe that something bad was going to happen. I had been unable to trust any one person, situation, or relationship—especially the one with myself.

The lessons of life pounded down. Began to refine me. Changed my course and direction. Forced me to look inside myself—deeply inside of myself.

At last I was opening a new world.

Chapter 14

Getting Ready

*S*aturday morning.

I knew I wouldn't join my teammates to cheer at the ballpark. It was the first day I'd missed since we began. The last three nights had been emotionally draining and I needed to rest. I felt exhausted in every way.

My cell phone rang shortly after I texted Colleen to let her know of my decision. My heart jumped. I'd hoped it was one of my friends checking in to make sure I was okay.

Instead? It was Jerry.

Oh no. I don't want to talk to you yet. I need to have a tough discussion with you and haven't gotten a chance to put my thoughts together. Whelp, no sense in avoiding what will only get tougher with the passage of time.

"Hi, Jer."

"Hey, Nick."

"How are you?" *Can he hear my voice trembling? Poor Jerry. What do I say? Do I begin with, "I've fallen for someone else, but I hope we can still be friends?"*

"Great! Just wanted to confirm our date on Monday, gorgeous *baby*," he teased.

"Um . . ."

What do I do? I can't go on a date with him. Do I tell him now? Or do I let him think everything is okay and wait until he gets home to reveal my feelings?

"Yeah." I couldn't decide on the right thing to do. I only knew that telling him over the phone wasn't okay. "Still hitting well?"

"Def." He was bursting with enthusiasm. "I worry about going into a slump at the wrong time, though. I'm so superstitious that I make sure to do all the same routines so I don't jinx it! I even wear the same briefs—washed, of course."

"Of course." I cracked up. "You've worked too hard for too many years. If you do slump, you'll make an adjustment. You're an awesome baseball player."

"Thanks for that. By the way, what's going on with your Facebook?"

"It's . . . I really don't know what to do with it, Jerry."

"Ethan Mathers? He's one of the Avengers' top prospects. I've followed him when he was drafted to semi-pro. When did you meet? When you were cheering, I guess?"

"Oh, it's a long story. I'll tell you when you get back."

"I feel like you're slipping away sometimes." His voice saddened.

Crap. What do I say now?

"No, I'm not. Cheering for the Goliaths allows for opportunities to meet a lot of people, that's all. You and I will be friends forever. Don't get down."

"I hope that's all it is. So . . . I've been doing a lot of online work, if you know what I mean."

"Yeah." *Shit. I know what you mean all too well.*

"Have you been doing *your* research?"

Before Jerry left for a week of summer baseball and on our last date we'd had a long discussion about all things sex: having it, protection, what form of birth control to use, and researching ways to pleasure each other, making our first sexual experience together more enjoyable.

He took no time in reminding me where we'd left off.

"Let me know when you're home." I ignored his direct statement. "We'll get together after you've had a chance to relax." *Then I can tell you about my feelings for Ryan.*

"I'll relax with *you*," his voice was low and muffled.

"Okay," I swallowed hard. "Bye, Jerry."

"Wait!"

"Sorry, what is it?" I almost hung up the phone.

"I want to talk for a while."

He continued, focused on his baseball life. He didn't ask too many questions about me. I was a good listener and didn't mind him telling stories of what had happened when he was away. Another hour and we said goodbye. Terrified when I revealed my feelings, he would become angry, I was even more afraid that after talking with him he'd never forgive me.

I wasn't ready to lose his friendship.

He was one of the last links to my grade school days and he knew things even my sister didn't know.

Jerry would show up to school with bruises on his arms. No one knew but me what had really happened. I was there for him when his dad got too physical and he was there when my household fell into an alcoholic's rage.

We ran away with each other and hid in the backyards of our friends' houses.

We'd bicycle to the beach or just around the block—sometimes ten circles or more—whatever it took to wait for peace to settle again in our houses.

Would it be automatic that we wouldn't see each other if I said no to having sex with him? *Could* men and women be friends, even if they were once attracted to each other?

When my cell phone beeped with a text around noon, I was certain *this* time it *would* be Colleen. A feeling came over me as if warm honey drizzled down my entire body when I saw Ryan's name.

He texted: *Where r u*

I responded: *Home, c u 2nite*

He texted back: *Can't w8. I have "!!!" 4 u*

I texted: ? *'!!!'*

He returned: *Surprise*

I sent: *Can't w8*

When I checked in with Jenise, I found her primping for our evening with the boys. She let me listen in as she practiced the important introduction of her African-American boyfriend, Sean, to our parents. We talked for more than an hour about how they were going to do it. I admitted to her that I was glad I wasn't in her shoes and admired their courage.

I'd just gotten a bottle of water from the kitchen when the doorbell rang. It was about three. I opened the door to find an attractive man dressed in black jeans and a gray muslin shirt, standing on our front porch. His smile alone made me understand how Jenise had fallen under his spell.

"You must be Sean." I extended my hand. "Nice to meet you."

Sean had incredible big, brown eyes, long eyelashes, and a

lean, well-proportioned body. His dark hair was short and thick, framing his high forehead.

"Same here." He shook my hand. "Sean Taylor."

"Nicky. Come in." I stepped aside to let him walk through.

"Your sister brags about you so much that I feel like I already know you."

"Likewise, she's—"

"There's my baby!" my sister shouted from the top of the stairs. She glided into Sean's arms.

"Wow!" I exclaimed. "You look beautiful, sis."

Dressed in skintight white pants, black heels, and a low-cut, sleeveless, shiny black shirt, Jenise was stunning.

"Thanks!" Jenise barely looked at me. She was only interested in her striking boyfriend. After they kissed, she took his hand. The time had come for the two of them to meet the judge and jury that waited in the kitchen.

"Good luck you guys," I offered hopefully.

My sister never took her eyes off her sweetheart as they walked down the hallway toward the kitchen.

The doorbell rang again. This time I opened it to find a delivery woman with a box and a bouquet of flowers. I signed her tablet and closed the door. The flowers had a card tucked into the tissue paper surrounding them. It was addressed to my mother.

"I'm sorry to interrupt." I dared to interrupt the serious conversation of my parents and their daughter and her boyfriend. "Mom, can I see you a minute? A delivery came for you."

She stepped into the hallway.

"Here." I handed her the flowers. When she looked at the card, her expression warmed. I couldn't wait to hear her read it. "What does it say?" I asked impatiently.

When I'd gotten my flowers on prom day, Mom had also been

anxious to know what my card read. I'd brushed her off. The memory made me realize how I'd chosen my own codependent path, burying myself in anything but my family.

My chest tightened as I thought about that moment.

She read it to herself and then said, "For a woman as lovely as her daughter—Ryan." She turned to face me. "Remember when I told you that you'd have to make your own decision about him? He doesn't miss much, does he?"

"No, he doesn't." *If you only knew . . . he's murder!*

I picked up the large box with my name on it and headed up to my room. Looking back quickly, I saw her bury her nose in the bright yellow roses. An obvious melancholy swept through her. I set the box on the step and walked downstairs.

"It's been years since I've gotten flowers." Her eyes glistened with tears.

"Now you understand, Mom." Although she had difficulty putting her arms around me when I needed her, I couldn't help but give her a hug.

She nodded. Carried the flowers into the kitchen.

I took the box up to my room, set it on the bed, and opened it. A card on top of the delicate paper read: *This is so you don't have to borrow clothes from your sister. If you'd rather not wear them, it's okay, Love, Ryan.*

I carefully folded the paper into a square and tucked it into my journal. In the box were a pair of flat, black ankle boots, a black knit top with long sleeves, dark blue jeans, and a matching short denim jacket with rounded edges. It came to my waist. I smiled as I considered how in tune Ryan was with my style.

I'm training him well. Or is he training me?

There was a smaller box that contained a pair of diamond-shaped emerald earrings; they matched the necklace he had bought for me earlier in the week.

You had this planned all along. What a sneaky boyfriend.

Still sleepy because of the dramatic events over the last few days, I needed to take a nap before we left so I'd have enough energy to last the evening. In what seemed like only a few minutes, my sister knocked on my bedroom door.

"Nick! You ready?" She barged in unapologetically. "It's six o'clock. Ryan is on his way."

"I need a few minutes." As I focused, I noticed that every part of her outfit, makeup, and hair was in place.

"Make sure you do yourself up right. This isn't a night for innocence and daisies," she chastised. "We're going to have a few beers and rock out! Take more than a few minutes, for God's sake. Do you need any help?"

I winced at her comment about having a few beers and hoped that number was all she planned to have.

"Ryan sent me an outfit—look. Isn't that romantic?"

"Does it fit?" My sister teased, watching me put on the jeans.

"Oh, man, I can hardly . . . let's see, if I squeeze this way—there. Damn, they're tight. I can hardly breathe. My damn ass—I have such a hard time finding pants."

"Gee, I wonder why Ryan got *that* size," she giggled. "Probably to get a good view of that gorgeous ass."

"You really don't think that, do you?" I asked with a look of panic. "He wouldn't, would he?"

"Uh, no, not your sweet little Ryan," she mimicked.

I was embarrassed at the thought and looked away.

He wouldn't be this bold so soon. We just agreed after our long talk this morning to take it slow. He probably misjudged the size.

"Sean and I suggested we go to a movie first. Afterward, we'll go to the Waterfront Café. You know, that club near the ballpark? They've got live music tonight. How does that sound?"

"When did you guys decide all this?" I fastened one of the emerald earrings.

"Wednesday, when you and Ryan went out. What happened that night, anyway? Something wasn't right."

"I'll tell you about it later." I didn't want to talk about our drama. "What if they won't let me in? God, how embarrassing." *Damn, more dancing.* "I'd have to take a cab home while you guys have your fun."

"You didn't have a problem at Gary's, did you?" Jenise reminded me.

"No, but that's a restaurant first and a bar with dancing second. It could happen. You never know how carefully they'll examine my driver's license. I—"

"Nicky, they're not going to question you when they see who your date is. Besides, if you had a problem he wouldn't stay without you. I mean, really, sis!"

"No, I know." *Would he really stay with me?* "Hey, how did it go with Sean?"

"Mom and Dad were a little reserved, but overall not too bad." She looked happy. "For our first meeting, we're okay with how they reacted."

"I'm glad." It was as if I breathed with her. "I'll get ready now. Close the door, okay?"

After she left, I freshened up and then pulled my hair back with a black headband. It lifted and tossed my long, wavy hair so it stayed off my face and cascaded down to my lower back. I finished the look with the other earring and the emerald necklace Ryan had bought for me.

The doorbell rang a few minutes later.

I heard my boyfriend walk in and greet my family. His rich,

masculine voice took every breath from my lungs.

Chapter 15

A Double Date With Sis

*S*tanding out of sight at the top of the stairs, I listened as Jenise introduced our boyfriends to each other. I could only imagine their masculine handshake routine and "bro" conversation. Taking several deep breaths, I walked to the area where I could see them and stood back to watch.

"We'll be out late, Mr. and Mrs. Young." Ryan's hand was on my father's shoulder. "Don't worry about your daughters. They'll be in good hands. I don't drink. I've taken lessons in race car and defensive driving and know how to handle a vehicle."

I wonder what Dad thinks about his comment. Hell, I wonder what he thinks about being touched? My family never does that.

Shades of judgment washed over Dad's face. Still, he seemed to listen to Ryan.

My sister held Sean's hand. Her eyes were bright and seemed filled with excitement.

Two strong men were taking his daughters out for an evening—possibly into another life.

The days of being subjected to his rage were over.

Every decision of how we moved forward was ours to make.

Mom looked at the yellow roses, now in a vase on the coffee table.

Never missing a thing, Ryan's eyes went from Mom, to the flowers, and back to Mom. I could read the satisfaction he felt by the look on his face as he realized she had been deeply touched.

"Do you like the roses, Mrs. Young?"

"I do. Thank you, Ryan. I was telling Nicky it's been years since I've gotten flowers—especially roses."

"You deserve them," he remarked.

How is Dad handling my boyfriend sending his wife flowers when he knows it's been forever since she's gotten any? Maybe he never let Mom know how special she really is.

"Wow, you look great, sis." Jenise noticed me standing to the side. She turned to Ryan, who spun to look at me. "Thank God, you got her something to wear. Otherwise, you'd have seen her running down the stairs in something of mine!"

"Shut up, Jenise," I kidded. "No I wouldn't. She's always saying stuff to embarrass me." I made the comment to no one, but then again, everyone seemed to have heard it.

Ryan wore faded blue jeans, a crisp looking white shirt with the collar pulled wide-open, black shoes, and a grey jacket. It was accessorized with a sharp looking black knit scarf, untied, hanging evenly on each side of the jacket. He walked over to me and kissed my cheek.

Oh, those lips . . .

Mom and Dad looked on cautiously.

Were they being concerned parents? Or did they finally realize their daughters were at the point of major transitions? They'd numbed themselves for so long—had they even seen it coming? Dad offered a simple goodbye. Mom reached for her cell phone to take a picture.

"You can trust me, sir." Ryan repeated his last statement and kept his hand extended until my father shook it.

"You *really* don't drink?" It was obvious from Dad's tone he didn't believe that a man like Ryan could stay away from alcohol.

"No, I don't," he reassured. "I haven't for a few years."

Our father accepted whatever silent agreement had just been made between them. We all said goodnight.

"Now that I know you like my arm around you . . ." Ryan's strong arm slid around my shoulder as we walked to his car. It felt natural. Effortless. He was mine and I was his. It was as if the heat from his body flowed from my neck, to my shoulders, and down my spine. I felt the soft whisper of two souls becoming one.

"Do you want to drive, Sean?" Ryan tossed him his car keys.

"Thanks!" Sean's smile told us he appreciated the gesture. "I've never driven a Land Cruiser. Handles nice?"

"Like she's on rails," Ryan flattened his hand and slowly moved it through the air, visually demonstrating the way he perceived the capabilities of his car. "Eight cylinders, 381 horsepower, Bluetooth, voice command, and dual controls for just about anything you want. Look at the screen and the menu will lead you through what you need."

I laughed to myself at the natural male bonding that seemed to form over cars and trucks.

"Sean's a good driver, don't worry." Jenise eagerly scooted alongside of him.

Ryan opened the back passenger door. He waited until I was

settled and then slid in next to me, holding my hand all the way to the theater. In some ways, it seemed as if we were starting over. He was careful about touching me, intent on being a perfect gentleman.

"Are you tired, Ryan?" Jenise asked. "Sean told me you pitched. I'll have to pay more attention to baseball. Of course your girlfriend fills me in on absolutely everything you do."

"Oh, really?" He turned to me.

Oh, God. Don't start the fire already.

"That's all I hear about. Ryan this and that, and he just got his fortieth save and blah, blah. Anyway, tough game?"

"Uh-huh. I need to rest on your sister it was so tough. In fact, I think I need to sit extra close so she can help me relax." His grin was wicked. "Maybe she needs to be on my lap."

They all laughed. I wondered what it was about me that was so entertaining.

"I talked to someone in my graphic-design class today," Jenise turned halfway around in her seat. "He's just reentered college and said he enrolled in one of your networking groups."

"Which one?" he leaned forward a little.

"The one for returning vets. When he was discharged, he was referred to SF State because of the support your group offers. When he told me, I said, I know that guy!"

"What's his name?" Ryan questioned.

"Hal Mesa."

"I remember him," Ryan stroked his chin. "Beautiful family, two little girls—his wife is Madeline?"

"Yeah, that's right!" Jenise clapped her hands. "Anyway, he told me he and his family came to a meeting you hosted. He said you were unusually humble for someone in your position. You made a big impression."

"Cool," he said. "Thanks for telling me. One of the requirements of being in the program is having a support network. They bring family members, friends, and anyone critical in their lives to the first meeting. We chart a plan for them largely dependent on the support they have."

"He's so good with people." I couldn't help chiming in. His generous spirit made me want to brag about him. "You should see him in public, you guys. Well, you will tonight, but he takes his time when he meets his fans. He makes everyone feel like they matter. He's so thoughtful."

"Nicky, what a nice thing to say. Isn't my sister a sweetie?"

"Yes, she is." Ryan kissed my hand.

I looked out the window, embarrassed that I'd made such a fuss over my boyfriend.

When Sean parked the car, Ryan got out before me.

I scooted to the edge of the seat to step out to the curb.

His hands went around my sides.

He lifted me to his body.

My feet dangled a few inches above the ground.

How can he hold me like this?

"I see you're wearing the earrings I sent you." He shot me a devilish look.

"And the necklace," I added. "Did you notice?"

"I noticed." He laughed his one syllable, low-toned, sexy sound, kissed my cheek, and then let me touch the ground. "So, you like the outfit?"

"I do. It's too tight, though. I can't breathe. I think the size is wrong and—"

"Oh really?" he winked. "Whatever could I have been thinking? I tried to get something that wouldn't accentuate your—"

"My what?"

"Your . . . beautiful . . ." He took a deep breath. "That curvaceous . . . never mind."

"You're making fun of my butt." The nerves in my belly fluttered. "Nothing fits right. I hate it."

"Oh, baby, there's nothing back there to hate. In fact it's uh . . . quite spectacular." His tone was suspiciously smooth. "Why don't you walk ahead of me so I can look at it—I mean, look at you. Um . . . *watch* you is what I meant."

"God, Ryan."

I don't need to hear everything that's on your mind.

Jenise and I sat next to each other during the movie. Our dates sat on either side of us. I watched how tender she was with Sean. Automatically, she slipped her arm in his, rested her head on his shoulder and gave him the occasional kiss on the cheek or lips.

"They really seem to be good together, don't you think?" I whispered to Ryan.

"They're in love," Ryan shared. He didn't attempt to kiss or put his arm around me. Although he was being a good Boy Scout, I wanted his touch. I couldn't wait any longer. After all, even a Boy Scout liked to hold a girl's hand.

"I don't mind if you put your arm around me," I hinted. "I didn't mean we couldn't touch when I asked you to go slow."

Immediately, he lifted the armrest and pulled me close so that I could put my head on his shoulder. Jenise shot me a glance and smiled. We were two sisters on a double date with our special men and another photo filled the memory book in my mind.

"Let's go party!" My sister stood up as soon as the movie ended. "I'm starving. I can't wait to hear the band, can you, Sean?"

"Can't wait, Neesee," he answered. "I'm looking forward to some slow dancing with you, babe."

"*Neesee*?" I raised my eyebrows.

"My nickname!" Her whole body seemed to come alive. It was as if she had an aura that glowed around her. "He used to call me Pima."

"How did you come up with *that*?" I asked Sean.

"Your sissy was a big pain in my ass," he laughed. "So, P.I.M.A. fit her. But then, well, she wasn't a pain after all."

They're so sweet together!

"Maybe you can sing a song tonight," My sister announced.

"I heard you sang the National Anthem at one of the Goliaths' games," Sean commented. "That must have been an awesome experience."

"Yeah, it was. It feels a little surreal now. When I went through the tunnel it was kind of traumatic for me." I looked at Ryan.

"I've heard you say that," Jenise commented. "But I've never known why. What happened?"

"Everything seemed to close in on me. I couldn't catch my breath." I pulled on my shirt as if it constricted my airflow. "Just in time, some nice fellow walked me all the way to the door to make sure I was all right."

"You never told me that story." She turned to Ryan. "She didn't tell me or anyone else too much until recently. In fact, you know, Ryan"—now she was rolling—"you've actually helped open my sister in a lot of ways. Now, if you can just get her to let you in other areas of her life you'll have it made."

Everyone tried not to laugh.

"You're not funny, Sis."

"Yes, I am," she lifted her chin confidently.

"I'm working on her." Ryan's lips quivered, revealing his amusement.

"Okay, I heard *that* comment long ago, Mr. Tilton. If I

remember rightly, it was after our first visit to Yountville."

Another one of his sexy laughs broke the sound barrier.

"Where did you get this necklace?" Jenise held the emerald that dangled from its gold omega chain around my neck. "I've never seen this."

"Where do you think?" I patted Ryan's chest.

"Aw," she made kissy lips. "Sweet gifts already? Hmm . . ."

I kissed his hand and we walked into the lobby. Several people recognized my date. The whispers and calling of his name began. As soon as a few people approached him, many others followed. I knew we'd have to step aside.

Waiting with my sister and Sean, we watched more than a dozen families and couples ask to pose with him. He knelt down for the younger children. One little girl kissed his cheek.

"You're my favorite," she said in a sweet voice. Her arms hugged his neck and her face blushed scarlet.

The look of endearment was all over Ryan's face.

It's obvious having a family is one of his dreams.

"Thank you," he said softly. "You know what? Your hug and kiss were just what I needed. Now I just *know* I'll pitch a great game tomorrow."

"See, Mama? It was okay!" the girl said excitedly. Her parents beamed as they shook his hand and thanked him.

He stood in the middle of young and old, grandparents who talked about watching years of Goliaths' baseball at the old stadium, and teenage boys who wanted to know how he pitched so fast. While answering their questions he signed autographs, posed or pictures, listened to their jokes, and discussed the team's chances for the playoffs.

"My friends won't believe this," a boy about fourteen said. "Thanks, Mr. Tilton."

"Ryan. Just call me Ryan. Do you come to any of the games?"

"My friend and I go once a month." The teenager was so excited he seemed to click his heels. "We sit in the third level. The seats are only eight dollars up there. Still awesome, though."

"Call this number when you can get to a game," Ryan pulled a card from his wallet, the same kind he had given to the woman waiting for her husband in Java House. "They'll upgrade you to a couple of box seats. Come to the railing and say hello next time you're at the stadium."

"I know you won't remember me," the young man's voice was laced with tones of self-imposed disappointment. "Thanks, though. This is really cool."

"Oh, I'll remember you," Ryan assured him. "Faces are my specialty." They talked for a few minutes and then he moved on to the last few fans waiting to speak with him.

"You're right," Jenise leaned over to me and whispered. "He *is* good with people."

"I know," I confirmed. "He's just . . . magical." I wasn't sure I breathed as I watched him walk over to me. He held my hand as we walked to his car.

"You're nice to your fans," Sean commented.

"Well, it's part of the gig. Without them," he shrugged his shoulders, "where would I be?"

"You make me feel good when you stop and spend time with people." I squeezed his hand. "The smiles on faces of those kids . . . the adults, too . . . you just made their night."

When we arrived at the car, I waited for him to open the passenger door to the back seat. Instead, he turned me around to face him. His look had gone from pleasant to sensuous. He pinned my back against the Land Cruiser.

"Tell me now if you don't want me to do this." His voice was breathy. "I can't hold back any longer."

Without waiting for my response, his mouth found its perfect fit. Slowly his lips opened mine. I let out a little moan. He fed me sugarcoated promises with every press of his lips and touch of his tongue. His body was on mine in so many places it was as if warm pulses and tingles lit up everywhere. Soft, muffled sounds of pleasure from his throat made the burn deep inside my body swell and alerted me to how much I wanted him.

"I guess you didn't mind." The desire within his sensual tone wrapped me inside it. "Should I stand with you a minute?"

"You get in the car first," I avoided looking at him.

"Why?" His voice was husky, alive, and beckoning.

"I need to keep my eye on you," I teased weakly.

His electric laugh raised every hair on my head.

I watched the way he moved as he got in the back seat and anxiously followed.

Looking at his butt wasn't too shabby, either.

Chapter 16

Waterfront Turbulence, Part I

𝒯requented by friends, families, and couples of all ages, the Waterfront Café was part of the Embarcadero area and waterfront. Located just a few blocks from the ballpark, it offered patrons two very different experiences.

Downstairs, a grill and sports bar was furnished with oversized TV screens and sports memorabilia—especially Goliaths gear. There were autographed photos of the ballplayers from past and present, along with their signed gloves, bats and baseballs. Families often went there after day games or before night games for burgers, salads or sandwiches. After ten, the over twenty-one crowd gathered for beer, cocktails and appetizers.

On the second level and accessed around the back was a

nightclub. The entrance was via an escalator, which was covered with an acrylic roof. At the bottom, two husky men guarded a rope that protected the entrance. Dozens of people waited in line on the weekends. At the top of the moving stairway were two more men made sure the *right* guests were let inside.

When we walked by, the whispering and speculating began. I heard Ryan's name bouncing through the crowd. The red leather rope was immediately unlatched for us. We stepped on the escalator and were carried to the entrance.

"Go ahead," the bigger of the two men opened his hand, gesturing us inside. Ryan gave each of them his soul shake and knuckle bump. I started to follow my sister but Ryan grabbed my wrist. I stayed at his side while he gave each man a generous tip.

"Where are we going to sit?" We walked through the doorway together and I quickly scanned the room. "This place looks full."

"They're in the back," a jovial and jubilant voice broke through the air.

I spun around to find a stunning red-haired hostess eyeing my date. She wore a formfitting bright pink dress that shimmered and caressed her hips. It dipped suggestively at her breasts. From the way she nodded and by her casual tone, it was obvious she knew the man at my side.

"Kevin's in rare form tonight, Ry," she giggled. "Have a good evening everyone!"

Oh yuck. Ry? Give me a break. I can only guess why she's so friendly. I want to ask how he knows her . . . should I?

The lighting inside was strategic and colorful, the decor was modern, the music blasted, and the volume of conversation was turned way up. There were people two and three deep, especially at the bar and dance floor. Everything about the place screamed for attention.

"I'll lead the way." Ryan raised his voice so we could hear him. "Jenise, Sean, follow us."

"You already have a reservation?" I stood on my tiptoes as if he couldn't hear me unless I spoke directly into his ear.

"In a way." His mouth angled in sin.

"You come here a lot?" *Ew, I know the answer. Why did I ask?*

"Don't start worrying, Nicky."

Too late to stop myself.

He held my hand as he led me through narrow openings between tables, crossed a floor crammed with dancers, and weaved through people smiling, shouting, and laughing.

How can anyone in here move?

Once we passed the bar and stage, we walked through a semi-private area, where multiple tables were put together for a few dozen men and women. I recognized the Goliaths players but didn't know any of the others. A few of the married men on the team were with women who were not their wives and I struggled with it immediately.

"Hey, Tilton!" Ryan's teammate and good friend, Kevin Reynolds, called out. "Over here!" He motioned to two empty seats near him. Kevin had introduced himself to the cheer team the prior year and also danced with me at the end-of-the-year party in November. I knew the two men were close. I had eavesdropped on a private conversation between them in the outfield and heard the deep concern and friendship the two had for each other.

Still, I was disappointed that it wouldn't be just the four of us out for an entire evening.

"Do you mind sitting here?" Ryan asked, perhaps noticing my expression. "Would you rather sit at our own table?"

Oh sure. If I don't agree, I look like an ass in front of

everyone. You might have asked me earlier.

"At the table with your friends!" Jenise's excitement made the decision for all of us.

"Ryan, do you think I could get in trouble with management?" I gently planted the suggestion, hoping he'd take my cue to sit elsewhere. "We're not supposed to fraternize with you guys."

"No." he waved off my comment. "That's management. No one here cares about that stuff."

"But what if someone snaps a photo?" I reminded. "I could be in trouble."

"Don't worry." He squeezed my hand. "I'll speak with management if something happens."

"Hope so."

Damn it. Oh well, I tried.

We joined the table of macho men and exquisite women. Ryan did his high fives and fist-bumping routine as did Sean when he was introduced.

They're morphing into boys . . . jostling and smacking each other. I wonder what Jenise thinks? Oh, there's Henry! At least I can talk with someone I know.

"Hi Ryan!" A woman with very short, stylish blond hair and blue eyes yelled to him. She stood and waved and then sat down to Kevin's right. Her tight, form-fitting dress seemed made of liquid copper and diamonds. The hem fell to the top of her thigh showing off her slender and petite body.

"Dana." Ryan's voice was flat. He squeezed my hand as if he'd come across a snake in his path and seemed undecided whether or not we should sit down.

"What's wrong?" I asked pointedly. "Should we sit somewhere else?" I tried a second time to steer him to another area.

"Uh . . . I'm . . ." He fumbled for the words.

"Come on you guys!" Jenise shouted. "Sit down!"

Ryan glanced at Jenise and then at me. He finally pulled out my chair as if surrendering to his peers. After he sat, he immediately turned to talk with my sister's end of the table.

What just happened? I know there's a secret going on here. I don't like being in the dark.

"Ryan." I tapped his shoulder.

"What, honey?" he leaned back.

"What's wrong?" I figured I might as well be direct, the same way he was with me. "How come you turned your back to me?"

"Nothing's wrong. Hang on a minute." Once again, he turned away.

Something isn't right.

"Hi, Henry!" I shifted to face him.

After I sang the National Anthem, Henry had followed me into the tunnel. We'd been friendly up until that point. When he saw me talking with Ryan, who'd warned me that Henry couldn't be trusted, something changed. I never asked why and instead chalked it up to male ridiculousness.

Henry smiled awkwardly and then looked away.

Okay, that was weird. This is all uncomfortable so far.

"Hi, Nick, how's it going?" Kevin nudged my shoulder.

"Good, Kevin, you?" *Finally, someone I can talk with since my date is ignoring me.*

"So far, so good. Beer?" He held up a half-full pitcher.

"No thanks," I shook my head. "I don't drink. Hopefully, there's water or iced tea or . . . something."

"I think we're fresh out." Kevin's eyes scanned the table. "I'll go get some for you."

"I can get it. You're all drinking beer, and—"

"No problem," he interrupted. "Sit tight. I think I see someone

I know at the bar. I'll say hello at the same time. Be right back."

Almost all of the people who sat near me were strangers. I tried to make conversation, but no one seemed interested in talking with me. I felt insignificant and immediately fell into my old pattern of withdrawing. I forgot to be attentive and in the present moment. To make matters worse, as I stood to check on Jenise and Sean, I heard whispering from Henry and his friend.

"She's so innocent," the stranger said, just loud enough so I'd hear him. "She must be tight."

"Only eighteen," Henry informed.

"Ryan's a lucky fucker," the other man commented.

I had nowhere to hide. Their nasty conversation elevated into disgusting banter. Even though I was hypersensitive to it, I showed no change in my expression.

I was always tuned in when conversations circled around me.

Forever insecure.

Forever vigilant.

Waiting to be validated.

I got out my cell phone and pretended to text.

Surprised? I shouldn't have been. I'd already witnessed their behavior at the ballpark dozens of times. Even so, I had hoped because of what I'd done with my business plan—creating something new for professional baseball—I'd be considered an equal. I reluctantly admitted to myself that in their eyes I was only pussy and nothing more.

My heart panged with a new fear—was *any* woman just sex to these guys—perhaps even to Ryan? I knew they browsed the railings with their "Alpha Male" game face on. I never imagined they would behave the same way when out for an evening.

Uneasiness fell on me.

The trouble I'd settled with Ryan earlier in the day began to rise up again.

Why isn't he saying anything to the guys? Didn't he hear?

When I turned to look at him I saw he was busy trying to flag down a waitress to place an order. The music and yelling was so loud that I gave him the benefit of the doubt he hadn't heard the demeaning conversation across the table.

Maybe when he's away from me he says those things, too.

Ryan finally got some attention, practically yelling to the nearby waitress. I couldn't hear him and I sat right next to him. Apparently neither could the woman trying to write down the items, as she cupped her ear to demonstrate the difficulty. When she quickly came to his side and squatted on the floor, he was given a clear view down her shirt.

I wish I could see his eyes. I wonder if he's wearing his flirtatious smile for her. Is this the way all waitresses dress in nightclubs?

"Sorry," she yelled to Ryan. She put her hand on his leg. "I couldn't hear from over there. Tell me what you want again, honey." She was almost in his lap when she'd made the suggestive comment. After jotting down his order, she winked at him, patted his leg again, and moved to the other side of the table to serve other people. As she waited on them, she kept her eye on Ryan.

"Come on, Tilton, you pussy, have some beer and Tequila shots," several men chided.

"I'm good," Ryan said calmly, seemingly unmoved. Just as he started to turn to me, an athletic looking Latino man yelled at him. I could see they knew each other and by their greeting, it had been a while since they'd been together. He grabbed Ryan's arm and escorted him to the bar.

Shit, there he goes again. Is that the man who kissed Cassandra when Jerry and I were admiring that sexy painting in

145

the Bellissima gallery?

"So Nicky . . ." Henry grabbed my attention while I was in the throws of worry. "How are you and Tilton doing?"

"Fine." Against my better judgment, I turned to face him.

"Tell us, does he really make your . . . uh . . . what I'm trying to find out . . . do you purr like a wild cat when Ryan strokes you in the sack? That's what he tells *us*, so . . . do you?"

Chapter 17

Trying To Keep A Lid On It

"*W*hat do you mean?" I hid my shock like the expert I was.

Oh my God! How do I respond? I can hardly stand to look at them. Keep your eyes open, Nick. Don't be a coward. He's actually asking me about sex with Ryan! Do I tell him to go fuck himself and ruin the evening or do I play stupid? Will I ever be invited to go out with his friends again if I make a scene? What will Jenise and Sean think?

Henry laughed sadistically. So did the man sitting next to him.

"You know—" *The hell with it. I'm going to call them out. This is bullshit.*

Just then Kevin came back with a container of something for me to drink. I stopped mid-sentence. Gathered myself.

"Here you go, Dana." Kevin placed the pitcher on the table. "And iced tea for Ryan's lady." He poured two glasses. "I hope it's okay if I join you. I figured it's time to cut myself off. Thanks for sitting next to me, by the way."

"Thanks, Kevin." It was like the darkness parted and allowed a rainbow to grace the sky. "Who did Ryan go to the bar with?"

"Carlos. We played together in semi-pro. That's who I saw at the bar and I told him Ryan was here, so . . ."

I nodded and took a long drink from the glass of iced tea.

"Did these guys give you any shit while I was gone?" He glanced at Henry and the others sitting nearby.

"Haven't heard anything," Dana remarked. "I would've told them to go to hell like they deserve." Her chin went up in defiance.

Most of the men and women shook their head, respectful of Kevin's seniority and dominance at the table. One woman sitting at the end seemed to watch my every move. Henry and his friend were silent, waiting for my reply.

Now that I had a chance to look closely at Ryan's friend, I noticed the flecks of gold in his brown eyes. It made them sparkle. He wore black slacks. A silver knitted mesh shirt covered his bare chest. It made his blond hair stand out and revealed his very fit body.

I wonder if Dana is his date. Does she love his chest as much as I love Ryan's?

Taking additional sips of my iced tea, I suddenly realized Kevin, Henry and the man next to him were still waiting for my reply. I knew my response could turn the entire evening unpleasant, possibly affecting the camaraderie in the clubhouse. Henry and Ryan not only worked together warming up in the bullpen, but also in the game. Kevin would probably defend me, being loyal to Ryan. It was important for the younger players to remain in good standing with those who had seniority—my boyfriend and his buddy definitely had it.

I debated my response.

I knew what I was about to say could set how Ryan's friends and teammates might treat me in the future. Shit disturber, whiner, or worse—a baby who needed to be treated delicately—could be some of the labels used to describe me.

I'd be ostracized.

Ryan would go out alone on nights like these because he'd be embarrassed to bring me.

I knew it meant the beginning of the end if I spoke up.

"No," I finally responded. "We were only talking about ordering some nachos."

"They better not." He gave them a look filled with serious messages. I thought I heard them sigh in relief. "Nachos sound delicious. Where's that waitress?"

I laughed, watching him raise his hand to place the order. I wondered if the same woman would stoop and put her hand on his leg as she'd done to Ryan.

"How's my sister doing?" I said to no one in particular. I was certain that Jenise sat at the other end of the table to stay away from my anxieties. Not having to worry about checking on me was probably a relief, but I wanted to be near her. It was what I imagined a double date would be. Not this current situation, which found me separated from her and ignored by Ryan. Plus, I was curious to know her in this new situation and also talk with Sean.

"Ryan," I yelled. He'd just returned from the bar and already engrossed in a conversation with the man next to him. I tapped him on the arm to get his attention. He put his hand on my shoulder, acknowledging that he heard me.

"Yes, sweetheart?" He finally leaned close.

"I want to be near my sister and Sean. Jenise doesn't know anybody and she's all the way at the other end of the table. This night isn't what I envisioned."

He yelled something to the man sitting next to him. It was like a game of telephone, one asking the other to get Jenise's attention until she received the message. She gave me a thumbs-up, a smile, and then looked away.

"Looks like they're doing fine," Ryan assured me. "I'll check on them in a minute." He kissed the side of my head. "Just relax."

"I can't."

You try sitting here with people you don't know making rude comments and see how you'd like it. All you have to worry about is fending off the waitress.

"Do you want to leave?" His tone was neutral. His eyes showed no preference for whatever my decision would be.

I couldn't decide if he was irritated, testing me, or really didn't care what we did. Taking the passive way out, I tried convincing myself the best thing was to stay put.

"Use your networking skills. Think of it as a business opportunity," he suggested loudly. "That woman sitting toward the end of the table in the yellow dress works for *Totemag.com* Maybe you could introduce yourself."

"Yeah." *Thanks a lot for the brush off. I feel like excusing myself and hiding in the restroom the rest of the night. Maybe I can take a bus home. None of them would miss me. Hell, they wouldn't even notice I was gone.*

Ryan turned his head and once again engaged with the opposite end of the table. His back was to me.

Why do you keep turning your back to us? Is it Dana?

I studied my sister and Sean. They'd obviously introduced themselves and were easily meshing with their end of the table, laughing, telling jokes, and pouring beer.

They've come in without any walls—what about you, Nick?

"Did you get something to drink?" Ryan finally shifted in his seat and faced me. "Here." He pushed a plate of appetizers in front of me. "I ordered some food. We could share."

"Kevin got some iced tea for me since you haven't been around." I hinted at him being late with his offer. "I'll have some of the appetizers. I'm so hungry."

"Sorry I ignored you. Something unexpected came up— with two people, no less." The peaceful look on his face showed he was now enjoying the evening. "I thought there was a pitcher of diet soda or iced tea near you."

"There wasn't." My response was clipped. "That's okay."

"Good movie, wasn't it?" He put his arm around me. He either didn't catch my tone or pushed through it. Whichever it was, it worked. Finally, I felt like my date was with me again. Only a few minutes later, however, his attention was taken away. He focused on the person sitting next to him.

Shit.

While I dealt with that challenge, another presented itself. Like the lounge at The Embarcadero Hotel, women poured by our table like the beer flowing from pitcher to glass—often and plentiful. Each woman who walked by our group didn't bother to hide their intention. They openly and brazenly flirted with the men as if it didn't matter their dates were sitting next to them.

Cleat chasers, Baseball Annies, Groupies, Gold-diggers, Fan girls, and *A woman who can go*, are among the less offensive names for women who try to have sex with athletes. These ladies know which jock is married, engaged, has a girlfriend, is single, and in each of those categories, which ones play around. They are skilled at drawing attention to themselves. They dress impeccably; making it known they are women on the hunt. They frequent all the strategic spots: nightclubs, bars, hotels, spring training venues, ballparks, neighborhoods where the athletes live and other places where they might run into men who make a living playing professional sports.

And here they were tonight.

Was it the possibility of a fantasy that made them so bold? Or perhaps the women dreamed of a chance to be taken from their every day lives and into something spectacular if only for a moment?

Maybe it was strictly lust and sex.

I didn't fault them for desire, but flaunting it to men who were already taken was hard for me to handle. On the other hand, wasn't it up to these men to say something rather than feign ignorance at what was happening?

Were these women she-wolves who could sniff out the weaklings of each litter, targeting the easy prey in front of them—men who were in the prime of their physical lives who ran on testosterone and adrenaline?

Physiques, influence, and looks were short-lived. Wasn't the point to have fun while they could, when they were young, no matter what? It seemed so. It wasn't hard to figure out why they might play it that way. Once the physical stuff dwindled, whether a man or a woman, no one seemed to give a damn.

Still, I hoped for better from my baseball heroes. The apparent lack of respect from both sides bothered me in a deep and profound way. Doubt seeded in my gut. Down deep, I knew I could never be part of this life. When it came to adult games and desire, I hadn't understood the agreements made when entering that kind of play.

Suddenly Ryan raised his voice.

It was loud.

He was irritated.

My head jerked.

My focus returned just in time to see an attractive woman turn away from him in a huff. She wore shorts cut so high that part of her ass showed. Her bikini style top barely covered her breasts.

No wonder these guys play around. There are endless . opportunities right at their fingertips. All but the strongest of them probably fall for the obvious charms in front of them.

Ryan's face knotted in frustration.

I have to burst this crazy bubble.

I turned his face and kissed him on the cheek.

His arm returned to my body and rested protectively on my shoulder.

"What happened?" I asked.

"She sat in my lap to have her picture taken with me."

"I don't mean her. Where have you been all night? Earlier—"

"I'm sorry about that. I'll tell you about it later."

I forced a smile.

How would anyone know you're with me when you've had your back turned all evening!

"Tell me now," I pushed.

"Glen was having a meltdown."

"Glen?"

"The guy who was next to me. He left. I'm not sure I convinced him to stay with the team. I had to make sure he was okay."

"He's sick?"

"His mother is. He's trying to decide whether or not to leave the team and he's right on the cusp of making it in the regular lineup. I feel so bad for him. She's his only family."

"What about Carlos?" I asked, somewhat defiantly. "What was so important you got up and went to the bar with him?"

"Kevin, Carlos and I played in semi-pro together but he didn't

153

make it to pro ball. He's kind of lost right now. Booze and women seem to be his solution. Kevin saw him earlier. He wanted to catch up. I should have asked him to sit down and introduce you, but he's pretty drunk. I called a cab to take him home."

So that explains it. I wish he'd said something earlier. Well, I feel a little better.

"You have my undivided attention now." He dipped a chip in the hummus and fed it to me. "You always do, babe. Sometimes I have to tear myself away, that's all." His lips were soft as they pressed into mine and the evening took a turn for the better.

That was until my third challenge of the night.

Ryan's past rose up from its grave and had come back to life.

Dana lifted the lid from his chest of secrets, bringing back from the dead a ghost Ryan had tried to bury—or hide—from me.

By the time she finished, I knew that ghost he'd hidden from me was all too real. She was alive and lived in San Francisco.

Chapter 18

Waterfront Turbulence,

Part II

"*S*peaking of Jesse, where has she been?" Dana had changed seats and now sat across the table. From the corner of my eye, I thought I saw the woman at the end of the table Ryan had mentioned earlier, straighten as if listening and attentive.

Jesse! I know that name!

"Who's Jesse?" I butted in.

"Ryan's ex—" Dana stopped midsentence.

If a look could be lethal, Ryan's would have stopped Dana's heart right there at the table.

"Who care?" Kevin interjected.

The woman in yellow looked at me.

What's up with you, lady?

I looked directly at her and shrugged my shoulders.

She took a drink of her white wine. When she wiped her mouth with a cocktail napkin, she failed to wipe off the smirk that went with it.

Who is that sarcastic grin for?

"No one. Well, me, I guess." It seemed as if Dana's whole body twisted and turned in nervousness. "I haven't heard from her in a few months. I thought if anyone had, it would be you, Ryan."

Before he answered, Ryan paused for what seemed like forever. He shifted purposefully in his seat to face her. Was expressionless when he finally spoke.

"I don't know what Jesse's been up to." His voice was cold.

"But you guys—"

"I don't keep tabs on her," he interrupted. "Never did."

"You two lost touch, then?" Dana asked, almost remorsefully. Silence.

"When you guys broke up, she stopped calling me."

"Call her, then," Ryan suggested.

"Her number has changed." She held her phone as if waiting for Ryan to update her. "You must know it. You're never apart for long."

My date only stared at her. His expression held no tell of what he was thinking.

"You and Jesse used to go everywhere together. What happened?"

"Was Jesse the one who called when we were going to Yountville last year?" I placed my hand on Ryan's forearm.

"I don't think so." His voice held no fluctuation.

She was, too. What's the big deal? The way you're reacting . . . I'm uncomfortable all over again.

"Who is she, anyway?" I pursued. "You still haven't told me."

156

"Monica Standwell," the woman in yellow suddenly stood up and reached across the table to offer her hand.

"Nicky Young," I shook it, aware of an introduction that seemed all-too-planned and very timely.

"I know," she responded as if all business, but some undertone of amusement danced in her words.

"You do?"

"I read your mention in SF Gate a few days ago. Impressive."

"Thanks." *Why haven't you introduced yourself until now?*

She pushed up from the table and walked to where I sat.

"Here's my card. When you're at Stanford give me a shout. I'd love to talk with you about doing a column. Something like, reporting from the college front."

"I'll do that." I eyed her suspiciously. "Thanks."

"Good night," she flirted and dragged her hand across Ryan's shoulder.

"Night Monica," he answered.

I watched her as she elegantly wove through the crowd and exited the club. I presumed the man who followed her was responsible for the diamond on her finger.

Ryan's eyes twinkled.

"Didn't I suggest you start a conversation with—"

"Yeah, yeah," I pushed his shoulder with mine. "You hang with her and Jesse?"

"Once in a while," he answered honestly.

"Well don't think she saved your ass. Anyway, who's Jesse?"

"Someone I used to know." Ryan squirmed in his seat. His eyes begged me to stop the conversation.

"*Used* to know?" I pressed. "Is she *dead* or something?"

Dana put her hands over her mouth and tried not to laugh.

A juicy story seems ready to circulate. I'm not sure I want to hear it—but then again, I want to hear it.

"We went to college together." It was obvious Ryan didn't want to continue.

"Oh?" I turned my body to face him.

She's the one he and Kevin were talking about that day I heard them in the outfield and they didn't know I was listening. You called her a fuck buddy. Kevin said she was in love with you.

"I've heard her name more than once and now here she is again tonight." I didn't want him to wiggle his way out of a pointed conversation. "In fact, when I overheard you and Kevin talking last year, you—"

"She's an acquaintance." Ryan answered quickly, still fixed on Dana. His blue eyes had gone cold.

"Oh, right," Dana snorted. "They were like the king and queen of the ball, Nicky." She waved her hands in the air like crazy, ignoring my boyfriend's glare.

"*Really?*" I encouraged her to continue. "How so?"

"Oh, they were seen everywhere! Any important event and the two of them were there," she informed. "I got to tag along and meet some of the hot guys that drooled over Jesse. They were so disappointed when they found out they couldn't have her." She cracked up. "Oh well, it worked out for me."

When I was checking on what Ryan's contacts could do for Jenise, Caden Blockley, the president/CEO of City Architecture had mentioned he wanted to meet one of Ryan's "acquaintances" at a function they attended. I wonder if that was Jesse?

"Jesse's leftovers are mighty fine. Another Cosmopolitan!" Dana shouted at the cocktail waitress.

"So apparently she *was* taken. By *you*, Ryan." I was devilishly aggressive. "You know, when I met your friend Caden, he mentioned you were with someone he was dying to take off your arm. That couldn't have been here, was it? After all, you never had girlfriends and you weren't exclusive with her."

Silence.

Awkward.

Uneasy.

Thick air.

"Ooh, I remember Caden! I tried to hook up with him but he only had eyes for Jesse. Ryan wouldn't let her out of his sight, Nicky." She sighed and turned to Ryan. "You guys were beautiful together. Does she still live in the city?"

"*Does* she, Ryan?" I pushed.

"She's a nice gal," Dana continued. "Tough to get to know, but once she opened up, I thought she was all right." She looked down the table. "I guess she's not around anymore."

A knot formed between Ryan's eyebrows. I'd seen it before when he was angry, frustrated, or undecided. In fact, I'd seen it only moments earlier with the woman who'd wanted his *photo* and sat on his lap.

"Excuse me." Ryan kissed my cheek and then got up.

I tugged on his jacket sleeve.

He leaned down.

"You promised," I whispered in his ear.

When he looked at me, his eyes seemed troubled.

Fear flashed inside of them.

He hesitated.

Seconds dragged.

Turned into minutes.

"Please let me go. Just for now. I don't want to make another mistake in front of you." He whispered in my ear. "I'm afraid I'll lash out. I can feel that I'm not handling myself well. I'll talk with you privately about all this. Please . . . just for now . . ."

I released his arm.

Watched him sit with my sister and Sean.

I wanted to be with him.

Spun around. Asked no one in particular, "He's uncomfortable talking about her?"

"Guess so," Dana remarked. "I didn't mean to make him leave."

"You didn't." Anger simmered inside me. "He did that all by himself."

"You're cool, Nicky." She smiled and winked.

I was overwhelmed that a mature, stunning woman like her gave me some words of acceptance—and was immediately suspicious.

Kevin sat forward and slammed his glass down on the table.

Both of us jumped.

"Why didn't you take the thousand cues Ryan gave to you and shut up?" Kevin's voice was as stern as a high school principle.

At first I thought he was addressing me, but saw his eyes were focused on Dana.

Quit beating her up. It's not her fault that Ryan couldn't finish the conversation.

"For fuck's sake, open your eyes, woman. Ryan's seeing Nicky, the woman sitting in front of you. She doesn't need to hear about anyone from Ryan's past."

"Oh gosh, I didn't realize he was dating anyone exclusive! I'm sorry," she glanced at me.

Really? We came together and . . . what did you think? I was Ryan's sister?

"I'm not upset." My stomach turned over. "Go on."

I have to know more . . . even if my curiosity kills me.

"Well . . ." She was obviously uncomfortable now that Kevin had pressured her. She avoided his stare and played with her napkin. When the waitress delivered her Cosmopolitan she looked relieved. After a long drink, she continued. "She was a spoiled rich girl, but then again, not so much. No offense, I always felt a little *something* for her. She had her sweet moments.

"Jesse tried very hard to live up to what her parents wanted. By all counts, her dad was an asshole and her mother's only plan for her daughter was a marriage to money." Dana stopped and shook her head. "I may be poor, but at least I'm free from *that* crap. The thing is . . . Jesse actually seemed happy with Ryan. I'm so surprised they're not together any longer. She thought she'd found her prince."

Ooh, I don't like that. Why didn't I take Kevin's cue to stop talking about all this?

"Why did they break up?" My stomach protested.

Kevin cleared his throat.

"Well, I'm guessing it's because of *you*." Dana's smile was warm and seemed sincere.

"How long ago was that?" I pressed on.

"Oh, about—"

"There was no breakup," Kevin interrupted. "Before you, Ryan didn't date anyone. He went on dates. That's all. He and Jesse were only friends who went to social events together."

What a doll you are, Kevin; I don't believe you, but still, that was gallant.

"I get that, but when was the last time they were together?" I looked at Dana. "If Caden thought she was taken, that means something, doesn't it?"

"Means nothing," Kevin interjected.

"Let's see . . . it was late April, I think. Maybe early May. Somewhere in there." She took another drink from her cocktail.

"Is she still trying to find money or did she find her calling?"

"She has a few art galleries in the city." Her hand waved and moved with every word.

Oh damn. Accomplished, smart, beautiful . . . I'm a sinking ship.

Kevin gave Dana another look. It was obvious it meant she should stop talking. She did—immediately.

"Like Ryan said earlier, he and Jesse were only college friends," Kevin repeated. "They saw a lot of each other at one time, but they were never serious."

"And yet, I just heard that apparently, she was very happy with Ryan," I recounted. "Obviously, he must have done *something* to make her feel that way, right Dana?"

"He treated her really well," she nodded.

"Uh-huh," I said suspiciously. "How well?"

"Well, enough of this!" Kevin tried to change the subject. I wouldn't let him.

"Was she the girlfriend who tried to kill herself?" I looked at the both of them for an answer. Their eyes were wide in obvious surprise.

"Where did you hear that?" Kevin's expression showed more than casual concern.

"I have my sources," I refused to give up Tara or Alex.

"I don't know the answer to that." Kevin looked away as if he were shutting down.

"I never heard, Nicky," Dana added.

"What are you thinking about?" I tapped Kevin's hand.

That look on Kevin's face says there's more to it.

"Just an evening I had a few nights back." He looked at me and then cast his eyes down at the table.

"You got caught with your hand in the cookie jar," I teased.

"No, Nick. You don't need to worry about her. There's nothing there, so . . ." I thought I saw him shiver.

"Thanks, but I worry about everything," I forced a laugh.

Kevin shifted into another gear and began telling jokes.

I was relieved the conversation changed direction.

It had become uncomfortable and tense. I was left more insecure than when the evening began. Ultimately, Kevin stole my attention with his sense of humor. I was glad we were sitting next to each other.

Even so, I couldn't shake the mention of Jesse.

She stayed on my mind a long time.

Chapter 19

Voices

𝒯he band's lead singer announced to club patrons the chance to sing a song of their choice onstage. It was about to begin. Jenise immediately stood and yelled for me to get up and sing, encouraging everyone at her end of the table to cheer.

"I'd love to hear you sing again." Ryan sat down next to me.

Well it's about time.

"Are you okay?" I tried not to show my frustration.

"Yes," he kissed my hand. "Thank you for understanding."

"I don't, though."

"I know." He caressed my hair. "This evening wasn't what you expected. I'll make it up to you and fill you in on everything after we leave."

"Is my sister okay?"

"She's doing fine; just drunk off her ass," he frowned. "I tried to replace the beer with O'Doul's but you can't fake the good stuff."

"Oh shit." I stood up trying to look at her. "I've never been out with her like this. That's why I wanted to sit next to her." I shot him a hard look.

"You really think being next to her would have changed anything?" Ryan returned the challenge.

"Probably not," I gave in. "Still . . ."

"There's no sin in letting go on a night out. She seems in control of herself. You can't drink like that consistently and hold it together at school the way she has."

"True," I agreed.

"Come on, Nick. We're here to have fun." He took me in his arms and gave me a kiss so hard that we smacked lips when he lifted off me.

Well I admit that was fun!

"I guess I could do one song."

The knowledge that Jenise had enough alcohol to get drunk unnerved me. But once again, I chose to stay passive rather than address it. No need to rock the boat—ever.

The things that others took for granted—getting buzzed, tipsy, or full on drunk—gave me extreme anxiety. When I went to parties with friends I became the person who made sure they were okay while they drank. Instead of holding a beer, I held a can of soda. And instead of holding a glass of whiskey or vodka, a favorite with my friends, I'd hold a beer so I'd be left alone and then pour it out somewhere when no one watched.

I was the bodyguard who made sure boys didn't take advantage of the girls or get carried away with their drunkenness. I saw to it that no one was made fun of or bullied when they had too much to drink. I'd hide keys, pull distributor caps, loosen car batteries and saw to it that no one drove home intoxicated.

When we'd visit friends of my parents or relatives and they had liquor cabinets or bars in their homes, I was on edge. I'd watch Dad the entire visit, hoping he wouldn't take a drink.

I was amazed that people had alcohol out in the open. Free for the taking around our house meant only for a short while *until it was gone*. There were no "cocktails." Dad drank the entire bottle—straight. He didn't need mixers.

Being tense around alcohol was my phobia—I knew that. My fear surrounding social drinking was so deep I wasn't certain I'd ever be able to enjoy a glass of wine with a nice dinner. I didn't know how. All I saw was the inability to stop once the first sip was taken. We couldn't even go out to eat and relax as a family. When the waiter's first words were, *Can I get you a cocktail*, we'd all cringe, hoping Dad wouldn't say yes.

I could see my mother tighten everywhere.

My sister and I picked up on it.

Her body language was definitely contagious.

I never could shake the bug.

I got up to walk toward the stage. Ryan spun me so that I fell back against him and into his lap. He tipped me over. His warm lips pressed against mine. The table whistled and hollered. After he released me, it was as if I floated across the floor.

"Do you know, *Not About the Money*?" I asked the bandleader.

"You got it," he said. "We'll give you four chords as a lead-in."

It was an upbeat song by Jessie J that wasn't about sex or romance. Instead, it encouraged people to shout out, have fun, and grab the hands of the people around them in friendship. What surprised me was how almost everyone in the club participated. Even the men and women at my table joined in. A new shot of confidence skidded through me. I finished the song to applause and a request for another.

"Guess you're up again," the guitar player said. "What's your next choice?"

"Do you think I could get away with an old Beatles song?"

"Everybody loves the Beatles, darlin'. What'll it be?"

"Nothing corny, just . . . well, I'm thinking of an early one, *I Should Have Known Better.*"

"Cool choice. I love that song—*Hard Day's Night Album*—classic!" He set his fingers in position on his guitar. "We'll come in and rescue you if it doesn't go over."

"Let me know if this is too old school," I announced. "If you don't like it, I'll do something else. When I discovered the Beatles, this became my favorite."

The rhythm was upbeat. The lyrics spoke of hopelessly falling in love, despite knowing better. I looked at Ryan as I sang. Sometimes I was coy and acted shy. Then I'd shake my hair, just as I'd seen in video clips of the Beatles.

Singing always made me lose my inhibitions. It was as if I'd faded from reality and was performing in private. Whether I was in my bedroom, at school, a ballpark, or this club, I loved it.

"Your voice is really good." A man who seemed to be in charge pulled me aside as I finished.

"Thank you." I felt heady. "I love singing."

"I can tell. I'm actually looking for a back-up female singer who isn't shy about taking the lead occasionally. Interested in an audition?"

"I'm flattered, but no thank you," I glanced at the stage. "Actually, I'm *really* flattered—I'm shocked! I'm not dismissing your invitation lightly. It's just that I won't have the time. Next spring is my first year at Stanford's business school. One of their conditions is to also continue my charity work and I'm afraid singing to too much time away from my goals."

"Too bad." He turned on the Karaoke machine and announced

the band was taking a break. "I'm surprised."

"Why?" I stepped to the side with him.

"Well, for one, you look like you're in your third or fourth year of college. Had I known you weren't twenty-one I wouldn't have offered you the gig. By the way, how did you get in? Those two brutes at the door are damn thorough about checking ID."

"My boyfriend." I pointed to Ryan. "You won't tell the manager, will you?"

"No," he laughed. "My real surprise is that you're studying business. It doesn't seem like a good match. You're creative . . . wouldn't a major in business kill that juice in you?"

"I'm actually studying an aspect of it that encourages creativity. Guess I won't know until I try it." I was embarrassed at the attention. When I looked away, I saw Ryan watching me.

Women are standing right in front of him, trying to get his attention with their dazzling bodies and skimpy dresses, and he's watching me—or did I just happen to have good timing?

"I also like to write," I informed. "Maybe I can write a song for you some day!"

"Writer, singer . . . here's my manager's card. My information is on the back. Call us if you change your mind. Some of the venues we play admit eighteen and over. I'm Gabriel, by the way." He extended his hand.

"Nice to meet you, Gabriel," I replied. "Nicky." I returned the gesture and put his card in my pants pocket.

On the way back to my seat, Jenise gave me a hug.

"That's my sissy," she said loudly to everyone around her. "Isn't her voice beautiful?" Her end of the table buzzed with congratulations. Sean hung all over my sister with drunken affection.

"You were wonderful up there," Ryan fawned. When I sat

down, he put his arm around my waist.

Because of my stage performance, it seemed I had commanded a different respect and attention from the people who sat near me.

Henry and his friend had long since vacated their seats and others filled in, condensing the table into a smaller group. Now when I joined their conversation, I heard *interesting*, and *hadn't thought about that*, and *good point*.

It was a small victory and helped me to understand that I'd made judgments too quickly. Just because a few jerks were rude, it didn't mean they were representative of the entire table. I needed to soften my harsh and protective first impressions. Glad that I hadn't lashed out earlier, I looked at the lesson in front of me.

I realized the brush that paints everyone shouldn't color in the same shade.

Chapter 20

On Stage

"*W*here's Dana?" I asked Kevin when I sat down.

"She ran into someone she knew."

"Are you and she—"

"No." He gave me a playful wink. "We're not."

As the evening continued, I spent a lot of time trying to get to know Ryan's friend. I found him both intellectually challenging and funny. The way he flirted with everyone around him wasn't offensive; instead I felt he was disarmingly warm.

"You know," I winked back, "if you were sitting at the other end of the table, you might charm one of those pretty ladies who've been trying to get your attention all night."

"Nah. Why would I be concerned with them when I'm having so much fun with *you*?" He rested his hand on mine.

"Well . . ." *Wow, fun with me?* "I'm just saying you might miss a connection."

"I've already made one. My new friend is more important than flirting with strangers, don't you think?"

"Thanks." I fanned myself. "Thank you."

"You nervous?" he prodded.

"Yeah."

"Don't be. Are you okay after what Dana said?" He looked in the direction of the front door as if she'd just walked through.

"Sort of," I admitted cautiously. "She seemed all right, but it was hard hearing about Jesse and Ryan. That bell of the ball stuff and how she'd found her prince?" I wrinkled my nose. "I'm glad he was nice to Jesse. Of course that's great to hear. I wouldn't expect anything else, it's just . . . oh well. My fault."

"I tried to stop her . . . and you."

"I know. Curiosity got the best of me, Kevin."

"She's got a big mouth," he said. "I dated her a few times."

"Dana or Jesse?"

"Dana." He paused. "And Jesse."

"Of course you did." I shook my head.

"Dana's nice enough. Actually, she's pretty bright. Just don't tell her anything you want to stay a secret."

"Blabbermouth?"

"More than that," he hesitated, playing with his glass of iced tea. "The way she fired off the questions? Spying for a certain girlfriend of hers, I think."

"Huh. I didn't sense that." I'd questioned the same thing, but in the end didn't agree with Kevin's summary. I dabbed the moisture under my glass from where it sweated on the table. "I don't think she meant to cause any trouble. She seemed to really miss her friendship with Jesse. On the other hand if she is spying, that sure doesn't calm my anxiety."

And *she didn't make any moves on the men at the table, which is a big plus in my book.*

"She's appealing to your innocence, Nick. She knows you're trying to fit in. By the way, you don't have to try. You already do, okay? Monica doesn't give her card out to just anyone."

"Yeah, well that was because I was with Ryan, I'm sure." I looked in Kevin's eyes, but he revealed nothing. "I hate to ask—"

"Then don't," he stated plainly.

"Don't what?"

"Fall into jealousy over nothing. What's past is past."

"I don't know that I've ever met anyone who talks on and on like I do." I offered my hand. "Nice to meet you, fellow talker."

"Nice to meet you, too." Instead of shaking it, he kissed it.

"Why did Ryan leave me?" I surprised myself that I had the nerve to ask him the question. Ryan still had his arm around my shoulder. Chances were he heard me. "Between you and me? I almost got up and left. He turned his back on me twice, Kevin. I get it, sort of. Glen and Carlos needed to talk, but . . ."

"I'm sure," he nodded toward Ryan, "he'll explain it to you. It was to talk with Glen, I know that much. But . . . the thing is, Dana, Jesse . . . well, Dana really doesn't know . . . I mean, Jesse can . . ." Kevin trailed off and stopped talking.

Ryan squeezed my shoulder.

"What was the kiss on Nicky's hand?" Ryan lifted an eyebrow at his friend.

"That's between us, shit face." He winked again at me. "If you'd been around, you would have known."

Kevin's a shit disturber! I like him.

I realized I hadn't talked to my boyfriend for more than thirty minutes the entire night. The evening at the Waterfront had begun with fear and hesitation, but after experiencing a few peaks and valleys, it ended with two business cards in my pocket and the enjoyment of engaging with a new friend.

See Nicky, it's okay to open up and let others in.

"I'll be back in a minute," Ryan said.

"No." I grabbed his hand. "You promised you wouldn't."

"I'm not leaving to talk with anyone," he said. "This is just for you. Something special for my sweetheart."

He walked over to the band, which had come back to the stage and continued the live performances with club guests. He spoke to Gabriel, the man who'd introduced himself to me a little earlier.

"You guys! I think Ryan's going to sing," I said excitedly. "Does he sing, Kevin?"

"A little," he smirked.

His friends at the table continued talking loud and paid no attention. I figured they must have seen him so many times it was old news. Since I hadn't, I wanted a better view.

"Where sha goin' little sistah?" Jenise's words were slurred. Her eyes had that familiar lazy and glazed look that comes with too much alcohol.

"I'll be back," I squeezed her shoulders. "Ryan's singing!"

"Ooh ur lovey dovey! Did you guys know Ryan and my sissy are loves?" Jenise had the men and women around her laughing.

Whelp, I guess we're not a secret anymore. I hope I don't get in trouble with management.

"Kevin!" I yelled. "Please watch my sister."

He nodded and sat closer to her.

I searched for an empty seat and found one near the stage. A table meant for four had only three people seated around it.

"Do you mind if I sit here?" I motioned to the empty chair.

"Not at all." One of the gentlemen pulled the chair out for me. "Is that your boyfriend?"

"Yes," I could hardly stand it. "I didn't know he could sing!"

174

"That's Ryan Tilton, right?" he asked curiously.

I nodded.

The music began.

Ryan's long, sensual stride carried him across the floor to me.

Oh no, what is he doing?

He stood at my side.

Waited.

Eyes beckoned.

A smile crossed his face that was filled with a devil's intention.

His hand reached for mine.

I took it and let him lead me to the stage.

My eyes were wide open that night—in more ways than I knew. I held my breath and wasn't certain I took another until the next morning.

Ryan's body seemed to get bigger. I was sure he filled the entire stage. When I heard his masculine voice begin to sing lyrics that were slow and sensual, it was as if they dripped onto my body.

We started at one side of the stage.

With each word, he backed me up.

One.

Step.

At a time.

He sung about being born for each other. Being sick for each other when apart. The longing in our hearts and the way his world was right only when alone with me.

I thought I might faint but kept walking in reverse.

He never looked away from me. His gaze steady. Full of lust. After what seemed to be forever, my back hit a wall.

His body pressed against me and his voice went lower.

Leaning on his elbow, it rested beside my head.

The song slowed.

He was only inches from my lips.

Suddenly he dropped to his knees.

One arm wrapped around my waist.

He looked up at me.

Sung about the helplessness he felt when in my light and it was only in my love that he came to life. Deep into the chorus he suddenly he let go. While still on his knees, he backed up. Pounded the floor with words that spoke of being desperate and bold in a life together.

The entire club was mesmerized.

No longer did anyone have to shout to be heard.

The waitresses stopped serving customers. The bartender looked up. The hostess ignored people near her who were waiting to be seated. I saw people with their mouths open.

Ryan got up.

My eyes were level with his chest—the chest I knew would bring me to the floor one day soon. If I looked in his eyes I'd completely lose myself. I focused on his lips. They opened. Moved. His tongue licked them and words dipped on the invisible bars of melodic bliss as he described how tasty I looked and how hungry he was.

I finally had to close my eyes and then had to open them.

His sensual laugh made the desire writhe in my belly.

As he leaned on his forearm, it seemed his chest expanded, pushing into my body. I wondered if it could push all the way to my heart.

He got down on one knee and held my hand.

It was as if people were tuning in to him, believing the words from his mouth were meant for them.

The music rose again.

He got up.

Took a step.

Pointed at me.

The intensity of his delivery, singing about lips kissing, delivering as only he could the lyrics of fingers caressing, bodies tangling and our souls melting together were perfect.

He was perfect.

His eyes were closed. His face, contorted. It was obvious he had lost himself. His passion came through like a heart on fire as he brought the microphone to his lips and fell to the floor once more, repeating "amen" several times and closing the song with his hallelujah.

When Ryan finished, he stood against me, breathing hard. He held me in one of his arms while I looked up at him.

Without words.

He spoke to me.

The club went crazy with cheers as he brought me to his lips.

Everything fell away in those moments. It seemed as if he could see only me, even in public and among his peers.

My heart had wings.

"Okay," I whispered weakly. "You've got me."

"I know." He slowly lifted off my body. "Forgive me for leaving you on your own tonight?"

"I forgive you. Yes."

Another kiss and he signaled to Kevin we were leaving. Little did my boyfriend know from the moment we'd kissed outside of the movie theater, any strength I had left had melted away.

Ryan didn't linger to say goodbye to the rest of the table. He didn't seem to care.

"M . . . my . . . my sis." I tried to pull myself together.

"Can you walk or do I need to carry you to the car, my baby?"

His fiery eyes seared my heart.

He was temptation: a sensuous devil danced in his eyes, deliciously waving his tail back and forth, its wicked tip ready to sting.

"Yes."

"What do you mean, yes?" His suggestive laugh rang out.

"No, I mean no. I can make it. But my Jenise," I muttered. "I mean my Sean and sister." *Damn it.* "Sean and my sister. They need help. Can you and Kevin get them?"

"You liked my song?" Ryan's voice slithered all over me.

"Mm-hmm," I purred. "It was willy," I cleared my throat. "Really good."

"Let's go," his spicy laugh taunted me. "Every part of me needs to be alone with you."

Finally!

"Don't you want to say goodbye to your friends?" I nodded toward the table.

"I already told Kevin we were leaving. He'll let them know." He stared into my eyes.

"So . . . this is it?" I looked anywhere but at him.

"It's enough of being here." His hand lifted my chin. "Why aren't you looking at me?"

"I'm looking at you." I glanced at him and then looked away.

I'm already weak. It won't take much for my knees to give out; nothing like falling to the ground in front of everyone.

"Here's the ticket for the valet," Ryan extended his hand. "Kevin will help me with your sister and Sean. We'll meet you outside. Open the back passenger doors for us, okay?"

I went down the escalator and turned in the ticket for Ryan's car. When the valet brought it curbside, I opened the doors as he'd asked and then waited for the boys of baseball to load and secure my sister and her boyfriend inside the car.

"Oh, my poor sissy." I patted her knee after I fastened her seatbelt and then secured her in the back seat. She and Sean were like large sacks of jelly.

Ryan said goodnight to his friend and then walked around to the driver's side. Kevin stood ready to close the door for me.

"Thanks for helping." I gave him a hug. "You know, I confess I was disappointed at first when I found out we were sitting with all of you. Now I'm glad we did. It's nice to get to know you."

"You, too, fellow talker." He leaned close to my ear. "Please take good care of my friend."

"I will."

Oh, how cute—bro love.

I sat in the front seat, feeling ready to burst for a variety of reasons: the way Ryan took care of my sister, the new friend I'd made in Kevin, the songs we performed, and most of all, my boyfriend's kiss and all-encompassing embrace.

Ryan turned on the same jazz station I'd set for him when we went to Sammy's in Half Moon Bay.

Other than that, we were quiet until we arrived at my house.

I wondered if he was as nervous as I was.

Chapter 21

Family

" *W*ell, Ryan, I guess this is goodnight." I kissed him on the cheek and got out of the car to help Jenise. "Are you going to take Sean home?"

"I'll get your sister first. Can you open your front door for me?" Ryan slipped his arms under her and I ran to open the door.

He's carrying her all the way upstairs! Damn, he's strong! Those biceps are bulging . . . oh, he's yummy.

"Let me get Neesee tucked in," I joked, using Sean's nickname for my sister. "I'll be down to say goodnight in a second. How will you get Sean home? Did you find out where he lives? I guess we can look in his wallet, right?"

"I'll help him to the sofa. He can stay the night at your place," Ryan's smooth voice didn't miss a beat.

"Okay, I'll be down with some blankets after I take care of my sis. Do you want some water or coffee? Or . . . I know—hot chocolate! I can't make it like you do, but good enough. Would you like some?"

Calm down, Nick.

"I'm good." He continued attending to Sean.

I rushed upstairs.

"Promise me you don't have an issue with alcohol." I stroked Jenise's arm.

She let out a moan.

"Let me help you into your pajamas." Although I spoke to her directly, I knew the words sloshed around inside her head and probably didn't register. By her pale look, I worried she might get sick. I was afraid to leave her. I'd heard of people who'd passed out from drinking and had choked on their own vomit.

My dad had almost been one of them.

After his incident, Mom purchased two baby monitors. She placed one in the bedroom and left the other downstairs. Even as she lay on the sofa reading her books she couldn't relax. There was no such thing as security nor was safety a given at our house.

I knew how to take care of someone who'd had too much to drink. I'd done it many times with my father. Now my sister was an addition to that list. I got her a towel, a glass of water, and some aspirin and set them on her nightstand. After I undressed her, I pulled the covers up and kissed her goodnight.

"Sissy, yube got lubby with that boy. Yur lub, too," she muttered. "Night-night." She grabbed my hand and put it against her heart. Although she was drunk, I couldn't help but smile at my beautiful sister. This seemed so different from all the times I had to take care of Dad.

When he was drunk, we all retreated.

Even the air in the house became charged with fear.

My mother withdrew, already exhausted from dealing with him

during the day. Jenise couldn't because of the way she clashed with him—their confrontations often ending in violence.

I'd take care of him when no one else would.

I knew how to be passive.

I became an expert at keeping the peace.

Tonight, however, I did it out of love.

Remembering how the stale alcohol in her body would saturate the air as she slept, I opened her window and then closed her door. I grabbed a pillow and blanket.

When I went into the living room I saw Ryan had taken off Sean's jacket and shoes. I noticed he'd moved the coffee table further away from the sofa. He held Sean's head as I slid the pillow underneath him and tucked him in so he wouldn't turn over and fall.

God, he's so gentle with people.

I put my arm in his and we walked to the front door.

He turned to face me.

His hand cupped my cheek.

"Now that they're settled," Ryan's eyes focused on mine. "Let's go back to my apartment and continue our evening."

My whole body fell into waves of warm, liquid sensations. A sweeping desire made my heart beat in erratic rhythms.

This wasn't what I meant by going slow. Guess after that sensual song and my obvious surrender that idea is over.

Suddenly, I was afraid to be alone in his apartment.

I wasn't ready.

It had been such a memorable night and all I could think of was our mistake in Yountville. Would everything come crashing down?

"Ryan, it's so late."

"What's happened between us over the past two days?" His thumb moved up and down on my cheek.

"What do you mean?" I wanted to close my eyes. Knew I had to keep them open. This was our turning point.

"Explain what you think our talk meant at Java House yesterday." His voice was steady.

"We had a long discussion about transitioning," I told him.

"What else?" His eyes filled with softness. "What did you say to me when I dropped you home this morning?"

"I invited you in. I know I did, Ryan. But then we agreed to take it slow. In fact, you insisted."

"Uh-huh. You just invited me in?"

"Well, yeah, more than that," I admitted. "If you want to talk, we can do it in the kitchen," I tried to stall for time. "I'm always up for one of our epic conversations."

"No, baby," Ryan corrected. "You invited me up to your room this morning and I refused for good reasons. Come home with me tonight. I need to be alone with you."

"What are you getting at?" *You and your questions and comments . . . they're exhausting.*

"You know what I'm getting at." He caressed my hair.

"I don't want to go to your apartment. Last time we were alone, things went to hell."

"I won't make that mistake again." His hand lay on my shoulder. "That's why I got up from the table at The Waterfront. I'm being careful. In Yountville, I misjudged your readiness for sex. I'm sorry I did that. Honey, I have no problem waiting for you to get comfortable. I respect your values and spiritual beliefs. What I need is for you to be honest with me. You've mentioned that you feel my life is too much. Then you reverse and tell me you don't want me to find the woman you insist is the right one for me. Please, Nicky. Be honest with me now."

He took me in his arms.

"If you really mean it, if I'm really not the man you want, tell me. I'm confused by your messages. If it's only that you're afraid to take a risk with me, we can work it out; that's different. I'm asking you to open your heart. Right now. Tell me how you feel. We're going to rise and fall for a while until we figure it out," he continued. "If you want to be with me, say it. If you don't want me, I'll respect your wishes and leave you alone."

"No!" My voice rose dramatically. Panic spread through me. I embraced him. Squeezed him as hard as I could. "Please, I don't want you to leave me alone."

"I don't either." He brushed his lips across my forehead. "I want to go to the next level in our relationship. We won't get there until we can be alone together. In Half Moon Bay when we got close . . . it was magical. I want that again . . . need it."

"Every time I think about us that way I go to some place that's stars and golden light," I admitted. My eyes stung trying to hold back tears. My throat burned as it tightened. I found myself grasping his wrists as if staying him. "It's just . . ."

"The night on your front porch, after you sang the anthem, I told you I could do things for your family. You found out they were true. You know I've begun helping your father."

"Yes."

"If I helped your dad and sister and then released you from your promise to give us a try, what would you do? You resisted me on the night of your party. You only agreed to go out with me because of what I could do. Now that you've gotten to know me, would our original arrangement be enough?"

"No."

"If I said, I'm sorry, Nicky. You don't trust me. You won't say you love me and I can't be with you any longer. And then I walked out the door, would you always wonder?"

"Yes," I whispered. "I don't want that. Please don't walk out." I buried my head into his chest.

"I won't. I'm not saying that. I only need to make sure I'm not misreading you again." His hand slid under my chin, lifting my gaze to meet his blue eyes. "I'm as sure about us as I've ever been of anything in my life."

"What if our sex is bad?" I had to confess one of my deep fears. "You've got all this experience and you'll be able to compare everything we do with women from your past. I know you have a fantasy of how it will be for us. The thing is," I paused. "If I'm a disappointment to you, I mean, what do I do when our time comes? You've got it all built up in your head—"

"We'll show each other what we need." His hands squeezed my waist. "I'm not waiting for *it,* I'm waiting for *you.*"

"Okay. Agreed. I believe you, but just for tonight, what about Sean and Jenise? I don't think we should leave them, do you?"

"You think your sister is in danger?"

"I think someone should at least be here to check on them. My parents have no clue they're home and it's a given my dad isn't . . . you know. Mom's has had enough of that crap and doesn't need to take care of a daughter that's had too much . . . I'm sorry, but I think we should—"

"Okay," he said with conviction. His hands fell by his side. A serious expression replaced the passionate one he'd been consumed with only moments ago.

"*Okay?*" I believed with all my heart he was a good man, but to put aside his obvious plan of seduction for me, well, my heart fluttered. Without hesitation, he put me first.

It was the night I fell deeply in love.

Chapter 22

Hall Monitors

" *We* should have pulled out the sofa so you'd have some room to rest." I was relieved we wouldn't spend the night together, and also secretly disappointed. "Now you'll be uncomfortable. Honestly, I wish you could sleep in my bed and not down here. You know, as company so we could talk."

"Me, too. Only to talk," he grinned. "I'll be okay in the chair. You can go check on your sister while I wait here. Come to think of it, I'll take that cup of hot chocolate after all. Do you mind if I make it for us?"

"That would be great." I started to go upstairs, but then ran back down and fell into Ryan's arms. I held on for dear life.

"Thank you. Thank you for giving up the evening you had planned for us. Fucking alcohol." *Whoops! I didn't mean to react out loud.* "Oh. Sorry. It's ruined everything in my family."

"If this is what you need, I'm here for you. Our flight doesn't leave until Monday afternoon. Tomorrow we can . . . would you come to the game tomorrow and we can do something afterward?"

"Yes!" I almost yelled my response. I was overly excited he wanted to see me again so soon. "Of course I will!"

"I'll make our chocolate while you check on Jenise." His delicious smile bloomed.

I glided all the way upstairs. I was about to open my sister's door when I remembered the monitors Mom had bought. Quietly, I snuck into my parents' bedroom and grabbed them from underneath her bedside. Sneaking out as quietly as I'd come in, I carefully shut the door, turned on the device and put it on Jenise's nightstand. Just to be sure, I put her pocket mirror to her nose and watched the glass fog. I placed my hand on her chest, making sure it rose and she took a breath.

While upstairs I decided I'd get out of my tight pants and changed into my pajamas.

Ah, so much better. I wonder if he might want some slippers. Dad is too small for Ryan to wear his stuff . . . maybe a robe?

"Hey." I walked into the kitchen. He was pouring the hot chocolate.

"Everything o . . . oh, Nicky." His eyes became hooded. "Is . . . is um, is everything okay?"

"Yeah. I remembered some monitors Mom bought for dad." I held up the one I'd brought downstairs.

Are my pajamas turning him on? Boy, he gets excited so easy! How am I going to handle him?

"I left one in Jenise's room and I'll keep this one down here with us. I want to know—well, here." I gave him the slippers and robe. "Do you want these?"

"Uh, not sure."

"Why not?" I wanted to understand his rationale.

"If your dad comes down and sees me in them . . . I'll take the slippers, I guess, but I'll keep my jeans on."

"I see your point." I grabbed one of the mugs of hot cocoa. "Let's drink!"

We clanked the mugs and discussed our evening.

"Your voice is incredible. You really should explore doing *something* with it, even if it's not professionally. Maybe the drama department at Stanford?"

"I'll be so busy." I braided my hair. "I don't want to screw up my first year . . . my charity work and all. We'll see. What's your relationship with Kevin? I know you two are good friends . . . he seems to have genuine concern for you. In fact, I felt like you were brothers. I think he loves you."

"We came up in semi-pro ball together. When I met him, his sweetheart back home had just dumped him."

"Oh, poor guy."

"We spent many a night in the bars talking about it."

"But you—"

"Back then we both drank some and at the stage when liquid courage kicked in, he opened up and told me his story."

"How come you don't drink now? I mean, I'm glad, but it's unusual for someone like you and in your position."

"My position?" His sly grin dared me to continue.

"Single, goes to social events, hits the clubs and all that."

"I don't like losing control," he confessed.

"Yeah, but—"

"Alcohol doesn't mix well with my body," he put his hand on mine, obviously not wanting to discuss it. "Anyway, Kevin's girl back home didn't trust that he'd stay true to her. I kind of took him under my wing—actually, we were there for each other. He did the same for me when I talked about my dad."

"Well, from what I've seen at the ballpark and at the table tonight, I can't blame Kevin's ex," I noted. "It's hard to have the kind of blind faith a woman needs to commit to you guys."

"What happened at the table?" He looked up as if he'd been smacked in his forehead.

Oh crap, I didn't mean to say anything. Do I tell him what a jerk Henry was? Should I change the topic?

"Well, you know . . . all the women." I covered my mistake.

"I know." He looked down. "Was there anything else?"

"No. Well, yes." I decided to be honest. "Um, a few of those guys, Henry for one—he's an ass."

"I know he is." His left hand fisted. "When we first approached the table and I stopped?"

"Yeah?"

"It wasn't only because of Dana. I told you to stay away from him that day you sang the anthem. He was after you and pissed when he saw us talking in the tunnel."

"You knew all that and yet you let me to face him." I shook my head, trying to understand his motives. "Why did you turn your back on me tonight? I mean for so long? I felt alone for so much of the evening."

"Two things." His eyes saddened and he looked away before refocusing. "I really did have to talk with Glen. He's battling depression because his mother is sick and considering a request to go back to semi-pro. I told him that was a death sentence and he shouldn't do that. I don't want to see a rookie make a mistake that could affect his career because of an uncertainty." He brushed a crumb from the tabletop. "It's one thing if management sends you down, but to request it?"

"Bad move," I agreed.

"Really bad. The other thing, well first on Henry, I knew you could handle him."

"Yeah, but he said some bad stuff, Ryan. I wished you'd been present and attentive so you could have stopped it."

"What did he say?" His faced flushed.

"I'm not going to repeat the words. You can imagine some of them, can't you?"

"I'm sorry. I didn't think . . . with Kevin and the others so close . . . I'll handle him."

"No!" I begged. "Please don't start anything on my behalf. I didn't want to say anything for just this reason. Promise me you won't."

"The other thing," he avoided answering me like a panther glistening in the night, his eye on his prey, aware of all that was around him. "I wasn't ready to face Dana and the history she shares with Jesse and me. She's uh . . ." he let out a long sigh.

"Did you sleep with her?"

"No."

"What about Monica?" *God, why did I go there?*

"Nicky," his shoulders dropped. "Do you really want to quiz me on every woman you meet that I happen to know?"

"I can't answer that yet," I admitted.

"I'm not going to keep doing this with you. You have to trust me and let my past go. The answer is no."

"*What*?" I mocked. "You mean there's a woman you know—"

"Please don't." Blue eyes stilled me.

"Sorry." *You don't understand the only way I can get through my fears is to joke or be sarcastic. How can I stop eighteen years of doing the same thing?* "Um . . . I'm a little pissed."

"I told Kevin to keep an eye on you to make sure you were all right. I knew Monica would be there and you could talk with her. If I had any doubt I'd never have taken the chance."

"Well, okay, but that's pretty ballsy. I mean you could have at least talked to me awhile before you turned away. And Monica was at the end of the table. Plus, she didn't introduce herself until things got dicey with the Jesse conversation so . . ."

"I'm sorry. I knew Dana would bring up my past. It bothers you so much . . . I didn't want to talk about Jesse. At least if I wasn't in the conversation I didn't have to go there." He paused. "Because I knew you'd make me go there and I don't have all the answers. I need to let you in on some of my past but those lines are blurred. I'm uncertain about how much is okay to share."

"Yeah, well, I know. I can't get a handle on you guys," I mused. "When you talk to me at the ballpark everything seems good. Henry was once a nice guy. We talked quite a lot in the beginning. And now, Kevin seems nice, but is he? Or is it an act the same way Henry's was?"

"Kevin's genuine," Ryan said. "Heart of gold. He's been hurt, so the walls are up. He really loved Maryanne. It was a complete shock when she cut him off. He took a long time to get over her. Too long, I guess—if there is a such a thing."

"He's one of the wild boys along with you. I've been warned plenty about you guys. What did he expect? The girl back home is nothing compared to the models and socialites that you guys attract in pro-ball."

"I'm not a wild boy," Ryan said disgustedly. "And Kevin's not either. Not really."

"Yeah?" I lifted my chin a little. "That's why you've dated—"

"You're doubting me?" He folded his arms on the table and rested his chin on them. The innocent look in his eyes was endearing. Still, I didn't believe him.

"What about Jesse?" I ignored his question. "Dana said you guys were *taken*. What does that mean?"

"We worked events together. We weren't looking to connect with anyone else because we were networking. We had a standing arrangement that way; Jesse knows a lot of people and so do I. We introduced each other at social gatherings and parties."

"And what about the way you treated Dana?" The look in his eyes seemed to convey he was telling the truth. Still, I needed more evidence. "She was a friend who was once close to you both or at least to Jesse. Now she's cast off because you two aren't together? That's cold and . . . irrational."

"I can't explain why Jesse stopped seeing her. I was never Dana's friend. We just didn't connect in any way. In fact, I think it was pretty rude she brought our history to your attention like that."

"I guess so. Kevin thought so, too, but I don't think she meant anything by it. On the other hand, sometimes I should be more suspicious of people. I don't trust easily, but then again I do, or I want to at least, and . . . I don't know."

Maybe she meant more than I thought. Now that I've reconsidered . . . even if she didn't know Ryan and I were seeing each other, she had to know we were on a date, right?

"I get confused about knowing who you can and can't trust, too." He held my hand. "I know I have to earn yours."

"You're doing a damn fine job." I smiled and stroked his thumb with mine. "I didn't know you could sing! You were, the way you did your song, you know—backing me up against the wall like that, you were so . . . well, I shouldn't say this, but um . . . *really* sexy. You know, you make me want to tell you everything. It's like I can't keep anything to myself. And you know what? I've said to myself so many times how I wish you wouldn't say everything that's on your mind, and here I am doing the same thing. Anyway, your voice, well truthfully, just your normal voice gets to me. You get me going. Did you know that?"

Be careful about revealing too much, Nick.

"I can tell by your body language when you're excited." his eyes danced with pleasure. "When I say something that stirs you up inside your pupils dilate and your body expands."

"Well that's not fair," I laughed.

"I hardly think I'm much of a mystery to you, either."

"No." I smiled in amusement that he'd admitted how I could sense his *sexual aura*, the same way he could mine.

"So, school is starting pretty soon." Ryan changed the subject.

"Yeah."

"Would you consider coming on a road trip with me? You know, I don't mean the entire trip. A few games maybe?"

"Possibly."

"You could bring Jenise if she makes you feel safer—or not. Whatever makes you more comfortable."

"It's not that I don't feel safe with you. It's . . . sex is a big deal for me. You don't understand how much it is. Sex shouldn't be so difficult; I know that. Everything seems easy for you guys. Crap, who am I kidding? Sex seems easy for just about everyone but me. I'm getting there, you know. You're helping and Jenise is helping, too. I understand that I'm not the greatest person for you to be with. And that bothers me, too. Everything gets to me."

"I understand you need time," he agreed simply. "I'd like to help you get there. Will you let me?"

"I want that."

Just then, Jenise started to cough. I ran upstairs and into her room. She had turned over and was already asleep. I checked to make sure she breathed freely and there was no vomit anywhere. When I went back down, I carried a blanket and pillow for Ryan. I placed them on the chair near the living room sofa where Sean was sleeping.

"Do you want me to stay down here with you?" I asked as soon as I walked into the kitchen.

"No, you can go ahead and get some sleep. I'll be fine. Once I know Sean's okay I'll take him home. I'll leave tickets—"

"No railings, please. I enjoy the bleachers with the real fans. Okay boyfriend?"

"Bleachers it is. Give your man a goodnight kiss."

"Gladly," I put my arms around him. "You're so, such a . . . I'm glad you're my boyfriend. I really appreciate how you stayed with me tonight."

"You're welcome." His arms returned the embrace, lifting me off my feet for a moment. "You're just upstairs, but in a way that's worse. I'll miss you."

"You're right about that. I might be tempted to sneak down here and take a peek at you. I promise I'll stay upstairs." I grabbed the monitor and looked back at him. "Maybe."

"Not sure I'll get to sleep. I'll be listening for you. Dress casual tomorrow my adorable girlfriend. We'll head out after the game."

"Dress casual; now that I can do. Can't wait, Ryan."

With a long kiss, we said goodnight.

It was the sweetest kiss ever.

Chapter 23

Church And Doughnuts

*A*s soon as I opened my eyes I threw on my robe and hurried downstairs. I'd hoped to catch Ryan before he left, but like a dream in the night, he and Sean were gone. The pillows and blankets were folded neatly on the sofa. I took them upstairs and put them back in the linen closet.

Dad came out of the bedroom, dressed and ready for wherever he was going.

"Where *you* headed?" I asked suspiciously.

"Church. What's with the blanket and pillow?" he asked with a tone of doubt.

"Ryan slept over. He stayed downstairs while I slept upstairs."

"Join me?" It seemed a look of relief washed over him as he asked for my company.

"Can you wait ten minutes?"

"Barely." He looked at his watch. "Hurry up."

I threw on some slacks and a blouse, brushed my hair, and quickly wiped my face with a cotton ball soaked in witch hazel.

"Ready!" I shouted while running downstairs.

"You guys got back late? Your mom and I didn't hear you."

Just as well. That way you'll never know Sean got drunk, which might put him in the doghouse forever.

"Yeah, we did. Are you going to the bakery after mass?"

"We could." He smiled at my question, possibly remembering earlier days when he brought home hot bread and warm doughnuts after church service.

"That would be great," I patted his hand and quickly turned away before my tears betrayed me.

"Did you guys have fun last night? Everyone get along?"

"It was a blast." *Especially when my boyfriend sang to me.*

We drove to a modest looking Catholic Church across town named Our Lady of the Visitation. The church was beige colored and had a large round stained glass window under the steeple. A bell tower made it quaint and beautiful. When we arrived the bells were ringing. The service was about to start.

Why he went all the way across town? I suppose it was that no one there knew of him or his addiction there. Maybe he considered each week a fresh start. Metaphorically, it could have given him some hope of overcoming his addiction.

Dipping our fingers in the holy water on either side of the entry doors, we made the sign of the cross, blessed ourselves, sat in the back pew and joined in the opening hymn.

I hadn't gone to Sunday mass with my dad for many years. Being with him when he was sober made everything seem possible. After the service ended, we drove to Hilda's, a bakery on Geneva Avenue. He picked up the twisty French bread Jenise loved and also a sweet loaf for my mother. I chose two glazed doughnuts and a coffee and downed them quickly on the way home.

"Thanks for inviting me." I gave Dad a kiss on the cheek, knowing on that day it might be the last time I'd see him sober.

"What are your plans today?" He avoided the emotion I'd just shown him, so typical of our family.

"Going to the Goliaths' game and then out with Ryan." When his face curled down into a frown, I added, "Don't ruin our morning with a speech. I know what I'm doing."

"I hope so." He gave in, letting drop whatever comment he had on his mind. Instead, he concentrated on making coffee.

It was barely eight in the morning. I had hours before Ryan's game started, so I decided to put on my sweats to go for a speed walk. I had to release some of my nervous energy. After a solid hour I build up a good sweat and when I got back took a shower and then opened my journal to try and catch up on the last few days. Around eleven, my cell phone beeped.

Ryan: *Can't wait 2 c u.*

I typed: *Me 2*

I couldn't help but break into a huge grin. Knowing that I was on his mind filled me up with happiness—too much to contain.

He replied: *Ticket 4 u in will call—bleachers, as u ordered.*

I sent back: *Thank u. Luv sitting there! Xxoo.*

He wrote: *Come any time, earlier the better.*

I couldn't wait to find out where we were going. I put on a clean pair of sweats and a T-shirt and tennis shoes, grabbed my backpack, jacket, and hopped the streetcar to the ballpark.

I'm meeting my boyfriend and he plays my favorite sport. How cool!

To continue on my mission of new possibilities, after I got my tickets, rather than go through the bay gate as I usually did, I entered the stadium from King Street near the souvenir store. It was a silly gesture, but doing it reinforced how I felt.

I wonder if that's why Dad goes to the church across town? Changing up the smallest of steps in his life might lead to change.

The Goliaths were taking batting practice and Ryan was in the outfield when I stepped into the stadium. I watched him a few minutes, admiring how his fit body and long legs were packaged neatly in his uniform.

No wonder he attracts so many women. *I hope he's telling me the truth when he says he's not seeing anyone else. What a cute belly he has—all those firm muscles protecting him—yummy.*

I grabbed a rice bowl and a bottle of water from one of the food kiosks and found my seat in the bleachers. As soon as I began eating, I heard my name. Ryan was at the railing. *Be careful . . . management might be watching. That's probably shot to hell after last night.* I gathered my food and water, and walked down to meet him.

"Hey!" I tried without success to contain my excitement.

"Good afternoon, darlin'."

"Darlin'," I cracked up.

The fans started to gather around, hoping he'd throw them a ball or sign an autograph. With his beckoning finger, he motioned for me to lean as close as I could to him. When I did, he leapt to grab the top of the railing.

"Meet you in the players' lot after the game. I left word to let you pass. Just show them your ID." He hopped down and continued his practice routine.

"What did he say?" a little boy asked.

"That he was sorry he couldn't sign autographs for everyone." I tipped his cap. "He'll try and get one to you later if you come to the gate after the game."

"Can we?" the little boy shouted excitedly to a man who I

assumed was his dad.

"He really said that?" his father doubted.

"He did!" *I hope he doesn't mind.*

"Sure we can, son." I was certain the little boy jumped three feet high as they left the area.

Watching Ryan come in the game to pitch the ninth inning was a special bonus. When he jogged in from the bullpen, his theme music, *Smoke on the Water,* blasted over the sound system. The entire stadium roared with excitement. The anticipation from the fans was almost unbearable. He was poised and stoic as he stood on the mound and stared in, ready to face the last batter. With every ball and strike the stadium roared.

Standing ominously at home plate, the opponent was ready to hit the ball hard, trying to tie the game with one swing. He waved the bat several times, honing in on the pitch. When the ball roared across the plate and the umpire yelled *strike three*, the cheers and applause thundered. My screams and claps for Ryan and the Goliaths were among thousands of others.

I talked with several fans that were regulars at the games and then exited the stadium. After showing my ID to security at the player's parking lot, I was let through the gate. I said hello to some of the wives and excused myself when I saw Ryan at the exit door. I started to walk to his car . . . until I heard the voice of the little boy I'd told to wait at the gate for Ryan's autograph.

Thank goodness he spoke up. I almost forgot about him.

"He'll be right out!" I shouted.

Please be okay that I did this, please, please, please.

The face of my lover seemed filled with eagerness. I worried he'd forgotten about management standing around, but then I wondered, didn't they already know? How could they not?

"There's a little boy at the gate. See him there with his dad?" I pointed. "I told him you'd give him an autograph. I'm sorry to commit you like that. I didn't know what to say when he asked me what you whispered to me at the railing."

"No problem." He took away my fear so easily it was as if he magically waived his hand and gold dust filled the air around us. "Kev," he yelled to his friend, "toss me an extra ball from the equipment bag, okay?"

"Hey Nick," Kevin tossed the ball to Ryan.

"Hi, Kevin."

"What's your name young man?" Ryan asked the little boy.

"Garth."

"Well, Garth . . ." Ryan signed the ball and took off the boy's cap. He rubbed the boy's head, messing up his hair. "Before I give you this ball, I need to be sure you're a Goliaths fan. Are you?"

He winked at the boy's father.

"You bet! Dad and I come to watch you guys play every home stand!" He was almost shouting. His dad's smile was so wide I could hardly see his cheeks.

"You said the magic words." Ryan tossed the ball playfully. "Here you go."

"Cool! Thank you, Mr. Tilton! Look, Dad!"

His father thanked Ryan and after a few words they shook hands and walked away.

"You bailed me out of that one."

"You owe me?" His grin dared me to respond.

"Guess I do."

He started to put his arm around me.

"Not yet," I said guardedly.

"Right. I forgot." He leaned next to my ear and whispered, "I don't think they give a damn, Ms. Young. In fact, I think you're safer than you know."

What did you do?

Chapter 24

Taken Away, Into The Night

$\mathcal{R}$yan opened the passenger door of his Mustang.

I love when he does this.

"What are we doing?" I couldn't stand not knowing.

"Four-wheeling."

"Ooh fun!" I exclaimed. "Where?"

"Pismo Beach."

"We'll never make it," I cautioned. "I hate to break it to you but that's a four-hour drive."

"I know."

"Are there bright lights on the beach? It will be dark when we get there. Won't we be late coming back? You have a day game and what about packing?"

"Just hang with me, woman. I'll get us there before sunset."

"I don't see how. Even with the way you drive," I kidded.

"Hey, I've never driven recklessly when my Nicky's in the car."

When he exited the freeway near the airport, I caught on. He pulled off to an area where small, chartered airplanes waited for their passengers.

"You're *flying* us down there?" I was shocked.

"Not me. Our pilot." The excitement in his eyes caused his eyebrows to lift. "Surprised?"

"Yeah, I'm surprised! I can hardly wait. How long does it take? Oh, how fun. Do you have everything ready, or . . . do we need jackets? How do we get to the beach? Is someone picking us up? Will it be cold there, and—"

"I have everything we need." He introduced both of us to the pilot. After discussing the flight and what we should expect, we boarded the small aircraft and buckled our seatbelts.

"How long does it take to fly there?" I fired off another question.

"Thirty minutes." Ryan nodded to the window. "Have you ever seen the coast line from this altitude?"

"Sure! I'm a jetsetter and I've seen it hundreds of times," I teased.

"It's beautiful," he laughed. "Sometimes you can see whales and dolphins, cruise ships . . . I've seen some spectacular sights."

The view in here is pretty spectacular all on its own.

"You've done this before?" I asked, fearful I was being taken to a spot that was the first step in his routine of seduction.

"No, honey." He put his hand on mine. "I didn't mean that. I meant when I've been in a small plane touring the coastline. I've never taken any woman to Pismo. Don't start spinning."

"I'm sorry."

He brought my hand to his mouth and kissed it.

We landed at San Luis Obispo airport, twelve miles from the beach. A Jeep waited. Two men stood ready to drive us to our destination. Fifteen minutes and we were there.

A dune buggy was outfitted with helmets, goggles, and jumpsuits that went over our clothes. After putting them on, we zipped over and down the dunes, spinning and making doughnuts, and skimming across the sand and tide lines. The cold wind tossed our hair in every direction. Water splashed our bodies. The wet sand covered our goggles and dirtied our suits. Like children, we screamed with new excitement. For a couple of hours we took turns driving fast, reckless, and without a care.

"Had enough?" Ryan asked as dusk began to settle.

"I guess we should call it a day but it was so much fun!" I threw my arms around his neck. "Can I drive back?"

"Actually, just take us down the beach a little further," he grinned. "Around the next corner."

Waiting for us less than a mile away was a roaring fire and a blanket spread out on the sand. A small, portable table was set with plates, glasses and silverware. The two men who drove the Jeep stood next to a small grill. It was lit and ready to cook something delicious.

"What's this?" I was anxious for my next surprise.

"Let's take off our suits first and I'll tell you all about it."

We unzipped them and put them in a plastic bag Ryan grabbed out of a small storage chest.

"They're cooking fresh abalone," Ryan informed. "Have you ever had it?"

"No."

"You're in for a treat. I love it with potato salad and sliced tomatoes. Will you try it?"

"Hell yeah," I smacked my lips. "I'm starving! What is it about being at the ocean that makes me so hungry? Does it do that to you?"

"Guess it's the fresh air." His arms slowly encircled me.

"Watch how they pound the abalone." His chest was against my back. His mouth at my ear. I felt packaged inside his body and the masculine essence I'd come to adore. "It has to be tenderized and pounded into thin steaks. Then they'll dip them egg and breadcrumbs, and fry them in oil until they're golden brown. I hope you like it."

Oh, I already like it. Maybe I'll enjoy the abalone, too.

When we settled on the blanket, we tucked our legs under the table and were served. The steaks looked like crispy chicken strips. A big scoop of potato salad and thick slices of beautiful beefsteak tomatoes that were dusted with salt and pepper, accompanied the shellfish. Two large glasses held freshly squeezed lemonade.

Ryan watched me take my first bite.

I closed my eyes to savor it. Perfectly seasoned, the abalone was tender and hot. When I took a bite of the old-fashioned potato salad—the kind with eggs, pickles and onions—I thought I'd gone to food heaven.

"Everything is delicious," I said after another bite. "You're right about these pairing together so well. All this is more than I could have imagined for one afternoon. What a sweet memory. You're so nice to me. Thanks for today."

"Makes up for last night?"

"Most definitely." I kissed his cheek.

"Do you want to watch the sunset before we leave?"

"If we stay, can we find our way back to the jeep? It'll be dark . . . do we use the dune buggy, or what? We'll need extra flashlights; do we have those? They took our jumpsuits. Will our clothes be okay? Where do we return everything? How do we get back to the Jeep? All those dunes . . . are they safe?" I was about to ask another series of questions when Ryan answered them.

"That's why these two gentlemen have flashlights," Ryan assured me. "Don't worry, we're taken care of. They parked the Jeep right over the hill."

Settling into his body, my back nestled against his chest.

"You think of everything," I prepared to enjoy sitting against Ryan and the spectacular sunset ahead of us. "Don't kiss my hair. It's filthy."

His laugh rang out. With it, the sun sprayed purples, oranges, reds, and pinks across the sky as it said goodnight.

"I want you to stay with me tonight." Ryan gave me a nice squeeze just before the last bit of light dipped into the ocean.

All the hair on my body must have stood on end. The air around us had become thick, as if saturated with the sensations of our afternoon and evening at the beach. It was almost as if a crackling static filled the air. Any moment, I knew lightning might strike us.

"We can talk here." My fears mixed with anticipation. As usual, I tried drawing a line in the sand before letting myself enjoy another possibility. He quickly blurred it.

"No, baby, you need to come home with me," Ryan insisted. "I enjoy your kisses but I'm not a boy who's satisfied with only that. I'm a man. I need to be with you. I promise I won't make you uncomfortable. I stayed with you last night. I leave again tomorrow and I'm asking you to stay with me. Will you?"

I knew this was another trust question—I needed to step through the barrier—the barrier that kept me in fear and shadows. Resisting would be a slap in the face after what he'd done for me—not only our spectacular afternoon at the beach, but also the way he'd taken care of Jenise and Sean.

"Okay." I agreed.

What have I gotten myself into?

I took his hand as we walked off the beach to the Jeep. We

were sandy, wet, full, and satisfied. As we waited for the two men to pack everything into the vehicle, my mind was dizzy with questions.

Within minutes we were at the airport.

When we got onto the plane, I knew I was on a new path.

Our path.

Thirty minutes passed in a blink.

I was still swirling inside, trying to steady my nerves.

We landed at the San Francisco International Airport, got in his Mustang, and drove to his apartment. I knew a night alone with him would be so much more than those few hours together. Entering a new life with an uncommon love . . . unique, powerful all encompassing . . . I felt it would take over me completely.

Although I surged with the unknown, I hoped his arms would surround me forever.

When it came to this—a relationship that seemed to offer me a chance for a different life experience—I needed to believe we could be loud and open together. We needed to endure the rewards, the dramatic rise and fall of our emotions, the beautiful joys, and all the important parts and challenges of love.

Making it as a couple, I was still uncertain. The hope I felt that night with Ryan made the possibilities seem endless.

For me, hope meant strength. I needed to see myself that way.

We pulled up to his building. Naveed, the valet, greeted us. We said goodnight to both him and the desk attendant and walked through the lobby to the elevator.

"I don't want sex, yet," I blurted.

"I told you I'd respect your boundaries," Ryan said calmly.

Breathing—I must have been.

Remember doing it? No, I don't.

My chest constricted, my face tightened, and my body became

drenched in sweat. My heart thudded.

The elevator doors opened.

We stepped in.

Ascending to his apartment one floor at a time, it was as if my own expectations rose, too.

"Where's your guest bedroom? You have one, don't you? Did you ever answer that question when we went to Yountville? I remember asking, but—"

"I have a guest bedroom." His low laugh made the ground I was standing on seem uneven. "And yes, I answered you in Yountville. I won't do anything you don't want me to do."

I'm afraid we'll blow it again. What does that mean—anything you don't want me to do? I don't know what I want. I want to go all the way with him and then something pulls me back. What a mess I am. Is this normal in new relationships?

It turned out his apartment was on the top floor; perhaps a metaphor for how he'd handled his love life—always in command, always in charge, and on top.

"To the left, at the end of the hall," Ryan said when the elevator doors opened.

A set of French doors guarded the entrance to his home. Several numbers into his keyless lock and the latch opened. He held the door and I stepped through. It was everything I'd envisioned about his life—sleek, bold, glamorous and sexy. I didn't look back at him. Rather than sit down, I immediately walked over to his kitchen island to make sure we maintained some distance.

When I heard Ryan close his front door, I was certain a chapter of my life had closed with it.

Or was it a new chapter that opened?

Chapter 25

Exploring Ryan's Apartment

*R*yan tossed his wallet and keys on a table by the door.

I could feel his desire coiled and ready.

The anticipation of his arms winding around my body, coupled with the intoxication of the masculine man who seemed completely focused on me, caused panic to well up in my throat.

He's ready for more. What was I thinking coming here?

He walked over to me in a stride that was blatantly sexual.

My arms seemed to lift themselves around his neck. Slowly, his fingertips outlined the curves of my body. They'd known the roadmap to my weaknesses the first time he'd held my hand to his lips. He stayed me. I let my body react to the sensations of his touch. For the moment, he moved me the way he wanted; the way I wanted. Certain our hearts were so close together they'd shared a silent and invisible kiss, warmth radiated with every beat.

An unrestrained joy had painted the room.

"You make time stop for me." Ryan caressed my hair and pushed a strand behind my shoulder. "I feel like I'm sixteen and a new girl has come to school. She's standing in front of me, questioning everything with her innocence that's so much more than being naive. She's the warmest light I've ever known. Without even realizing it, you call to me in a tone that sings only to me. Do you know what I hear from your body?"

"No," I said faintly.

"You're ready for me; us; our next step. I don't mean intercourse." I could feel his mission unfolding. "I mean finding out what makes this connection special. Reasons we've come together and the emotions that keep us grasping for each other. I'm ready. I want to be with you. I need to feel everything about you. My spirit is ready to soar with yours. Let's take the steps we need to take and crash into our unknown. Do you want that?"

"Yes."

"Tell me how you feel," his voice lowered. "Describe the sensations that come from deep inside, like I've just revealed to you. Will you risk telling me what your heart wants to say?"

I want you to know, but another voice keeps whispering, be careful.

"Well . . ."

I breathed deeply.

Closed my eyes.

Put both hands on my stomach and then dropped them to my sides. It was as if I was letting go of my defenses.

"I see you as this innocent boy." I opened my eyes once again. "The things you do—Pismo Beach, sleeping over without pressuring me for sex, giving me a daisy on my birthday because you saw it when you were jogging—all of those are being tender and being in love for the first time. And then, there's this very mature and experienced side of you that stayed with me last night, and—"

"First love?" The corner of his mouth curled into a slight smile.

"It's how I see us. Like the first serious relationship each of us has had and, well . . ." I was stumbling and nervous. "You know, I don't really understand a lot about having them, but you and me— it's like we're shooting stars."

"I know." He took a deep breath. "I feel like I'm exploding whenever I touch you, see your smile or hear your voice."

"We're sweethearts," I shared boldly.

"And if we are sweethearts, how can we reach for love? Imagine us still in high school. What ways would be available to us at that age to explore each other?"

"More dating, continuing our deep conversations about everything, hanging out," I thought seriously. "And—"

"Yes, all of those," His voice sizzled in the air. "And nudging you gently, testing each other respectfully, and following the cues we give to each other for deeper intimacy."

"Hmm."

"I want to help you get there, Nicky."

Oh, I love his deep voice.

"I want that, too." I steadied myself on the kitchen island. "But we need to talk about what it all means."

"Sometimes . . ." He leaned close. His lips touched my ear. "Sometimes sex doesn't talk—it whispers."

Yes, whispers . . . kiss me now.

"Relax and make yourself at home while I go change." He kissed me on the forehead.

Oh damn . . . I was hoping to taste those moist lips.

"I can't relax wearing these dirty clothes." I tugged on my sand-spotted T-shirt and sweats. "I think my suit had a rip in it." As I

215

gathered myself, I sped up. "Can I shower in your guest bathroom? Do you have something I can borrow? Maybe a robe? I'll wish it later. You have a washer and dryer, don't you?"

"Sorry. I should have taken you home first." He held my shoulders. "I was afraid you'd get in your pajamas and want to stay put. Yes, I have a washer and dryer."

"I would have come with you," I smiled and looked away.

He started toward his bedroom, but then turned around. His expression warmed. With a determined look, he stepped close. His belly was against mine. My breasts pressed to his chest.

My heart pounds way too hard around him. I wonder if I should make a doctor's appointment.

"From the moment you left me to go up to your sister's bedroom early this morning, all I could think about was having you here to hold." His eyes were bright and seemed to take in every detail of my face. "Let me get something for you to wear."

"Thank you."

"Of course . . . you can always hang around in your birthday suit," he suggested. "I wouldn't mind."

"No, no, I'm not—"

"Kidding, Nick. Although . . . it wouldn't be the first time we were naked together, would it?"

I looked away. Embarrassed. Secretly kept an eye on him. I couldn't get over how he was able to say everything so naturally as if it was normal conversation.

It is. It can be.

"I'll be right back," he informed.

My legs, face, and chest . . . my entire body seems to be pulsating. Please don't call me into your bedroom.

I looked around Ryan's apartment, admiring his style. His furniture was modern and coordinated with the walls in shades of grays, blacks, and olive greens. Accents of purple and red were in the pillows, draperies, throws, and other accessories that complimented the décor. Several interesting paintings hung from the walls. Two sculptures of some modern interpretation of the human body sat on top of columns that were waist-high. His kitchen, dining, and living room areas were open and flowed together. He'd strategically arranged his dining table, sofas, and other furniture to create separate spaces within the large room.

Two oversized matching chairs covered in purple suede framed a large, black leather sofa. An entertainment center, put together from individual pieces of dark wood and glass, was arranged against the largest wall in the room. It was polished to a brilliant shine. On its sides, glass shelves held various photos in decorative frames. In the middle was a large, curved-screen TV. Speakers were mounted throughout the room for a theater style experience.

God, what a guy he is. Leather, dark, masculine colors, speakers everywhere—this is a big fat trap for naive and unsuspecting women . . . or not so naive . . . or unsuspecting.

There was a balcony and sliding glass doors to the left of the entertainment center. A large picture window to the right showed off a stunning view of the city. Perpendicular to the sliding glass doors was a gas fireplace. A small loveseat was placed in front of it. I visualized sitting there together on some chilly night, warming our souls and bodies, a cup of hot chocolate in our hands.

I looked more closely at some of the photographs on the glass shelves. Another introspective side of Ryan revealed itself.

One was a picture of a mother and father standing with their two little boys. I assumed it was Ryan and his brother. Both of the boys looked so innocent. It was difficult to glance at their sweet faces, knowing the tough times that had been ahead of them.

The innocence in the family photo made me think back to the

first time I became aware of my father's alcohol addiction—back to a time when none of us knew how dark our days would be.

It was a night when my eight-year-old sister and I transitioned.

How?

I still didn't understand the dramatic and subtle changes. I wouldn't really know how growing up in a family battling alcoholism would impact my life until one day in the future.

Chapter 26

Only An Undershirt

*U*nlike Ryan's father who was killed in the Middle East, mine was alive.

In many ways, however, like Ryan, I'd lost him, too. Dad's dark descent into alcoholism began even before I was in kindergarten. The beginning was somewhere just shy of five-years-old, when Jenise and I came to *know* his friend, Ernie.

Ernie started showing up at our house twice a week when my mother worked the night shift at juvenile hall. Gradually his visits increased. With each visit he brought a bottle of whiskey. Sometimes the bottle was a pint; other times a fifth.

Why didn't a man with two children and a wife of his own know any better than to bring alcohol to our house on the nights Dad was responsible for watching his two young daughters?

He was addicted.

Diseased the same as my father was.

He craved it.

Needed it.

Lived for it.

Ernie was a big man, well over six feet and 230 pounds. At that time I didn't know he used that strength to abuse his wife and beat his oldest son.

Unfortunately, Dad's peer was his first co-dependent.

Maybe on some of the nights when dad was late, he was doing the same thing—drinking a bottle at Ernie's house and preventing his friend from watching his own little boys.

I didn't grasp the deeper layers of what I had experienced for many years, but I became aware of two absolute truths: an addict has no conscience and addiction has no heart.

It turns on family.

It's greedy.

It wants what it wants.

It won't stop until it's satisfied.

The problem?

It's *never* satisfied.

Ernie and my father sat on two grey recliners in our living room in front of our big picture window. They pulled the heavy, beige curtains closed, as if locking themselves in cages of drunkenness.

They looked like giants sitting in the middle of the room.

Was the purpose of them sitting there to block my sister and me from escaping? Without actually being jailed, they trapped us, holding their bottles and our freedom in their hands.

The secrecy of our family's sins had begun.

The pure joy of being children, something my sister and I had previously taken for granted, ended in a blur of sloppy dysfunction that night.

Afterward, we never looked at being secure in our home—or having the protection of our father—the same way.

It began when Jenise and I were getting ready to take a bath. I had trouble removing my cotton undershirt. For some reason, I couldn't pull it over my head, nor could my sister. We both ran out of patience. I stormed out of the bathroom despite the protests from my sister.

I *knew* my father would help me.

There was no doubt in my mind. Problem solved.

Venturing out to where Dad and Ernie sat, I was bare-bottomed and uninhibited. I didn't think about being naked.

How did I know it wasn't okay to go out there without wearing any underpants?

I'd never been aware that being naked was wrong; I'd been around my parents plenty of times without clothes.

"Can you get my undershirt off?" I whined to my father. "I can't get it, and Jenise can't—"

The full force of Dad's hand smacked my butt. The burn screamed. Pain rang out like church bells ringing in Sunday mass.

"Get in the bathroom!" he screamed at me.

Even though it hurt like hell, it wasn't Dad's hard wallop that tore open my wound. It wasn't the handprint that remained in white against the crimson of my behind for hours.

What hurt was his words and the choices that followed.

"Are you *stupid*?" he shouted.

I felt as if he'd killed the two of us. Hearing my father call me stupid with his slurred voice and in front of his red-faced, drunken friend was far more painful than the burn on my bottom.

I felt dirty.

Ashamed of myself—without knowing why.

The experience changed me in several ways.

First, I was determined I would never feel *less than* ever again. Ultimately, the encounter drove me to pursue a higher education so that no one could call me stupid and have meaning behind it.

Second, I vowed not to be helpless or made to feel weak by anyone again—man or woman. I surrounded myself with the people who helped me gain strength and intelligence: teachers, higher ups at the places I volunteered and the parents of my schoolmates.

Third, I became sensitive to the *cute* words used to describe women. For whatever reason, the experience caused me to believe that some men tried to make women believe they were helpless little girls to be dominated and made submissive.

Fourth, it marked the beginning of my bashfulness and shame about my body. I came to adore sweats, sneakers, T-shirts, and high-collared sweaters. I covered any bare skin at all costs—and added additional weight to my body when I was an adolescent. I hesitated when I had an opportunity to share myself verbally and physically, not wanting to draw attention.

Because my father was horrified when his little girl showed her immature nakedness, I learned baring myself was dirty. It was better to hide. Stay unnoticed and invisible.

That night was also the beginning of my fear of boys. To be a naked girl was bad. Touching was a sin. Sex was for marriage only. It was the defining moment of how I shaped my thoughts and associations about having a physical relationship.

If I could make my own father and his friend react that way at only five-years-old, what did that mean? How would boys my own age react? If I made them uncomfortable, would they scream or hit me, too?

I couldn't take the chance that I might get that kind of rejection or be made to feel ashamed ever again.

Then Jenise was raped six years later and I learned being a flirty girl only brought trauma. My beliefs that sex was dirty were reinforced in every way. Even as I started to explore my own body and masturbate, I knew I was sinning. Turning on sexually was dangerous—and might bring violence.

During my weekly confessions at church, my priest told me that sex without marriage was a mortal sin—an offense to God. So much so that according to their teachings it meant I'd be cast to hell if I hadn't gotten the chance to confess my sin.

My naked body was bad.

Period.

After my father spanked me, I ran back to the safety of the bathroom in tears. Jenise locked the door immediately.

"I told you not to," she cooed. Her little arms surrounded and comforted my very soul. When she was able to settle me, my sister was able to take off my undershirt. "It's okay. They can't hurt us."

We sat in the bubbles hugging and playing with our bathtub toys. Washed each other's back. Let the water run down our bodies as if we were washing off the shame.

Not too much later, the conversation in the living room between my dad and Ernie quieted. We heard our father snoring. It was the same rolling, sinus-filled, raspy-throated snore we'd heard coming from down the hall when Dad drank too much whiskey and was asleep in his bedroom.

"Dad's snoring," I said in as quiet a voice as I could. "Do you think Ernie is asleep?"

Footsteps came up the stairs.

The bathroom doorknob turned back and forth a few times.

"Shh." My sister put her finger to her lips.

We sat in the bathwater without moving.

It seemed we weren't even breathing.

It wasn't hours but seemed like it when the footsteps went down the stairs and out the front door.

We heard Ernie start his car and drive away.

Neither my sister nor I told Mom what happened. We didn't purposefully withhold telling her, it was more that we didn't understand the sick, twisted man who tried to get into the bathroom and see two little girls bathing. We knew something was off about it, but like other children in families battling alcoholism, we didn't know what to do with our feelings.

After that night, we made sure we slept in the same bed together whenever Ernie visited. Our little arms hugged each other's body. We kept the light on and the door locked.

We believed, as children do with undying faith, our light would protect us from the darkness.

Maybe it did.

You would think that all two little girls could do with a father who chose the bottle over them was wait for Mom to come home and rescue us.

Not so.

During all those nights of being left alone, we learned survival.

It wasn't purposeful.

Nevertheless, we studied the lessons.

The options for two little girls weren't many. As if some power combined when we were together, we learned to hide, be quiet, lock the doors and try not to be noticed—we learned that being passive and invisible could save us.

What also happened that night was Jenise went from being an eight-year-old-child to my protector. She grew up instantly without knowing it. It brought the notion of survival into our house—another worry to our already sick and dysfunctional family.

In many ways, she became an adult in a matter of seconds.

The way she sheltered me?

She was my big, brave sister and my hero forever.

Like it did for Jenise, transition also came for me.

I wasn't fully aware of all the subtleties of what had just happened, but I *knew* my life was different. Something felt different about my body—and also the way I felt about Dad.

He had allowed his disgusting friend, Ernie, to witness how he's punished me for baring my bottom. I hated that Ernie sat there with a smirk on his face. I felt like I didn't matter.

And I was right.

The struggle to separate the drunken man in our house from the loving and sober one was an ongoing battle that lasted years. It was bad enough the raging demon took my father into the disease of addiction, but in choosing his friend over me, he put me second, the same way he'd done to Mom.

My father choosing to befriend someone as wretched as Ernie . . . what did that mean?

Yes, Ernie was another monster in our house. He hid under the cloak of friendship.

The other reveal?

My complete and unquestioning faith in my parents was gone forever.

The battle that raged without me . . . I knew I should challenge my father's decisions. But question my own father? No—how could I?

I stuffed down that question as far as I could. It was too difficult for a little girl to face. If I admitted my love for him had been damaged, who would I be? Who would *he* be to me?

I *had* to love him.

I *couldn't* hate him.

What his actions told me was I wasn't good enough for a father's love and protection.

Ernie made sure to leave every night just before Mom came home. He crept in and out of our house as if he were some dark spirit going underground. He never tried our bedroom or bathroom door again. Still, we made sure it was locked whenever he visited.

Jenise and I were left alone as our parents continued to deny our family's struggles. It wasn't an accident that we grew up quickly.

My sister and I . . . we *dealt* with it.

That evening changed the way I trusted—forever.

If I couldn't trust my father to keep me safe or choose me over their friends, how could I trust anyone?

If my own father would rather numb himself with a buddy and at the same time make a joke out of one of his daughters, he couldn't really love me, could he?

And now, wouldn't Ryan, with whom I was trying to form a beginning, a man who seemed to promise safety and love, a good man, let me go just like my father had?

Hadn't my father also been a good man at one time?

Chapter 27

A Photographer's Eye

*M*y dark memory faded as I studied the beautiful photographs Ryan had displayed on the glass shelves framing his entertainment center.

There were magnificent thunderstorms against Mid-western summer skies, dramatic ocean vistas, historic covered bridges, mountain lakes, and several tender shots of children.

Did you take these? Am I seeing another side of you—a side that's even softer than what I've seen so far?

Lush intimacy was evident in the emotion he'd captured. It was like he'd found the very secret of what each moment meant. I especially liked one of a little boy and a small rabbit. The boy held the bunny to his face. His smile seemed to show his inner joy. I imagined Ryan's gold dust had fallen on him.

I held the picture to my breast. The tenderness captured by the photographer came through like a brilliant wish of hope. To me, it spoke of his longing for calm and family. Respect for nature. The innocence I believed was in his heart.

There were no other pictures of Ryan, whether alone or with family or teammates or at events.

Where are all his trophies? He must have dozens from little league on up. With all his success, why doesn't he have them displayed? He wants attention only when in the public eye? Or is he so secure he doesn't need any of it? I wonder what his bedroom looks like. Oh, that's where the trophies are! A trophy room for trophy women! No wonder I wasn't invited in there.

I walked toward a shining, gray marble dining table, which stood between the living room and kitchen area. Eight high-backed chairs surrounded it, all covered in heavy black cloth.

Dark cherry wood cabinets and black granite countertops filled his kitchen begging to be touched. I couldn't resist. I ran my hands all over them, sliding along the polished surfaces without catching a rough edge. A Viking six-burner gas range with a large copper hood was centered in the long counter and an island workstation stood in the middle of the room. Its surface matched the countertops in the rest of the kitchen. It had a sink, a cutting board and outlets for small appliances. Four stools were tucked under its granite lip.

I imagined us sitting there someday, eating breakfast and having coffee. With such a beautiful gourmet kitchen at his disposal, I wondered if he cooked.

Curious what he had in his refrigerator, I opened the door. It wasn't stocked with much. He had basic items like milk, water, cheese, eggs, and some fruit.

"Do I pass your inspection?" Ryan came up behind me.

"Oh, damn!" I jumped. "You scared me. How long have you been standing there?"

"Oh, Nicky," he sighed. "Long enough to take you in completely. Watching you go through my apartment . . . I have a vision of you in bare feet wearing a robe with nothing on underneath before I ravage you."

I feel like I could sink right into his body and disappear.

"I wasn't expecting." I cleared my throat. Kept my back to him. Refused to look in his eyes. "Inspecting. I was looking over the design of your place. I like the color scheme a lot. Your furniture and all the matching accessories are nice. Everything is so shiny and clean. I love the feel of the granite. I've never seen a place so coordinated. Did you hire an interior designer or . . ." *Talk fast; change that look you know is on his face.* "Do you cook a lot? It doesn't seem like you have much in your refrigerator. On the other hand you have a gourmet kitchen . . ." I took a bottle of water. "Here's what I was looking for. May I have this? I'll pay you back."

"Please." Ryan's laugh was muffled as if trying not to laugh at my nervousness. "Help yourself. Just make sure you pay me back. I'll need that money tomorrow morning. Or . . . we can work out a trade tonight."

Sure easy for you to laugh. I'm a mess.

"I will." I tried to swallow the lump in my throat. "I mean, okay, I'll get it to you tomorrow."

"Slow down, Nicky. There's not need to protect yourself every second." He put his hands on my shoulders. I let him rock me gently back and forth.

God, his hands are big.

His voice sounded different. It was relaxed and comfortable. Now that he was safely surrounded by the comfort of his home, I wondered if a layer of protection had fallen from his body.

"I'm sorry, I can't seem to stop doing it." I closed the

refrigerator door and had no choice but to turn and look at him.

He wore a pair of gray, drawstring sweatpants. They were tied low on his hips and paired with a white, form fitting T-shirt. It stretched across his chest and hugged his biceps and torso. The man standing in front of me became hard-stamped in my brain. He was a vision I knew I'd remember forever.

As I looked into the cool blue of his eyes I was sure I heard them invite me in for a swim in his carnal waters. A basic and primal part of me answered their call.

I woke up standing right in front of him.

"Wow, Ryan." I commented out loud.

"What?" His sly grin might as well have translated to "I know I take your breath away."

You know exactly what I mean. I'm a gooey mess and there's nothing I can do about it. All I can feel is the aching—God, that feeling again . . . I want . . . I need to have fingers relieve me— Ryan's fingers.

"Nothing, I'm just . . . oh, man." I stammered like a fool. The sight of him was beautiful.

"Here you go." He held on to the clothes he'd brought for me from his bedroom. When I reached for them he wouldn't let go, as if encouraging me to play tug-of-war.

I struggled to pull them away.

My arms felt heavy. I was weak from his sexy looks and hooded eyes.

Turning away, I grabbed as hard as I could.

He finally let go.

I didn't notice what kind of clothes he brought for me. I didn't care. I needed only to catch my breath and get away from his simmering energy.

"Did you took, um, take these pitters? I mean, take *pitters*?"

I stammered. "Damn it—*photos* is what I'm trying to say. Are you the one who took them?"

Come on. Speak up Nick. Open your mouth and pronounce the words. My head, my face—everything feels red-hot.

"Yes, I took them." He nodded toward the photos. "Does that surprise you?"

"No. It's not that. I've seen your soulful side. I thought it might be a friend or whoever did the artwork in here. I was thinking maybe it was Chris, since he's an artist type with his music. They're beautiful. Congratulations, you have a great eye."

He stepped in close.

"Whelp, I'm going to shower and change." I tried to avoid his face, eyes, and lips. "I'll be right back." I started to leave the kitchen but didn't get far. "Um, where's the bathroom?"

Jeez, I must look like a complete idiot.

"Let me show you." His voice was smooth and slippery. "It's straight ahead and to the left. Follow me."

"Where are we going?" I had to look at him to see where I was supposed to follow.

"Through my bedroom." He held his arm straight. His long finger pointed the way.

It felt like a drizzle of hot rain had slipped down from my belly. Nerves that were hidden inside me and had previously lay dormant now hummed with an electric current. My legs hid the throbbing between them.

"I'm not going in there." I battled my smile. "The guest bathroom is fine." I didn't want him to know how I enjoyed his teases. "Where is it?"

"Through the door to the left of the kitchen pantry." His sweet, seductive laugh was hypnotic. I dreaded him knowing that when he used it, I could easily give into whatever he wanted.

Locking the door behind me, I turned on the shower, undressed, and stepped into the warm water. After I dried my hair, I put on Ryan's clothes—a man's large-sized, yellow T-shirt, and a pair of black, drawstring shorts. I leaned on the bathroom counter. Took one deep breath after another.

As I studied my reflection, I wondered: which woman would look back at me in the morning? One who was strong, in control and still a virgin? Or would it be my Evil Twin—the woman who had recently come to life and encouraged me to give in to the sensual world waiting for my discovery?

And what about you, Nick? What is it you want? Aren't you finally done with old beliefs that will condemn you to hell if you're not married when you have sex? Can't you trust this man in front of you, who's promised to help your family, revealed his secrets, and stayed because you asked?

Filling up with one more deep breath, I pursed my lips to slowly let out the air. When I felt brave enough, I opened the door and turned off the light.

Ryan was sitting in the middle of the sofa.

He watched me as I sat down.

I scooted as far away from him as I could.

"Thanks for the clothes." I tightened the drawstring on the shorts. "It feels good to get out of those sweats. They were all wet and sandy."

"Well, sand does get into warm, moist places." He looked me up and down. "Damn, you look good in anything. Is my T-shirt too tight on you?"

"Kind of. I'm embarrassed to tell you, it's just . . . this is a large. At least the label says so. Can you even fit in a large? I would think you're XXL or at least XL, aren't you? Anyway, it's um . . . I think it shrunk, Ryan. You should probably toss it. I don't see how you'd fit in it any longer. Anyway, thanks. Why do you ask if it's too tight?"

"It looks like your . . . um . . . it stretches across your . . . uh . . . your . . ." His eyes drifted to my breasts and then back to my face. "Do you want something to eat or drink?"

Oh damn! He gave me the shirt on purpose. I can't answer. I wish he'd keep some things to himself.

"I've got this bottle of water. If you're going to make something, I could eat. And tea would be good, too."

Watching his body move as he poured water into the teapot, put it on to boil and then reach into his kitchen cabinet, was a fantastic show. The way his arms and thighs bulged and then relaxed—I felt like he was a bakery of treats—buns, cakes, and sweet rolls ready to taste. Standing at his kitchen sink, his shoulders and arms flexed as he sliced some cheese and fruit. He plated the food and walked over to the sofa.

"That looks delicious." I felt hypnotized. I closed my eyes. Little by little I knew he'd suck every bit of me into his world.

"Mm-hmm." He sat next to me. "Certainly does look delicious."

It was easy to see how Ryan enjoyed his dominance and experience with seduction. He had an ability to knock me sideways and seemed to delight in every moment.

"Where did you take these?" I put a piece of cheese and fruit on a napkin and walked over to the entertainment center before he could settle in beside me.

Phew! It's hot in here.

"They're from all over." He took several strides toward me and then stood behind me. His head rested on my shoulder. The evening scruff on his face rubbed against my cheek. All those luscious muscles in his hairy arms wrapped around my waist.

My hands rested on top of them.

It was as if a big bear hugged me.

I could feel the light vibrations of his voice with each spoken word. They were so thick with desire it was as if my shoulder resonated with warm ripples. Every note that kissed my cheek was smooth, even, and relaxed. My resistance—and perhaps the first layers of my defense—peeled away.

"The one with the twin girls was in Atlanta." He took my arm up with his and brushed against my right breast as he pointed to the photo. "See how sweet they are sharing their cotton candy?" His hips moved a little. "The pink in the spun sugar matches the color in their cheeks. They were so happy. They didn't fight or bicker, they were just giddy to have their treat." He slowly turned his head. I could feel his breath fall like a snowflake on my face. His mouth was open, lightly touching one ear and then the other. "Can you see the color? See what I'm trying to capture?"

Yes, I understand completely what you're trying to capture.

"Uh-huh." I forced a whimper with the little strength I had left. My throat felt dry.

It was difficult to catch my breath.

His chest pressed into my back.

I thought I might need CPR just to get through the next few minutes.

Ryan constantly moved and shifted.

Hands, arms, hips, and legs all seemed as if they were trying to feel my body in subtle and not so subtle ways. His right arm stretched across my breasts and his left hand moved to my navel. It flattened against my rounded belly. Slowly rubbed it in circles.

"Oh baby . . . God, you're . . ." He let out a moan.

At times it was all I could do just to look at him when he talked. But when that voice of his deepened and he groaned?

My body squirmed as if my sensual core was trying to come out of me. My natural reaction to his hand on my stomach was to step backward into his hips. When I did, I pushed against his erection.

A breathy sigh escaped his lips.

My bottom felt his hips move into it.

I closed my eyes as I listened to the sounds of his lust and tuned into the language from his body. Like a lasso of invisible magnets, he pulled me in. His grip tightened. I was helpless, caught in his masterful seduction. He held me firmly against his chest and stomach. Although I couldn't see behind me, his masculine body was obvious—hard and plain against my back.

Chapter 28

A Child's Innocence

"*T*he picture of the little boy and his rabbit was taken in Colorado." Although he was describing his photo, Ryan's brooding sensuality moved all over me. "We were playing in Denver. I drove to the country to relax and there he was on the roadside at the end of a long driveway with his box of rabbits. I'll never forget when he started talking. He broke into a big grin. Both his front teeth were missing. Do you see how wide and beautiful his smile is?"

That's because you hypnotized him just like the rest of us.

"Mm-hmm."

"Do you think I captured the essence of the moment?" he whispered.

I wonder if I have high blood pressure.

"Nicky?"

"Hmm?"

"What do you think of the photo?" he asked softly. "Do you like children?"

Once again, he turned his head so that his cheek lay against mine. Instead of whispering in my ear, he kissed it. His lips moved purposefully and with a light touch.

I wonder if skin has ever melted off of anyone's body. I could slip into the grooves of his hardwood floor and no one would ever know what happened to me.

"Yeah," I swallowed.

I can't talk right now. Don't ask me any more questions.

I could feel his feathery eyelashes tickling me, delicate as a spider's web. His cheek, studded with evening whiskers, snuggled against mine. When his head moved, I was sure his mouth was searching for my lips. I turned to receive his kiss. It was simple, yet profoundly intimate; far more complicated than any discussion we'd had so far.

Could he sense my heart was opening?

Is this what being vulnerable feels like?

"Nicky?" he whispered.

"Yeah."

"What do you think about them?" His throat was against my neck. The vibration of his voice made me feel like I was at the start of the Indy 500; engines roaring through me, ready to take off, pedal to the metal, open and ready to go full throttle.

"I think . . ." I took a deep breath and tried to expand my chest so I could say something that made sense. "All your photos show . . . well they show that you have a soft spot; like your soft belly. I really like it, you know."

When Ryan laughed, I laughed, too.

My comment finally carved our bodies from the thick, sexually charged air.

It seemed to be glowing.

"The tea and fruit sure sound good." I patted his hand. It rested on my stomach. "I'm ready for more." I needed to move before I went over the edge and acted on my desire. And yet, I wanted to stay right there with him.

Ryan held my body against his, perhaps savoring how it felt to have me tucked into his maleness. When I turned to walk back to the sofa, his hand dragged across my belly. I felt so off balance I thought I might fall. Somehow, I managed to sit down.

He went into the kitchen to get the mugs of tea. "Here you go." He placed each on a coaster, protecting the polished glass table and pushed the plate of fruit and cheese toward me. "You still hungry?"

"Yeah. The ocean just . . . well, we already talked about that. Something in the air, I guess. I mean, dinner though—it was delicious! Just because I'm hungry, it doesn't mean that it wasn't filling, it was awesome. It's just time for little something. Do you sleep better when you've had a little snack before bedtime? The time really flew by, don't you think?"

"Mm-hmm," he agreed. "I counted down the minutes until we could be alone together. Aren't you glad it's just you and me now?"

I nodded. Nibbled on a piece of melon.

"I love being alone with you, Nicky. It lets me see more of who you are. You had fun at Pismo?"

"Oh, yeah, so much fun. It was like we were kids. I haven't felt that carefree in a long time. You have no idea the gift you gave me today. To play and have fun was . . . thank you."

"I'm glad. Hey, what did the bandleader say to you last night? I never did get around to asking you." He had one eyebrow raised. "He seemed uh . . . friendly."

"Auditioning for a backup singer," I shared. "He gave me his manager's card. I told him there was no way I could do it with college on the horizon. Plus, he needs someone who's at least twenty-one."

"I thought I was the one you accused of spilling gold dust on people," he teased.

"He must be desperate," I giggled. "In fact he told me he was."

"Uh-huh," he kidded. "Desperate for what?"

I shrugged my shoulders and quickly stuffed six crackers, a piece of cheese and three pieces of pineapple into my mouth. I washed it down with several gulps of the tea. Followed with two more pieces of cheese and two crackers.

"Easy there," he directed. "I don't want you to get sick. Not tonight."

"I know." My mouth was full and I let out an awkward laugh. "I won't." I chewed some more. Laughed again. Finally swallowed. "I'm a noisy eater. I chomp instead of chew. Help me with snacking, okay? I love them, but not I realize they were substitutes for other things. Old habits, you know . . ." I tried to break the moments that were flying by me and package them into small, manageable bits. "The photo of the two children with the man and woman—is that you and your family?"

"Yes."

"It must be hard being so far away," I supposed. "Living on the opposite coast and all."

"It is." He fiddled with a few pieces of cheese and wrapped them around a piece of melon. "Although sometimes I'm glad to have the space. Keeps Chris and I from killing each other."

"So . . . here we are." I shifted nervously.

"Here we are," he chuckled. "Something on your mind?"

"Well, you were insistent I come here and I was just wondering what all the hubbub was. You need to talk about something serious? That was my impression."

"Oh, I'm very serious." He scooted closer. "I need to spend an entire evening with you."

Oh God. I wonder if I'll really go to hell. That's got to be bullshit, right, Evil Twin? Is that why you came to life inside me?

"For one night I have you to myself. I'm leaving tomorrow. Already I miss you," he said sweetly. "Do you miss me when I'm on the road?"

He's murder.

"Yes. It's almost . . . kind of, well, frightening when I think of being without you. You're someone whose company is easy to get used to. Have I ever told you how much I love your check-in calls and texts?"

"I like hearing that. Sometimes I worry that I'm too much."

"No, not too much." I thought carefully before revealing more. "Your life and what you've done so far is a lot for me to handle, but when we're one on one, I feel we're perfect."

"Amazing how things slow down when it's only me and you, isn't it?" He sipped his tea.

"Yep."

"You'll tell me if I do something that puts you off, won't you?" he checked. "Don't keep it to yourself, okay?"

"Okay."

"In my world . . . being around so many men, our gross habits and rough language can take over. I need to hear your voice, views and opinions. It's the calm that surrounds me when I need it most."

"God, Ryan. The things you say."

"What do you mean?"

"You know." I looked toward the balcony. "You have a way of undressing me even though I still have my clothes on."

His eyes hooded.

"Shh." I put my finger on his lips.

"So why did you *really* come to my apartment? You could've stayed home."

"Not really. I mean, yes, but what you said . . ."

"What?" he asked purposefully.

"You scared me." It took everything I had to admit my feelings.

"Why?" His look changed to concern. "What did I do?"

"Last night, you said you'd go if I didn't want to come to your place because that meant I didn't want you—I thought you would leave me," I confessed. "I don't want you walking away forever."

"That's not what I meant." His eyes went soft and he put his arm around my shoulder. "I'm sorry; I didn't—"

"I mean, logically, I was pretty sure you didn't mean you'd walk away," I interrupted. "Your words sliced right into my fears. Not having you to talk to, well . . ." I played with my fingernails. "I can't imagine my world without you."

"So you *would* wonder about us," he said with his wry grin. It was as if he needed reassurance that I wanted him.

"I already said it would be terrible."

"Because you love me," he took a chance with his assumption.

Dear Lord, say something, Nicky. Just don't let your vulnerability show too much or he'll take advantage of you.

"You know, staying up late like you do can't be good for you." I began tearing apart the piece of cheese on my place, avoiding his statement. "The club last night, Pismo today . . . what if you have to pitch in today's game?"

"I'll be okay." His voice was slow and sultry. He walked over to his sound system and took several CDs from his storage tower. I watched his body as he moved.

"You like CDs?" I was curious.

"Does that surprise you?"

"Yeah, it does. I'd think that someone like you would just dock whatever music device you have and then select a song from one of your playlists."

"Someone like *me*?" he repeated.

That low voice is going to make me faint.

"Yeah, well, I mean you have the money for what you want . . . I guess. I don't track the money part of sports, it's . . . I would assume, that's all. Plus, the Internet makes it easy to get music; when do you have time to shop for CDs?"

"I have time." He sorted through his collection. "I use an MP3 on the road so I don't clutter my phone. When I'm here relaxing, I like CDs. I already told you. I'm an old-fashioned boy. I have a vinyl collection, too."

"Oh that's right," I smiled. "I remember hearing you were old-fashioned when it came to your hot chocolate." I giggled and couldn't help but reminisce back to the first night he spent at my house when he'd bragged about the way he made it.

"My hot chocolate is classic, though, isn't it? Totally old school," he laughed. "Do you—" He stopped when he caught me checking out his body. He smiled and popped in a CD.

I can't believe he caught me checking him out! Nothing like letting him know my green light is blinking on go.

As I looked him over, I noticed his sweatpants were loose enough to hide his thighs and his butt. The other thing . . . wasn't hiding—and there was no mystery about what it wanted.

What did I do to cause that? Just from standing together looking at his photos? Is that all it takes?

"Do you like children?" He walked back to the sofa and sat next to me. "You never answered."

"Love them. I volunteer with Tara at Children's Hospital. Didn't I ever tell you about that? You should see the faces of those little boys and girls, especially when Tara comes in. She's like this earth mother or something and . . ." I stopped, fearing my rant went on too long.

"Please don't stop," he reached for my hand. Ryan smiled as if he were a child who'd found warmth in his mother's arms.

"I'm rambling."

"I love it when you ramble. It's so sweet when that smart mind of yours spins and you get lost in your thoughts and dreams. I want to hear everything you have to say, no matter what it is or how long you talk about it."

"All right, then. You asked for it." I lined up on the runway and took off, telling him about all the charities at which I volunteered. "By the way, do *you* like children?" I asked, wrapping my story.

"Mm-hmm." He looked over my face. "I can't wait to have my own; it's one of my dreams."

"I see." I stopped talking.

The air was still.

We sipped our tea to the sounds of soft jazz playing in the background.

"This is relaxing. George Benson. You like this kind of music?" I picked up the CD case and read the list of songs. "You played it when we were at Half Moon Bay, too."

"I like just about every genre, but mostly because you set this kind of music in my car when you went into Sammy's. Right now? I'm in the mood for some soft music to go with my soft belly."

He waited for my response.

I couldn't hold back my giggles.

"I'm just laughing at the image of you with a soft belly. Ha! With all your workouts I hardly think . . ." I poked his stomach. "Still, you do have a nice give there. Ooh, I love it."

"Speaking of . . . I'd like to take a look at *your* soft belly."

244

He traced the corner of my mouth with his thumb. "Isn't it time we relaxed? We can come so close . . . so close."

He put his mug of tea on the coffee table.

His blue eyes focused on me.

I sensed something in my core tightening.

He reached for me.

"Kiss me, Nicky."

Chapter 29

Exposing Soft Bellies

"*R*yan." My breathing was shallow and fast. "Wait." He kissed me on the cheek. "Wait, I—"

His soft lips kissed mine.

"Can I love you?" His hands outlined each of my arms.

"You know, I mean, you're . . . wait." I put my hand over my face. "Wait a minute."

It was sublime as his fingers squeezed and massaged the back of my neck. All the knots loosened inside my body. The boyfriend-infused *stress* in my body, however, continued to build.

"Okay. What I'm saying is that I know you're in a soft-belly mood. But I've been going non-stop three nights in a row and the only mood I'm in is tired. Where did you say your spare bedroom is? Let's talk tomorrow after I get some sleep. Okay with you?"

I know sleep isn't on his agenda. I'm struggling. I don't know what I want to do. Oh crap, look at him. He's making his move and I'm too weak to resist. It's over.

"I had a great time tonight, but you know I don't go out and party like the other women you date. Well, that's judgmental, but, if you do. I'm not a cool girl. I know you like your clubs, but I can't last all night like you can. I don't know how you do it, Ryan. I'm tired and just . . . beat."

That sizzling look of passion returned to his eyes.

His smile was now full of desire.

All the talking was done.

His invitation was mailed, I RSVP'd, and Ryan's party of two was in full motion.

"Nicky, you're the coolest girl I've ever met." He twirled strands of my hair around his fingers. "You can handle me or you wouldn't have come here."

"I'm not sure what you mean," I fibbed.

"All you had to do was tell me you wanted to stay home." His thigh pressed against mine. "We both agreed we should explore our relationship on a deeper level. Now uncross your gorgeous legs and wrap them around my hips. I've waited long enough to feel you."

Wrap them . . .how . . . where?

Everything about him seemed to open.

I was sure a light had begun to illuminate from him.

"Didn't we both agree to take this slow?" My breathing was suddenly labored. "Ryan? Didn't we . . ."

He ran his hands through my hair. I was drawn to him immediately and moved closer. His mouth descended to mine. I knew his lips were going to devour me.

I realized . . . I wanted his passion.

The sounds from his throat and the way he touched me were a testament to his lust—he was giving himself over to our most basic need.

Urgency, lying dormant inside of me came alive and brought intense pulses between my legs. I felt like I was a riverbed, filling with pools of warm, liquid light. Little fish covered in gold were swimming in my belly.

The sensual wonder I'd only experienced when touching myself seemed ready to climb up to a new level of pleasure with the man at my side. I wanted to be one with his visions—to feel, embrace, and live them.

He caressed my shoulders.

Pulled me close.

Eagerly, I pressed my lips more deeply into his.

Uncrossed my legs.

Straddled his thighs.

A few moments earlier, I'd been nervous and afraid of losing control. But now our kiss, enchanting and welcoming, brought me closer to him than ever before.

Ryan brought my left leg around his hip. With a quick turn he moved on top of me. I was underneath him just like he wanted—like I wanted.

"How does it feel to have me between your legs?" His voice slithered inside me.

The paralysis of desire had hit.

I couldn't answer.

He gently bit, licked, and kissed my ears. His tongue licked the ridge of their outer curve. The vision of Ryan penetrating my body crept into my mind, almost forcing me to tilt my head back.

I hoped the perfection of our entwined love would stay suspended in time.

The feel of him against me, the warmth, the whispers . . . all brought waves of invisible sparkles surging throughout my body. They tingled and coaxed my legs to tighten around him. His caress was gentle on my cheeks. When kissed, I was overcome with the stored power inside of him, bulging and ready to be released on me.

I shivered.

A photo he'd displayed in his living room—capturing one drop of water hanging precariously from a pine needle, seemed made for our moment.

I imagined a freshly melted snowflake had settled there. Hand in hand we approached the perfect crystal. It hesitates. Suspended. Delicate.

I was there.

He was with me.

We embraced.

This magnificence was meant for us.

I felt wrapped in the scene as Ryan and I held on to each other inside his apartment and inside our hearts.

It was a scene that had played out millions of times.

Simple.

Stunning.

The clarity that presented itself was sudden.

I understood differently—we'd been frozen in our fear, watching the beauty and also the challenges of life pass by us.

It was time to thaw.

I needed to fully engage. Melt my defenses and let go of my protection. Expose the tenderness underneath the steel around my heart—like that perfect and suspended forest crystal.

The tip of Ryan's tongue curled. He flicked it against my ear as if he were a snake, stabbing at the air, smelling, tasting, and trying to sense his surroundings. His tongue opened my lips. The inside of my mouth felt as if he had a special tool that explored me. Having it inside my mouth tasting and exploring made me hyper-aware of my body. All I wanted was to close my eyes and fly away in my fantasy. Sensations came fast—Ryan's hands, muscles and the deep sounds of his voice—brought me to a place of complete and pure enlightenment.

Move me, kiss me, and touch me any way you want. Don't make me talk.

"Nicky," Ryan whispered.

"Mm-hmm."

"Are you okay?" He lifted his head to look at me.

"Yes."

"Do you want me to keep going?"

"Yes."

Yes, yes, yes!

He put one hand on the back of my head. His legs tightened. They captured me. His lips sealed my mouth. We were joyously melting into our forest floor just as I'd imagined moments ago. Ryan held me so that I couldn't move. It was undeniable—he was ready to make the flames rise between us.

Our voyage had started.

I tuned into a language I'd never understood until that evening.

Moistening my skin, his tongue moved up and down my neck, tasting my salty wet flesh. My body was in delicious agony. I was aware of and enjoyed the feel of his body as it pushed, strained, and flexed. I imagined his muscles would move the same way when he made love to me.

I felt as if his soul drifted into me, swirling with my spirit, dancing and twirling in pure joy.

Although I weakly resisted when he lifted my shirt, I didn't mind. I made low sounds of my own. Our sensitive pleasure burst like a thousand butterflies swarming into the air. A million little voices whispered, "*Give in, give in, give in.*"

"Relax and let me pleasure you. The more you think about us

and the slower I've been with you, the farther you've drifted from me. Let's begin a dream together right now."

Take me away.

"Put your arms around me." His request was gentle and yet commanding.

I raised my arms.

He removed my shirt completely. His mouth inched from my neck to my stomach, searing my skin in hot, tender kisses. The sensations between my legs made me ache and throb—oh, the delicious throbbing. My logical mind disappeared. I felt the magnificence of my woman's body become moist, preparing me to be with a man.

Ryan unhooked my bra and flung it across the room. He never looked away from my eyes. He said something I couldn't understand. My head was filled with too many heartbeats. And yet, I sensed what it was.

His eyes contained the blue of the ocean as they looked at my breasts and then back to me. I adored the way they hooded, widened, warmed and held love inside them. Squirming under his desire, those eyes watched my every move. I wanted to shed my bashfulness and become one with the primal male on top of me. My breasts pushed up to him. I wanted him to hold them in his big hands. My nipples were long and hard almost as if stretching so his mouth could taste them.

"You're my exquisite woman. Did you know I've always thought of you that way?"

I moaned.

As we rose up together, his chest against my breasts, my body touching his little stones on his pecs, the two of us rejoiced together. Our hearts pounded.

Love waited patiently to join two bodies in a physical way.

His tongue slid into my mouth.

Kisses covered my neck.

Lips touched my shoulders.

Chills rushed over me.

"Ohhhh . . ." I moaned from some deep place that was swollen with my previously hidden woman who now begged for more.

He lifted his head.

The loving look on his face was overwhelming.

He took his shirt off.

Beginning to wrap around me, was a man who'd become a predator ready to eat his prey.

Oh his chest . . . his beautiful chest is against my breasts . . . goodbye world . . . I'm floating away.

Both of us knelt on the sofa, seeking more. I rubbed against him, purposefully trying to experience his masculine body and the passion underneath his skin. My woman's essence cried for release. Everything about him filled me with pleasure.

I imagined lying together on a tropical beach, each of us caressed by a silk cloth scented with the finest oils as it lifted in warm breezes.

His hand held my breast; my body now in a state of complete and total gratitude. Lowering his head as if to kiss me, he suddenly stopped to look in my eyes.

"Would you let me make love to you tonight?" Ryan asked.

My body rippled.

Chapter 30

Primitive

"*Y*es," I answered without hesitation.

Was he *really* asking for full on sex or had he only tested my desire?

Was I *really* as close to going all the way as I'd just inferred?

"I love . . ." I started to speak. Instead, I succumbed to his hands and let the chills flow up and down my back. "I love . . ." Ryan's chin gently nudged, lifted and directed my cheek to turn so he could kiss me. I locked my hands around his neck. Let him lower our bodies down on the sofa.

He was on top of me.

The curves of my feminine body accommodated him perfectly.

His belly moved in and out, the same way his tongue slipped in my mouth. I felt as if he was urging me to follow rhythms of erotic abandon. My breasts felt his nipples rubbing them. Acting as an anchor, his feet pushed against the sofa. He became long and aggressive.

We gave each other permission to escape.

Our hips danced as if we were at the mercy of a siren—some exotic Polynesian call filled us.

Our backs arched into natural bridges.

My body softened as it was meant to, preparing for a man to enter me.

The sounds from our desire became laced with urgency.

"Nicky." Another strained whisper fell at my ear.

"Hmm."

"I'll make love to you so sweetly."

"Hmm . . ." I could hardly answer him.

"Will you let go?" He caught my earlobe in his lips and then slowly pushed it from his mouth with his tongue. "I'll be gentle and respect every one of your stop signs."

I have no stop signs. They're all down.

"Do you ever look at your breasts when you get excited?"

"No." I said weakly.

"I'm looking at them now. Shall I tell you?" A kiss on my lips and a nod from me was all he needed to begin a narration of the visual blush he saw from my desire. "When your nipples harden the flesh around them shrivels." His tongue traced the little bumps that ran around my pink circles. "Your areola darkens." He kissed the area he'd just described. "The sweet little pink becomes full as if your breasts are telling me to take them in my mouth. I'm the one, Nicky. I'm going to explore them in every way. I'll whisper to you softly about the delicious connection I feel inside your body. I need to know how it is to taste every inch of your skin as I lick and suck your curves and moist places. Your signals are visual and obvious. You don't have to say a word; I'll know everything."

He'll know . . . everything.

"Take them." I pulled on the back of his neck, coaxing his mouth closer to my swollen breasts.

His fingers held me reverently. Squeezed lightly. He rolled my pink tips with his fingers and circled them with his tongue. Nipping at each hard pebble, he moaned in pleasure as he suckled them. The way his body stretched and twisted on top of me encouraged me to embrace my fantasies, as well as the ones I imagined played in his mind. Lifting up enough to make a little room between us, he untied the drawstring on my shorts. I was his roadmap to explore.

Oh yes.

My body struggled with the dual sensations of pleasure and resistance I felt against him. My natural response was to tighten my legs, but they were open wide around his hips.

His hand slowly moved against my belly. Gripped the waistband of my panties. Slid inside of them and reached my furry pelt. He played with my pubic hair. Tugged gently. Twisted it in his fingers. His eyes never left mine.

"I'm going to open the nest of your wet curls and feel the soft lips so carefully protecting you. I'll circle the opening of your vagina with my finger and feel the tremble between your legs as I work your clitoris."

My head went back.

"Look at me," he ordered gently.

I forced my eyes open.

"I'm going to slide my finger through the split of your body so I can feel the part of you I know is moist and ready for me. Your pubic hair is so silky and wet. Can you feel how your body prepared for me so quickly? You had no decision or control, your vagina moistened with only your expectation and desire."

His fingers gently pushed my lips apart. They caressed my labia; the delicate softness revealed only when my legs opened. My garden was alive and blooming as he stroked my inner passion. Feeling him play with the opening to my secret areas was almost too much to bear—almost. It was a hypnotic bliss I never thought I'd be able enjoy with another person.

My legs loosened.

I opened.

Let him feel me the way I imagined he wanted.

His finger slid easily over the liquid heat of my pleasure.

My excitement mounted quickly.

When he pinched shut my outer folds, the moisture between them trickled down to my buttocks and inner thighs.

I moaned.

He twirled his finger around my opening. Slid along my swollen, hidden place—the soft little spot carefully tucked away. Ryan changed the gentle stream that flowed from inside me into a waterfall of wonder.

"You're ready for me," he breathed heavily. "Do you understand what I mean?"

I nodded.

"Nicky?"

"Uhhh," I moaned and then closed my eyes.

"Look at me, sweetheart."

I opened my eyes and found intimacy.

He had me.

I couldn't know that being so completely vulnerable with another person was real. I'd fought against it. Now? I welcomed it. His finger was at the opening to my core, the pad of his thumb stirring my clitoris into frenzy. Although I was afraid, another part of me felt complete as if being in his arms was meant for me.

At least for one night, I trusted him.

It was a golden moment.

We whispered without words and fell into another world. Anything . . . everything we could be for each other flew in front of me with light speed.

"I love you, Nicky." My sensitive pearl hardened. It was swollen. Ready to feel the rush of blood in my body against his finger as moved over it I trembled. "Don't be afraid. I love you." His finger provoked. Urged. Made my hips want nothing more than to move and adjust, surrendering to his touch.

A new kind of pleasure waited. It was coiled tight and deep in my belly. I hungered for its release. My hips rose, wanting to meet his body. Resistance disappeared. I stopped questioning our evening, our togetherness, and the man loving me.

"Nicky, you're so . . . mmm . . . baby, so . . . tender." Every muscle in his body seemed to bulge. The veins in his neck throbbed, as if trying to gain impossible control of his sensual pain. "My finger is circling the opening of your womanly body. So carefully protected," he whispered. "I'm deep into our first time, imagining I'm inside you. I want to feel the liquid you make on my penis. I want to be painted with it and enjoy the way it makes the entrance to your body smooth and easy for me. My semen is spilling over. I'm wet and glistening in anticipation. Are you ready to experience my love?"

"Yes!" I answered with all the strength I had left.

"It's like I've dipped my body into a new universe. My wish has been granted. I'm swirling the stars with my fingertip. Tell me. Tell me you want everything: my fingertips, hands, mouth . . . all the parts of my body that will join the intimate parts of you."

"Yes." I grabbed his sides and pulled him down. "Yes."

"I'm yours." He pressed hard on my wet, aching spot.

I could hear his every breath. All the little sounds in his throat and chest were like music. My hips met his; they arched and rocked to get closer to his body. My stomach jerked and screamed, announcing, *I'm open, I feel you,* and *Yes! I'm yours!*

Every consciousness and control I ever had, abandoned me.

Desire rolled in crescendos.

I started to climax.

"Aaaahhh . . ." A yearning like I'd never felt before pushed into the air, drifted up and made its own song as I came into orgasm. There was no stopping my responses. The blood rushed down, first filling and engorging my belly and then flowing between and down each of my legs.

My river had rushed to her ocean.

"Let my body and heart love you," he exhaled the words.

I whimpered.

He kept the pressure of his finger on my body, his skilled motion polishing me, while his belly pressed against mine. It moved in rhythms. My body fought to push through the unbearable seduction of the man on top of me. I wanted the freedom to open wider and shout for the joy I'd just experienced. I broke jaggedly into his arms, his torso and thighs, calling out in a new language, approving of what he'd done.

My spasms ceased. New rawness settled in. The entire area of my opening and clitoris felt as if it was on the edge of hurt. Ryan's continued devotion to my wet little bump made me rise and fall dramatically and in a kind of tender pain.

"Okay, Ryan." It was like having too much. He wouldn't stop. "Ooh, I . . ." It was as if my body's strings were plucked everywhere and too many tunes were playing all at once. My legs and belly were sensitive. Even the air around me felt heavy.

"I want you to know what you taste like." He pulled his finger from my swollen lips. Withdrew from my panties and opened my mouth so I could experience what my body had made. He put the same finger into his mouth. Closed his eyes and sucked on it. "Mmm, delicious. I can't wait to taste more of you."

All I wanted was collapse into the sofa. With my energy drained, I felt soft and lush, as if I was sinking deep into billowy clouds. Just as I was falling into my sated, dreamlike state, Ryan slipped his hand inside the waistband of my panties again.

"Oh . . . please . . . no . . ." I gripped his thick forearm. "I'm—" I tried hold his arm from going any farther with all the strength I had but he was too strong to hold back.

"I'll get you ready again." The muscles in his arm tightened. "I know you're tender. This time I'll move your orchid more carefully. Relax for me."

His lips, chest, arms and stomach connected everywhere with my body. He had me at the exact place he wanted me. Once more, the pad of his thumb began shining my diamond. He left one finger at the opening to my core.

It was completely still.

I tightened and pulsed.

"What . . ." I needed to understand. "What are you doing?"

"I need to experience the way your vagina clenches so I can understand the way you move. I want to sense the way you grab at my finger when you get excited. Your moist walls squeezing me—I want that, Nicky. Your inner thighs yearning to achieve the position that gives you the most intense orgasm . . ." drew in a deep breath. "I have to sense your body in every way as it surrounds me so I know how to make love to you."

My head didn't have to tell me what was happening. Ryan's delectable and criminal smile let me know. That night, he was the captain of my body. I gave myself over to the way he wanted and he charted his course. His finger drew magical colors.

My body gathered and sparkled, ready for my second orgasm. I wondered how it would feel to have his penis inside of me.

Chapter 31

Finger Food And Off To Bed

*S*pellbound.

I was unable to speak or move. Ryan's touch caused the basic need of my body to respond in every way. The deepest recesses of my femininity felt full.

I moaned gloriously as he played with the spot I'd come to life only minutes earlier. As much as I resented him having so much of it, I knew I'd received these gifts because of his experience. Could I learn to appreciate that part of him instead of being fearful?

A candle had lit inside of me. Its flame flickered upward, urgently reaching for more oxygen.

I was weak from his kisses. My sounds of pleasure—soft and hard, loud and then hushed—escaped my body and released into exquisite musical notes. My vagina squeezed. My stomach tightened. I felt as if my uterus had contracted into a hard ball.

Between the aching and the jagged spiking of my body, I began to understand the conflict of pain and pleasure during sex.

Ryan braced himself on one elbow so he could move his hand with ease and the other flattened to feel my knotted belly. I heard him moan and wondered what kinds of thoughts might be circling inside him.

My next orgasm was even more intense.

The man whose apartment I'd agreed to visit was making familiar the places on my body that brought me to life. I thought him to be an artist who intently brushed a canvas he'd prepared and had come to know well. The imagination he brought into my world resulted in a blend of glowing, magnificent colors.

"Uaahhhhh . . . ooh . . . I . . . Rrrryan!" My orgasm burst from me in a kind of joy that was unrestrained.

My neck stiffened.

My mouth opened wide.

Desperate for his lips, barely touching, gaping open, the symphony of breaths from my mouth filled his. Sublime heat moved down as if I was a wishbone—through my pelvis, sizzling down my inner thighs and legs, finishing in the arches of my feet to the very tips of my toes.

"Baby." Ryan groaned and collapsed on top of me as if he'd also climaxed. His body seemed exhausted.

Seconds.

Calming down.

Minutes.

Long sighs.

Deep breaths.

"One day soon, you'll want me to take all of you," he reminded, gently caressing my cheek.

"Mm-hmm," I mumbled.

"How was that?" he whispered.

"You know how it was." I kept my eyes closed. "The advantage you have over me isn't fair. You make me squiggle all over."

"Squiggle?" His voice was filled with suggestion. I knew by the way it dipped low he understood how excited he'd made me.

I placed my hands on the back of his head.

Brought him down to my lips.

Kissed his soft mouth.

Needed it.

Had to . . . as hard as I could.

Delicious.

I fell back into his sofa.

Finally relaxed.

Ryan took his finger out of my moistness and put it in his mouth.

"What a succulent dessert you are." He closed his eyes.

Just be quiet, Nicky. The more you talk, the more trouble you'll invite. On the other hand, do I want more of his kind of trouble?

"Let's go to bed. Now that you're relaxed you can squiggle more." He smacked his lips. "On top of me would be fine."

"Give me a minute," I begged.

I didn't want to move.

My body had emptied.

I wanted to lie in peace after the blood rushed down hard, away from my brain, leaving me weak.

Beautiful exhaustion held me captive.

I didn't care my breasts were naked and displayed to him.

My arms were lifeless and rested loosely above my head.

Just as I was coming out of my numbed brain, his muscular arms scooped up my body and held me inside them. It was enough to stop my heart. When I opened my eyes I thought I might some weapon of love he was so skillful at using, circling above me and ready to strike.

To my surprise, I found his gentle smile.

"I've pictured carrying you into my bedroom for more than a year." His eyes were fixed on mine.

I let him take me inside his vision.

Can he feel my body shaking?

When he lay me down on his king-size bed, the covers had already been pulled down.

Holy God, I'm in his bedroom—in his bed!

The way I felt in his arms, tucked away safely . . . it was as if love itself had carried me. The intimacy I had dreamed of and had always hoped for seemed possible. It was lovely, lovely, lovely.

"God, Ryan, I could have made it on my own."

"I know, but . . ." He walked to the other side of the bed.

"But what?"

"You're my blossoming flower and I couldn't resist the opportunity. Looking at your body filled with pleasure because of what I did . . . I'm caught in your net."

My net?

He began taking off his clothes.

"What are you doing?"

"I can't sleep in pajamas." His corner-of-the-mouth grin reflected complete mischief circling inside of him.

"You slept in your sweats in my bedroom," I reminded him, feeling the blush on my cheeks.

"Yeah, well . . . I had to be a good boy then." He turned to walk into the bathroom. "I'm going to brush my teeth. I have an extra toothbrush if you want it."

Why does he have an extra toothbrush? Is it for other women?

"You go ahead." I was still dizzy. "I'll be right back." I went into the living room to put on the T-shirt he'd previously taken off me and then returned to his bedroom.

I can't get over it—I'm going to share a man's bed.

When I walked into the bathroom, I couldn't help but look at his naked body. I was overcome with the power that lay just beneath his skin simply watching him stand in front of the sink. His shoulders were broad. His back was muscular, defined, and curved beautifully into his buttocks. His firm behind looked like two rounded shelves. I thought they could be waiting for my hand to caress them and giggled silently at the thought of keeping my trinkets there. Of course, his erection was something I couldn't help but notice as well.

I walked by him quickly, aware of feeling and wanting too much too soon. I grabbed the soap and lathered my face so I wouldn't have to look at him any longer.

"That T-shirt?" His voice probed my belly.

"Yeah?" I continued washing my face.

"It isn't safe."

My knees . . .

"I'll be a minute." I held the luxurious towel against my cheeks and patted them dry.

"Can I help?" He wore a shit-eating grin.

"No. God, Ryan."

I closed and locked the door.

I was soaked between my legs. My underwear was completely wet. I wanted to examine everything.

Chapter 32

Jam For Jelly

What the hell is all this? It's like . . . jelly! It's milky. Oh, God is this normal? What if I'm a freak? I need to wash off my underwear and hide them. Damn, lying next to him without my panties on . . . I hope we're going to sleep.

There were some washcloths in a basket on the counter, so I used one of them. After I wiped off, I panicked.

Where was I going to put it?

I didn't want to ask Ryan where his dirty laundry went.

Opening the bathroom door as quietly as I could, I tried to sneak out and put both the washcloth and my panties in my backpack. Holding them behind me, I was one step away from my escape when I saw Ryan on the bed.

"You okay?" He lay on his side watching me, his arms hugging a pillow. It was easy to imagine being underneath him. His smile sent waves of breathlessness through my chest.

"I need something in my backpack." My hands shook.

"Like what?" His voice made my throat tighten.

"Um . . . a pen." I couldn't think fast enough. My brain wasn't functioning at one hundred percent yet.

"A pen?" He cracked up. "You're going to write on what . . . toilet paper?"

"God, Ryan, must you know everything? I'm going to take this washcloth home and clean it. Please don't ask me anything else."

"There's a laundry room with a hamper to the left of the guest bath," he nodded. "Behind the green shuttered doors. Do you want me to show you?" He had a playful smile.

"No."

I walked out of his bedroom. Found the hamper with nothing inside. I didn't want my washcloth to be the only item in there for his poor housekeeper. Folded on the shelves above the washer and dryer was a stack of clean towels. I wrapped the washcloth and my underwear inside one of them and tucked the package inside my backpack with my bra, which Ryan had earlier tossed across the room.

My overwhelming anxiety was temporarily relieved—that was, until I walked back into the bedroom where Ryan lay bare-chested. His long body was spread out like a lion relaxing on the Serengeti.

God, he looks so good. Maybe you're a lioness on that hunt, Nick!

"Come lie down with me." His voice carried notes of temptation.

I'm dead meat.

"Move over to your side." It was ridiculously naive of me to assume we'd each go to sleep, especially since we'd spent three nights together prior to this one.

After my orgasms, I was ready to rest.

What everything meant and what his expectations indicated, I didn't fully understand. I was only used to spending the night with a girlfriend and when tired, went to sleep. When that damn smile came over his face? I knew my sleepovers with Ryan were about to be defined in a new way.

"Come lie against me, baby. I'm waiting," Ryan motioned to me with his finger. "I've waited a year for you." He threw the covers off his naked body and invited me to swim with him in the deep end. "Your feelings have overtaken you over so fast, you don't understand how it's possible we could be together this way. Although you never planned for someone like me in your life, you to have him. And now you're wondering how you can control this when you haven't a clue."

I know—it's making me insane.

He looked too inviting . . . those arms; blue eyes; a body of muscles that bulged and flexed for me; mischief that filled his body and a heart of love. Playfully, I jumped on the bed, complying with his request. I wished I could be a slithering minx and crawl all over him.

He grabbed for me.

Pulled me down on the bed.

Stayed me against his body.

"Mmm," he rubbed my belly. "My baby."

"You're my baby, too, but I need sleep and I know you do, and well, what I want to know is . . ." I counted to ten. "How you, I mean, I did, but um, how could you be, uh . . . did you—"

"Have an orgasm?"

"Yeah."

"Mm-hmm."

"How? We didn't, that is, I didn't do . . . um, you didn't—"

"When you came as my finger moved your clitoris, I watched

your expression, felt your body under me—"

"I hear you. What I'm asking is if you're um, if you're expecting me to do something for you or—"

"Yes," he said.

"Yes?" *Oh, God. What does he want me to do?*

"I mean no, you don't need to do anything. I'm satisfied. Yes, I want more, but for now what I want is for us to lie next to each other and have your loveliness against my heart."

His voice settled like the evening around us. The way he said things was like a rhythmic seduction from the most beautiful of poems or sonnets, read aloud in a lost language.

Heavenly bells rang in my ears.

Even in those early days, I knew gold dust was my destiny.

It was so strange I lay in bed with a man who had filled his arms with me. Only a few months ago, I had been thinking about my first kiss with Jerry.

Awakened with a gentle pull to Ryan's body, I was blessed with the moves of man who wanted me. His head was in the spot he'd come to love on my shoulder. His cheek rested on mine.

"Next time," his voice dropped. "I hope you'll invite me in the bathroom with you. I'll wash you off, dry your thighs, your belly, and your wet . . ."

His unspoken words seemed to hang invisibly in the air above us, suspended like our snowflake that had melted in our forest. I relished the feel of his skin—rough and hairy in muscular places, but in others, he was soft and smooth. I became aware of the way his chest moved as he breathed, broadening with a deep breath, and falling as he exhaled.

The intoxication from his touch caused me to focus on the complete lusciousness of his muscular frame—especially his large penis. His erection was long and thick. Although I'd felt him before, my focus had been on his big body, not the part of him that seemed destined to be inside me.

How would his penis possibly fit inside of me?

The veins on it . . . were they always purple and prominent?

It stood up clear past his navel.

What was the average size of a man?

Was it always dark, thick, and moving on its own?

Was he normal?

Of course, I knew women had babies, and if they could fit through a vagina, certainly a man's penis could. I also knew pregnant women produced hormones that relaxed their joints, allowing the whole area to dilate and expand when the baby was ready to be delivered—I wouldn't have any of those benefits.

How tight or loose was the average woman's vagina?

What was I like inside the warm, moist areas of my body?

Would Ryan moan with pleasure as I surrounded him? Or would he instead deflate with disappointment and compare me to other women he'd been with? Perhaps he'd want to get it over with as soon as possible and make some polite excuse to leave me.

Teasing and pretending to undo the drawstring from my shorts, Ryan's voice vibrated against my neck. My meltdown began once again.

Oh, no. Keep control, Nicky. You can't let yourself go there. If he feels between your legs . . . you have no panties . . .

"Please don't." I fought to stay present. "I'm not ready for sex."

"I just gave you sex," he explained patiently. "You were, uh, most definitely ready for it."

My body writhed in the warm chocolate of his words.

"You know what I mean. When I go to the next step, I want my brain functioning right, not numbed or in a dream state because of what you just did for me."

I want to. What about all those other women? What if I don't satisfy him, he turns over, pats me on the back again and starts snoring? What then? How can I really compare to the gorgeous bodies he's been with? I can't. But I want to. Oh how I want to.

My other fight was my need for control. When I went all the way with Ryan, I wanted to set up a special romantic night for our first time, planned perfectly and resulting in absolute beauty.

What kind of scene had I visualized?

I wasn't sure.

I only knew that when the picture came to me, I needed it set to the last detail.

"I hate to break it to you, sweet woman. When we make love, your mind won't be working the way you think it will. You'll go where she tells you, because she'll have given herself over to the sensual pulsing I'll bring to your body. You told me I could come inside you when we were on the sofa and my finger was driving you to orgasm. That's all it took for you to say yes. Now that we're in my bed, your curvy, round feminine body is moist and ready . . . don't you think—"

"Good night, Ryan."

After his masculine laugh slithered across my chest, he hugged me tightly and kissed me on the cheek.

"I want to feel you against me." He tucked my hair behind my ear. "Remember how we lay close in Half Moon Bay and felt our hearts beating? Lie naked with me now."

Yes, but all you need to do is lie on top of me and I'll disappear. I need to catch my breath, write about this, analyze this . . . oh shit, do I really? Shouldn't I just—

"Not tonight, okay, Ryan? I just need . . . I'm on the edge. When you come back, okay?"

"Okay," he surrendered to my hesitation. "You're a love."

"I don't feel that way." I was disgusted that I couldn't move any faster with sex. "Why do you say that?"

"Because when you talked about keeping your shorts on, instead of saying what I did to you, you said *for* you. And the way you moved for me—oh, Nicky, it's obvious you've enjoyed fingering yourself; you know where you like to be touched. It makes me so excited knowing that you like sex. Just thinking about us that way gets me going."

"Ryan?" *I have to say it. He needs to understand I'm not rejecting him. I'm afraid. Even though I told him he could do whatever he wanted earlier—now that my brain is coming back, oh hell—I'm a mess.* "I don't know how to give you the sex you want." I pulled the covers up to my neck.

"We'll figure everything out as we go." He sighed and his hand rubbed my belly.

"Ryan?"

"Yes, Nicky."

"I don't think you'll fit." I turned my head slightly to watch his expression.

"What?" He opened his eyes wide, apparently surprised by my comment.

"What I mean is, I don't think I have room for your thing," I whispered.

"You'll be okay." I could feel his chest move up and down as he tried not to laugh. "Just relax. You need your rest, little Nicky, especially since you're not a cool girl."

I started laughing and had a hard time stopping the giggles.

He started laughing.

I couldn't stop.

He couldn't stop.

We laughed like children, loud, silly, and joyful, as if we were still skipping over the sand on Pismo Beach.

Finally, after teasing some more, we settled down.

He held me. My back was against his chest. His hands were on my belly. He didn't press me for more. The part of his body—the mystery that my mind was most definitely focused on—pressed against me off and on throughout the night.

I fell asleep quickly, trusting he would stay true to his word.

Ryan wrapped me with his body, the same way he was wrapping around my life.

Chapter 33

Trophies

*C*offee. The smell was in the air when I awoke the next morning. I was alone in Ryan's bed. The clock on his nightstand read 8:09 a.m.

I could hear the water running in the shower.

Unable to resist the chance to luxuriate in his bedroom, I stayed in his bed rather than get up like I knew I should have. Feeling his bed covers around me, enjoying his lingering scent . . . all were lovely pleasures. Having these sensations all to myself . . . I just had to revel in them.

Shortly after the water stopped, the glass shower door opened. His towel rustled as he dried his body. When he walked out with it wrapped around his waist, my eyes couldn't look away.

Oh, damn. That incredible chest is coming at me. Put your shirt on—please!

"Morning." He sat down next to me on the bed and gave me a

nice bear hug.

"Good morning." A wave of tingles rushed in my belly.

"You seemed to sleep okay; did stirring your little button help you nod off?" From the smile he wore, he knew I felt lovely being in his bed.

Is he on automatic 24/7?

"I slept great." I couldn't acknowledge his statement. I feared he could go from first base to home plate in mere seconds. "How about you?"

"The best since Half Moon Bay when your naked body was against me." He shifted his hips to face me more directly.

"Oh, sure." My cheeks felt warm. "Thanks for saying so. You're really special."

Just say the words, Nicky.

He laughed. I responded with one thousand flames between my legs. Liquid fire surged through my body all the way to my eyelashes. Ryan's laugh was one of the most defining things about him. I never tired of hearing it—apparently, neither did my woman's body.

"I'm *special*, huh? You mean I'm a close friend?"

"Yeah." *No, but that's all I can give you right now.*

"Well baby . . . I've never seen a friend's body jerk for me like yours did. And I don't recall seeing a friend writhe and moan from pleasure like you when I brought your soft, wet, little flower to climax last night.

"Nope, I don't ever remember doing any of that with my buddies," Ryan continued. "And I've never had a friend stay the night with me in my bed, safe in my arms, talking about a certain thing fitting into a certain place inside of her. My friends don't give a damn about my penis."

He paused to gauge my reaction.

I looked away, but in reality, I wanted to grab him and bury my head in his chest. My very happiness called—no pleaded—to be released and say, *I love you, Ryan*!

"You look beautiful this morning. In fact"—Ryan put his hand under my chin—"it's hard for me not to eat you up right now."

Oh, God, please don't. I knew I should've gotten up. Once you came out, well, I should've gotten up, that's all.

"Coffee should be ready in a minute." He pushed up from the bed. "I'm almost through in the bathroom. I'll wait if you need it. There are some clothes in the closet"—he stopped in midsentence. It seemed he was suddenly confused about continuing. "Uh, there's some old stuff from a while ago. You're welcome to look through them instead of wearing my crap."

Is he actually suggesting I wear other women's clothing? Is this real? God, I feel like one of his castoffs. Our night was spectacular and now he casually tells me about former lovers' clothing still in the closet . . . is he nuts? Why are we always in turmoil? Aren't we doomed when it comes down to it?

"Thanks. I don't want to wear anybody else's stuff," I snapped.

As I got out of bed, Ryan stood in front of me, blocking the doorway to the bathroom. He closed the space between us, once again pressing so close it seemed there was no air between our bellies as they touched each other.

God help me, I'm so weak.

"You used *my* stuff last night," he said as if I'd forgotten.

Yeah, your stuff, Ryan, don't you understand the difference? I thought you were . . . maybe you're just a jock after all. No wonder you had an extra toothbrush. Now I understand.

If I spoke up in the way I'd just done to myself, would he throw his hands in the air and give up, finally understanding that I was too afraid to be comforted? Or perhaps he'd scream and rage like

Dad did whenever Mom, Jenise, or I took a stand.

"So you already used *other people's* stuff, right?" he challenged.

"That's different," I challenged meekly.

Why don't you understand the difference?

"Why?" He folded his arms.

Just speak your mind, Nick. Now is the time before you fall any harder. Maybe you're discovering his dark side. Maybe your own darkness is ready to lash out!

"Ryan." I looked at the floor. Took a breath. "I can't believe you don't understand why it bothers me. If I have to explain," I took two beats to continue. "All I can say is that I don't want to touch clothes worn by the women you've been with. Those are the clothes you're talking about, right? Women you've had sex with who left their stuff?"

"They're not all—"

"You know what? You just made me feel like I'm one of your hookups in the tunnels. It's as if I've just been told to hurry up and grab something so I can get out fast," I continued. "Is that how it is? The women you've been with are still here in spirit because after sex you say goodbye as you hold the door open? Do you usher them out of your apartment so quickly, they don't have enough time to grab their belongings? Or do *they* leave in your shorts and T-shirt, the same way I'm dressed?"

"No, that's—"

"The thought of getting into their clothes is awful," I cut in. "And that you'd still have them here, it's . . . I thought you were more sensitive than this."

"I'm sorry." He stared at the floor and looked defeated.

I felt badly he seemed emptied of his fight. Now that I had mustered some bravery, however, I had to keep going and explain my feelings. Maybe, by the time I was through, he'd finally understand the battle it would take to calm someone who wasn't using him, had her own focus and goals, and wasn't only after an exciting life with a professional baseball player.

Just as it would be for me with Ryan, perhaps he finally understood being together meant facing a steep climb. Trying to make me feel secure against all the women of his past would be the challenge of our lives.

"Maybe they're my mom's." He suddenly rose from the ashes, ready for another round. "You're judging pretty quickly."

"Okay," I drawled. "Show me. If they're your mom's, I wouldn't expect you to have her clothes in your closet—at least not piled in a corner or a box. So let's see them."

He hesitated.

His eyes darted everywhere except my eyes.

I knew the answer.

"Didn't think so." I heard the disgust in my voice. "What you just offered, to actually search through the clothing of former lovers, you *really* say that to women who have spent the night? Oh, wait. Let me take that back. You just did."

"I didn't mean—"

"What I'm trying explain," I interrupted, "I'm supposedly *special* to you . . . this is what you say to the woman you love? I mean, obviously you don't care about your former lovers as anything more than a sex partner and I accept that. Actually I'm kinda grateful for it. What I don't get is how you can be so callous as to suggest she *find something* to wear the next morning?"

I paused to see if he had anything to add.

He didn't. His eyes were focused and serious.

"And let me get this right—I'm supposed to casually sort through other women's clothes and not feel anything? I may be naive, but I'm not stupid." I thought back to my father's friend, Ernie and felt the same as I had thirteen years earlier.

"I know you're not stupid." Ryan's face knotted. "You don't have to repeat that to me. I respect your intelligence. I do have Mom's—"

"Don't." I waved my hand in the air. "What you just did is pretty screwed up. I'm pissed you'd even say it."

Ryan's head jerked back as if I'd coldcocked him.

He didn't understand the way his past affected me because he never had to with any other woman. They'd only been happy to be a part of his present. For me, I had to be clear about all of it to move forward. How long that would take? I didn't know. No longer did I want to accept the way things were because I was afraid to speak up. No longer would I be passive only to keep the peace. I had to begin taking small steps so I wouldn't remain in the same fearful life of my childhood.

"Move out of my way." I stepped around him. Went into the bathroom and closed the door. My first thought was to go through his closet and look in the box of clothes, bring them out, toss them in his face, and then leave his apartment. After I took some time to freshen up, I reconsidered.

I began to second-guess myself.

I forced myself to stay put.

Was it wrong that I pressed Ryan and that I was having a hard time dealing with it?

Why did it turn my stomach? Because it showed me the way I'd also be dismissed if we didn't work out?

I needed patience. Just as I was changing he was, too. Jenise told me he didn't know how to change since he hadn't been challenged to do so. Okay. I had to admit that might be true.

Was he afraid that he'd just shown me how he had conducted

his one-night stands?

I tried to shake the feeling of being used. Couldn't.

Wasn't he taking his past too casually?

Jenise told me I'd overreacted when it came to Ryan's sex life, but this—surely even she would be surprised.

I turned off the light and opened the bathroom door.

Ryan sat on the edge of the bed.

I sat next to him.

"Why do you still have those things, Ryan?"

"Did you look through them?" He didn't look at me. "Now you want to leave me?"

"I didn't look."

His blue eyes became lasers and focused on me.

"I don't want to leave you." I twisted my body to face him. "But I might have to. Help me understand."

"Why does it matter?" Ryan asked defensively, his voice shaken. "I can't seem to anticipate the things that make you upset. I can hear your agitation and see your body language, but I don't get it. You haven't committed to me exclusively. *I'm* the only one of us who has said I love you, so why is your reaction so strong?"

That was a comeback I wasn't expecting. I've tried to stay calm and objective. I'm already exhausting him. He's exhausting me, too. I suppose we need to let loose and see where this goes.

"Because I—"

"I need to hear your explanation. I don't understand your reaction." He ran his hands through his hair. "I'm not trying to be flippant or dismissive. I've told you I love you a dozen times or more and haven't heard you say anything that lets me know I'm yours. You've told me I'm your boyfriend. You like me a lot and have strong feelings for me. The newest one is I'm a special friend. Yet, I'm supposed to ride my life of all and any evidence from my past so you're not upset. I feel as if I need to take a course on relationships so I learn how not to offend you.

"Sorry, I don't mean—"

"The thing is," he caressed my hair. "I'm happy to do it. I wouldn't hesitate if you'd only . . . we're friends, right? So tell me, *girlfriend.* Why does my comment upset you?" He stood up. "I need to finish getting ready. I'll only be a minute. I'm not avoiding our conversation. If you want to come in the bathroom and talk I'll continue. Otherwise, when I'm done, okay?"

I nodded.

Tears flooded me.

He just used sarcasm. The same sarcasm I'm so used to flinging around whenever I feel threatened. God, that hurts.

While he finished getting ready I gathered my sandy sweats and T-shirt and put them on. I walked into the kitchen and grabbed some coffee. I sat at the kitchen island, sipping it from one of the two mugs Ryan had set out earlier.

Was I about to lose him?

I shouldn't have pressed him. This always happens when I speak up—everything falls apart. What was I thinking?

Maybe he was gathering himself, getting ready to say goodbye. I couldn't blame him. It would be sad, but perhaps the feelings I had from LA *were* right. We'd tried a few times and had fallen short. Were we destined to circle in these misunderstandings?

He walked wearing only a pair of sweatpants. His feet met the hardwood floor in deliberate steps.

"I poured yours," I told him. "It's right here. I thought you needed to get dressed."

"Thanks," he kissed the side of my head. "Just finishing my hygiene stuff. I like to get my coffee before I dress."

I appreciated the effort. Even though we were still confused, he made sure not to turn his back on me as he had in Yountville.

"Continue." He took a long sip from the mug. "Why do those clothes make you so upset?"

"It's like . . ." I tried to say it as unemotionally as I could, without falling apart or starting to cry. "It's like a reminder of what I'm up against. I know you'll get tired of hearing this but my fear of abandonment . . . it's as if you've been toying with me. Maybe you let the women of your past believe they were something more. I mean, if they can leave something at your apartment, doesn't that imply they're welcome to return? You may not be now, but weren't you're stringing them along? Worse . . . " I closed my eyes, daring myself to finish my deadly thought, " . . . maybe the *clothes* are your trophies."

Chapter 34

Skeletons—His & Mine

"*M*aybe, because of the sweet words you used on all those women, they purposefully tucked something away so they'd have an excuse to come back." I sighed when Ryan's cell phone rang. "Is that why you have them?"

"Sorry; just a second. What's up?" He listened to the caller. "Do I—" he paused again. "Okay. An hour. See you then." He ended the call. "Coach reminding me of my training session. We still have time. Please go on."

"Do those clothes remind you of the life you say you're giving up for me?" I rolled on. "They're like your black book? Do you keep their panties to sniff at night?"

"Oh shit, Nick." He shook his head in protest. "No. No, of course not. I don't even know what's in there. They're in a corner of my closet I don't even use. My housekeeper, she, they—"

"Stack up?" I pushed even more, albeit not too forcefully. After all, I didn't want to sever us and I felt he might be on that edge.

"Jeanne, my housekeeper. She tosses them in a box or a bag." His face was in turmoil, knotted, twisted, and fearful.

"How often?"

"I'm not answering that," he said firmly.

"Okay, then, I need you to hear me and hear me clearly. I don't want to be reminded of all the sex you've had before, so . . ."

"Why not?" Now he had changed tactics. He pushed to get me to say the words he'd been waiting to hear.

He was on the offense.

"Because of the feelings I have for you." I gave in a little.

He pushed up from the stool and lifted me from my seat. His arms surrounded me and brought me to his body.

Don't even start. I'm mad at you.

"I'm not letting you off that easily," he said boldly.

"Yeah? Well I don't feel like letting *you* off so easily, either. In fact, you—"

"I know you're upset." His hand fell gently on my shoulder. "I'm sorry for what I said about the clothes but I want to hear why it affects *you*. I need to hear you say the words. I need your reassurance, Nicky."

"Reassure you in what way? What words?"

"Tell me why, really tell me, why keeping them bothers you. Down deep. I'm a strong man but my heart is vulnerable and you need to give it hope. Those clothes? I don't look at them the way you do. They're only clothes. I don't identify them with sex or the woman who once wore them.

"I'm sorry I wasn't more sensitive to your feelings. I don't mean to hurt you or be callous to anyone. You're the only woman I've ever responded to like this or waited for. When I'm with you, I'm helpless. I lose control. I need you to understand how desperate I am for you."

"I thought I knew what I felt. I thought . . ." my bottom lip quivered. "I thought I knew you. Now—"

He swept me into his arms.

Walked back into the bedroom and put me down on the bed.

He lay next to me.

"Can't you feel my love?" He kissed my cheek.

"I thought so, but—"

"You really don't think I'd play games with you, do you?"

"I'm not sure now." I planted my feet.

"Don't you hear how fast my heart beats when you lay your head against my chest?" He reached for me. I rested against him.

"Yes, I do—"

"Don't you think we deserve a chance together without all the analysis and what ifs?" His arms rested on the small of my back. "Can you put aside your doubts? Just for now, can you believe I'm telling you the truth?"

"I'll try." I began to give in.

"Don't you think we deserve to have a special love?" Each of his hands framed my cheeks. "Am I special to you?"

"You are."

"I want to be the one who brings everything good to your life." He looked over my face. "I'm trying to understand you. You have to help me and trust that I'm present with you and no one else. I'm waiting for you to shout, *I love you*. Your lovely woman's body—seems like *she* loves me. Last night she made her announcement two times, in fact."

He gave me a shy look that was only pretend.

"Don't say that." I knew I turned bright red.

"Why not? Your responses were natural and beautiful. The way your body arched for me and your vagina grabbed my finger, it was—"

"I couldn't help my reaction last night." I looked away.

Ryan lifted me on top of him. Placed one of his arms on each of my hips. My thighs were against his. My belly felt the soft parts of his body and also the hardness of the primitive male under me.

"Nicky, I know you're not experienced but if you weren't into me, your body wouldn't have reacted the way she did, your legs wouldn't have opened wide, and your lovely hips wouldn't have risen up to me last night. I didn't even have to guide you. Your body moved and came close to me all on its own. More than once you pulled me down to kiss you. Although you haven't claimed me as your man, I can see you and I know you see me. You want more, just like I do. I know you love me, just say it."

Yes, yes, yes, I do!

My brain went to gel, leaving me with only a blob of random and rapidly misfiring neurons.

Come on, Nick. Regroup and get it together.

"You say all the right things. I can't believe . . . you seem to have a talent for it. The way you're inside my head—I'm mad at you, Ryan. I want to stay mad for a while. But then you start talking and—"

"Don't be angry." His arms tightened around me. When he kissed my lips, everything softened. The room spun like a camera on wheels circling two lovers as it filmed a scene for a movie.

"I know this shakes you." He kissed me again. "I want to shake you hard. Whenever I've been easy on you, you've drifted."

He flipped positions. Now his body was on top of mine. He slipped off the sweats he'd put on earlier. No boxers or briefs covered his erection. I felt as if I was bending to receive it like a succulent flower reaching for the morning sun. His hips persuaded me to imitate their motion, accept his invitation to drown in the liquid of our bodies—dripping desires, moist, and exquisite. His hands gripped the waistband of my pants.

I wanted to forget about the clothes in the closet.

Sweep it under the carpet.

Don't talk about it.

That's what I'd always done.

No! Don't give up. You promised you wouldn't give in.

Although I wanted him badly, I knew we didn't have time for a lovely sex adventure—not the way I wanted and thought I needed it. I'd fantasized about relaxing in our afterglow and wanted to discuss the sex as I lay in his arms. Waiting an entire week to see him again after my first experience didn't feel right or good.

Forget all of the controls and childhood beliefs.

My Evil Twin didn't want to let go. She pushed and urged me to stretch myself, and step over my self-imposed boundaries.

You're not a child any longer.

I'd always felt like an adult in so many ways, but this—this was something I knew I had to insist on doing my way—for now.

"Ryan, I need to get home. I have plans today and you have your game and coaching lesson."

"Are. You. Sure. You. Want to. Stop?" Long, slow breaths were like pauses in each spoken word. He opened his eyes. Lifted from me. Created space between us.

Let him pleasure you! When he gets back, you'll be ready to go deeper because you'll understand what it's all about! Think of what you could offer him! Love, Intimacy, Vulnerability, Validation, Acceptance, Commitment, Reassurance! The same things you want for yourself and never get at home.

"No, but yes," I affirmed.

Oh, Nick. My Evil Twin whispered her disappointment.

He rolled off me and lay on his side. I sat with my back to

him. My hands were loose at my hips.

"Come to my game today and let me see my sweetheart a while longer before I have to leave." He scooted close and tucked my bottom against his stomach. His thighs folded me inside them. My hips were held snugly in the V of his body. His head now rested against my back. I felt packaged in his love. "I can't bear to part with you so soon. I'm already sad just thinking about being away from my woman."

Panic went through me like a fire alarm—blaring, warning loudly, coming closer and reaching the very inside of me. What I refused to admit was so obvious—it had been obvious from the beginning—it was why the clothes, his past, and the bold women who vied for his attention bothered me.

I was in love with him!

Every protection I'd built around me crashed down.

I wanted to be with him.

Didn't know how to say it.

"I have other plans today." I grasped for excuses, stalling to gather my thoughts. One of my legs was on the floor as if ready to run away and the other was on the bed wanting to stay.

"Please cancel them." His eyes twinkled.

"I can't."

"What are they?" He was going to make me own it.

"I'm going out."

"With?"

"A friend," I blurted. "I haven't spent much time with them lately and college is almost here." *I know it sounds contrived.*

"Won't she understand? Unless . . . if you called Jerry and put him on speaker, would I hear the voice of a guy who's excited about seeing you today?"

Chapter 35

Friends

"*Y*ou know Jerry and I see each other as friends. We hang out with the same people. I've known him all my life. You don't want me to give up my friends, do you? That's not a working relationship."

"If you're only friends, why did you lie about your plans?" He avoided my question and shot an arrow of truth right through me.

I don't really know. I guess . . . oh damn, I don't know.

"Because you keep pushing me to stop seeing him. I don't want to talk about it anymore." I rushed my answer. "I'm still trying to figure this out. I wouldn't ask you to give up your friends. It's not right you're asking me to do it."

Hasn't Ryan gotten right to the heart of it? Jerry isn't only a friend.

"What would you think if I kept seeing my women friends?"

"Do you even have women friends? Haven't you had sex with all of them?"

And now you *avoided* his *question, Nick. Seems like the two of you are very well schooled in this game.*

I waited for him to answer. When he didn't, I assumed it was an acknowledgment.

"Tell me who, Ryan. Who *are* your women friends? Friends like *Jesse*? Oh, wait. Maybe it's Monica or Ms. Tabitha Sable?"

"Monica is married and I already answered that question." His eyebrows knotted.

"How many women friends—I mean *real* friends—do you have? Let's see, I've heard you say Jesse's a friend. I've also heard you say she's someone you *used to know* and that you have no clue as to what happened to her. I'm confused since you can't seem to get it straight. If you grew up with a woman and you wanted to keep her friendship, I'd try to understand. The thing is, I haven't had sex with Jerry. Are there any women from your past like that?"

You're holding him to a double standard. If you expect him to stay strong and committed to you, you need to show him the same.

"You don't need to worry about Jesse." He sat next to me. "We weren't serious in any way, even at college. I've never lied to you about being with other women before you."

"How could you?" I asked pointedly. "Your reputation speaks for itself."

"Please stop doing that," he requested.

Silence.

"Well . . . Dana said Jesse was happy with you. How did she phrase it? Oh yeah. You treated each other lovingly. You say you're in love with me. Yet, someone at our table thought you two were in love. Jesse told Dana she'd found her prince. How do I believe, just because you're treating me *lovingly*, I'm any different?" I carefully formulated my thoughts. "I guess on the one hand, it's good you treated her well. So well that others noticed. If you got along so great, what's to say you're not taking a break from each other while you figure it out?"

"I'm not—"

"Are you *really* over her? Is she *really* over you? If you're in love with me, why didn't Dana catch it? She certainly caught the cues between you and your ex. If you guys ended in such mutual agreement and were friends, then why don't you know where she is or where she lives? Doesn't sound amicable to me, Ryan."

"She's not my ex. She was never my girlfriend." He hesitated while assessing my body language. "She still lives in the city."

"Why did *you* lie? You just asked me why I wasn't truthful about Jerry and yet you did the same thing last night."

"I didn't want to carry on a conversation about another woman in front of you. I was afraid of blowing it again. It's none of Dana's business what I know about someone's life."

"Why not? Why are you so defensive? You were friends, or so you say. Dana was her friend, unless . . ." I looked at the ceiling and then back to his eyes. "Unless you were more."

"No, we—"

"Sorry. Let me correct that—unless *she* thought you were more and now you're uncomfortable about it," I interjected. "As intuitive as you are about people, you must have known Jesse felt something for you, didn't you? The day I heard you and Kevin talking when I was behind the fence he said she loved you."

"Then you also heard my response," he replied confidently. "I replied it was never love between us. If she was telling others she loved me, she never said that to me. If she had, I would've made sure she understood I only looked at her as a friend."

"Then Jesse would've been there last night. When we volunteered together last year in Yountville . . ." I stopped when

Ryan's nervousness became visible. He shifted. Wrung his hands as if he couldn't decide whether to continue. Held me so I wouldn't run. Planted his feet so he wouldn't run. "What are you so nervous about? *You're* the one who started this."

His face flushed.

You're not used to being pressed. It's okay to question me and insist I answer your *questions. Can you do the same?*

"How do you measure your relationships? Which ones are special? Someone you once saw regularly—like Jesse, you say you're over her now, right?"

"There wasn't, it wasn't . . ." He cleared his throat. "I never cared. I wasn't in love, or . . ." He grasped for the right words.

I finally shook him.

"I know, I know. You were never committed to her. I've heard you say that a few times. You and her, you go all the way back to college and you were out together at every important event, I'm told. Even Frances said you were seen together a lot. In fact, Alex mentioned that she and Darrell ran into the two of you. Dana said you guys were like the king and queen of the damn prom, Ryan. I'm supposed to brush that off?

"Obviously you made a habit of taking her to places where you'd be noticed—she meant *something*." I continued to probe, and I admit, push. "Would you take me to any of the same places when you need to have a beautiful, rich woman of society on your arm?

"Face it, Ryan. What can I really offer you in those situations? When the next someone you want to *see* for a while, what do you say? *Sweetheart, you're so special and like no one I've ever dated before*? Did Jesse hear the same words I'm hearing now? Haven't you really just tossed an invisible baseball to me?"

"Yes. I mean no. Yes, I saw Jesse a lot at one time." Ryan sighed deeply as if he were holding his breath throughout my discussion. "We had an arrangement. After college she moved here and—"

"Wait—she *followed* you here?" *Now I'm really nervous.* "Was that so she could be *close* to you?"

"I can't answer that, exactly." He scratched his cheek. "I don't think so. We ran into each other—I thought accidentally. I've never considered anything more until now."

How naive are you—or maybe more appropriately, how naive do you think I am? Are you kidding me?

"Jesse never called to tell me she was relocating here. I always assumed she moved to be near her brother. He's an attorney and helped her set up her business. Between her brother and me she met a lot of contacts for her business."

"And thanks to her, you were introduced in society," I added.

"That's . . . partially, yes." He was careful in his response.

"And yet, at the social event where you two you ran into each other, you didn't waste any time, did you." I laughed disgustedly.

"It wasn't like that." Frustration wove through his voice.

"Oh, no? How was it, Ryan? Others saw you both as loving. If you weren't into her, why would other people misinterpret your signals? I mean, why start up with her again if whatever you two were was in the past? You can't fake love. Not to someone who saw you both so often like Dana."

"How would she know?" he said angrily. "I put on a different face when I was out, that's all. If I went out with a woman, of course I treated her lovingly. What the hell am I supposed to do?"

"I don't know," I waved my hand through the air. "You told me at the Embarcadero how careful you were not to show emotion in public and now I hear how loving you were."

"I never kissed or took her in my arms in front of anyone. You're the only woman I've kissed passionately in public." He tried his best to reassure me.

"I don't know what to think. I don't get why either of you would continue with each other in that way. Why not get on with your life and try to find someone who really loved you?"

"I have." His blue eyes were fixed.

Stay fierce. Don't let him make you weak. Keep pressing.

"Yeah." I stared right back. "Whatever. Now I can't be sure."

"It was, I was . . . I wasn't looking for that until I saw you last year. With Jesse, I had familiarity, some type of security—I don't know how to explain it other than we were never exclusive."

"Seems like *she* was," I snapped.

"No," he snapped back. "She saw other people just like I did. I'm an asshole for this . . . oh, shit, I don't know how to . . . you're so sensitive about all this, and I'm—"

"Just say it," I insisted. "We're on a roll, so let's get it all out."

"It was that, um, her family is wealthy. Like you said, she introduced me to her society friends and associates."

Oh crap, is Alex right? He used her for money?

"So you went with her for . . ."

"No, I don't mean that I wanted to tap into her family's riches or use her for money. It was only to meet her family's connections so that I could make inroads with them. She wasn't bashful about flaunting *me* to make a gallery sale, so . . ."

"So you took advantage of her?"

"We used each other for what we needed. I can say with absolute confidence, I never took advantage of her. Jesse benefited from me as much as I did from her."

"Is the art in your apartment hers?"

"Some of it."

"*And* you had sex with her," I pushed uncomfortably. "Plenty of times and over several years. Are some of those clothes in your closet hers?"

"No,"

"How do you know? Oh, wait. She had a special drawer and she can, um, *grab* something from the closet after taking off her gown from an evening at a social event with you and have sex?"

"No." His voice was growing colder.

"I get it now. She's over here so often she just gives orders to your housekeeper on how to clean her clothes, where to send and leave them for her next visit?"

Ryan's face flushed. His brows knotted.

"If I asked Ross, *do you see Jesse anymore*, would he know who I meant? And oh, let me just get this straight—you have her art pieces here, easily worth thousands of dollars and you don't *see* her any longer? That's because . . ." I waited for Ryan to complete my thoughts.

"Because I supported her as a friend, just as I expected her to support me as a friend," he answered plainly.

"Some friend. And yet you said she had art contacts already. So why did she need *your* charity?"

"It meant something to be my friend, and—"

"I thought so, too." I put my head down.

"Nicky," he sighed. "It's . . . when other athletes saw I was a patron, they made their own purchases," he continued without wavering. "I helped her with her gallery events."

"Yeah. What did she help you with? She—"

"Listen. You've had plenty of time to express yourself and I've answered your questions. Let's turn the tables a bit. Jerry needs your support. Or another friend wants your help. Wouldn't you be there for them regardless of having a physical relationship?"

"Yes, but spending that much money just because you're a pal?" I shook my head. "I don't believe you. I'm sorry. I don't believe any of your stories. I know that's insulting to say. I'm sorry."

Chapter 36

Settling For Now

" *F*uck!" Ryan clenched his fists. "You have me turned around. I'm not explaining myself right." He looked as if he were trying to figure out how to proceed, redirect, answer, and reassure me all at once.

I was being hard on him—really hard. I felt with absolute conviction if I didn't understand his past and his ideas and beliefs about women, we'd be over before we started. Why he was so casual and comfortable about all the sex he had—especially dismissing this important person he tried so hard to make me believe was no longer a part of his life—I couldn't understand. I had to keep digging for answers.

She seemed to be the only female he'd known from his youth—almost an anchor of sorts—like Jerry and me. Jesse was so key to him he rekindled their relationship when she relocated. There was something hidden he wasn't admitting—either to me or to himself. Of that I was certain.

"Turned around or not, *Mr. Tilton*, I know where my friend lives and I don't deny it or avoid his calls. I know what he's up to and claim him openly and proudly as my friend, not an *acquaintance* or someone I *used to know*, the words you so conveniently use to address a woman from your past.

"You've known her since college. In a way you grew up with her. Because you've had sex, once you're done you can't remain friends? When it comes to having relationships with women, it's sex or no relationship at all?"

"No, it's—"

"Excuse me. I have to understand why. You were so flustered last night you couldn't even stay at the table. In fact, you couldn't face my way and could only ask Kevin to keep an eye on me."

He hung his head.

"I'm supposed to be okay with that? Come on, Ryan. Admit it. That's more than just *someone* you *used* to see. Are you so torn apart you can't face her because you're with a new woman?"

"That's not it at all. I stopped seeing her and anyone else I'd had a physical relationship with because of you."

"You must've sent out *hundreds* of announcements," I said coolly. "How did you *ever* afford the printing bill? I'm amazed the post office could handle it."

"I'm asking you to stop doing that," he reprimanded. "I've asked a few times. You're making me feel like this discussion is a joke and you're discounting my feelings."

"Sorry."

"Can we stick to the issue at hand without your sarcasm rising up to attack me?" he shot back.

"Why? Seems like you're used to rising up in a lot of ways, especially for your women friends—at least the ones who've left their clothes in your closet."

I don't know why I can't stop attacking.

He let out a deep sigh.

He looked at me without saying anything, as if trying to reboot.

"I stopped seeing women to reassure you. I did it before I even knew if you'd agree to go out with me so that when you did, you wouldn't have to worry. I did it to comfort you. I don't believe it's good having a close relationship with her or any woman who's single. I understand what you're getting at. I hear all your barbs. Shit, I *feel* them as they go through me. I'm not some freak on demand when it comes to sex. You're the one I want with me."

"Oh yeah?" My chin lifted. "From all the women I've seen trying to be with you, it seems like you're in big demand."

"I'm not pretending to be serious with you or confusing lust with love," he continued. "Since you've pushed me, I have to say it and you'll have to listen. You opened this door, so . . . ."

Crap, I know I did.

"No matter how good the sex was, I've never been in love— until now. I've had enough physical relationships to know the difference. I know what I feel for you. I'm not going to screw it up being close with another woman. Women will be around me. I have to meet people on behalf of the team at various events and at charity galas. There will also be women who are uninvited, like Tabitha. I'm saying—actually, *promising*—I can control myself.

"Tell me you want me. Say you're mine and you love me. That's all I need to hear," Ryan pleaded. "I won't seek out a woman from my past, no matter how well we got along."

"Is that the right thing to do?" I posed. "I'm asking, if you and Jesse are truly friends, all the way back in college, why cut every tie with her? Isn't having a link to your past valuable like the one I have with Jerry? What that tells me is either you can't abstain from your desire or there's more to it."

I started to get off the bed.

Ryan wrapped my waist and held me to his body.

He kissed my lower back.

"Stay." His hands squeezed me. "Let's finish this discussion."

"Okay."

"Hanging around the opposite sex invites trouble," he posed.

"You just said you're not a caveman and can control yourself," I challenged.

"Yes and I can," he answered. "But why take a chance that you'll misunderstand a situation, or she might? It's easier to stay away completely. Remove temptation from the equation. Why chance it. Jesse and I had a business arrangement. I no longer need that. Our friendship wasn't deep like the one I have with you or Kevin."

He rubbed my back.

"Let me pose this to you. You won't like it."

"Go on," I encourage.

"If you think you know everything Jerry's been up to, you're fooling yourself."

"No, he wouldn't—"

"He's a young man," Ryan interrupted. "He's eighteen-years-old, entering the beginning of his sexual life, playing competitive sports and his hormones are raging. I know. I've been through it and I'm telling you it's a strong urge. The biological pull of it is powerful and it's no joke. When I was his age, I was jacking off and having sex with any girl or woman who was willing— anything to get *that* feeling—it was all that was on my mind. Shit, every minute it seemed like."

I can relate. I think about it night and day. Are we really helpless when it comes to desire?

304

"Your so-called innocent friend, Jerry?" He shot a defiant look my way. "He's playing baseball away from his parents, right?"

"Yes."

"Dozens of young women are available to him. It's no different in summer league ball at that age. Girls, women . . . they're around. I'd bet money he's not waiting for your decision while he's away."

"And you could?"

"Yes."

"I'm sorry. I don't agree. You're either a good person or you're not. You talk about how you control your reactions? Well, Jerry and I are close and he'd never lie to me."

Oh really? And yet . . . here you are with another man. And at the coast not too long ago . . . maybe they'd never lie, but you're doing a fabulous job of it, Nick.

Thanks a lot Evil Twin. Why won't you shut up? Yes, I need to be honest. But I'm not like Ryan having sex all the time. I just wanted some experience—or at least . . . I thought so.

"As soon as we were in trouble, you sought out a male friend. As soon as you felt your distance in LA, you ignored me and went out with Jerry. Isn't that right?"

I turned to face him.

We looked into each other's eyes and perhaps . . . our souls.

Each of us was afraid of saying the wrong thing.

"You're partially right. I admit Jerry and I were seriously thinking about having sex. I wouldn't do that now. Once I tell him, he'll understand and we'll just be friends. Temptation won't be in our way at all."

I hope so, anyway.

"I appreciate your honesty, honey, but still . . . I'm telling you that it's naive if you think you can be friends with a guy who wants you," Ryan educated. "Men aren't good at having women friends. At some point one of you will be tempted or he'll overstep. It's all friendly until it's not."

"I don't agree." I practically crossed my arms. "And that doesn't make my opinion any less valid than yours."

"I know it doesn't. I understand you don't agree with me. You and Jerry have a vision of going to Stanford together and being friends forever. You'll find out for yourself it won't work."

"That's because you've forgotten what it's like to be with regular people," I chastised. "Everything is either competitive or a sexual situation for you. It's not like that with me and my friends."

He took my hands in his.

"Please believe me and give me credit for having lived a little. I know something about people." He looked in my eyes, his expression pleading with me.

"You mean trust *your* instincts above *mine*?" I couldn't hide the edge I was feeling in my comment. "I don't think so."

"Your innocence is beautiful. I love that quality in you. I'm not trying to make you upset or dismiss your opinions. However in this case, yes." He took a breath and then gave up the discussion. "Let's table this and pick it up when I get back."

"This isn't over," I warned. "I can't let this drop and I won't."

See, Nicky? You're not as weak with him as you think you are.

"Can we please hold on to the possibility of our today?" he asked sweetly. "When I come back, I'll stay up all night talking it through with you; as long as it takes. Today, I'm leaving and we don't have the time. Won't you please come to the game with me? Just give me a few more kisses before we move into our day."

No, I'm mad at you . . . I'm . . . mad . . . I'm . . .

"Don't you want to hold onto us a little longer before I leave?"

His voice was breathy and shallow. Once again, he pulled me on top of his big body. He lifted off my shirt. His lips went into a pout. "Won't you miss me, Nicky?" He kissed my nose. "Don't you want to see me again before I have to go?"

"Yes." I looked down at his face. *Oh damn do I ever!* "I'm having a tough time letting go. I need to finish this discussion. I can't have you leave while we're in turmoil."

"Oh, baby." The northern lights seemed to fill his blue eyes. Waves of color sparkled inside them. "We're not in turmoil. It's a point of discussion, that's all. If we disagree, that's okay. It doesn't mean I'm going anywhere."

"Okay." I gave in for the moment.

We got off the bed and stood against each other.

My breasts pressed against his chest. We breathed in long sighs, as if trying to come back to our center. The intense feel of our skin sticking together was static and little shocks of pleasure sparked between us. Our hearts beat with a desperateness that made me want to lie on him again—and much longer than only the few minutes we had left together.

"I'm only asking you to come to the game with me," he repeated. "Will you?"

He pushed away from my body.

His nakedness filled every space.

His arms gathered me inside them once more.

"I don't know." I looked down at the floor.

"Nicky, I know your responses scare you. I'm only asking for an afternoon with you before I leave. One day. Next week will be hell and too long before we see each other again."

Just as he'd given in to me, I gave into him. I didn't want to fight any longer. We'd worn each other down.

"Okay, I will. I have to change, though. I heard everything you said. I'll come to the game. I just want to go home and change into some clean clothes."

"I'll drive you." His face seemed to relax. "It'll give me a chance to say hello to your folks."

Sometimes it's best to avoid doing that.

Ryan went into the bathroom to change. He came out wearing light blue jeans and a red T-shirt. His body showed the definition of someone dedicated to maintaining it at a high level.

If you just stand still, I can run my hands all over you.

"Do you want a coffee for the road? I'm going to turn off the coffee maker."

"Sounds good."

"I'll get the commuter mugs so we can take them with us. You're already dressed, but do you want to wash here? I've got plenty of washcloths for you."

"I'll do it at my house, where I've got all my junk. *God*, Ryan."

"Wait for you in the kitchen," he chuckled.

"Thank God."

"Don't forget to leave my pen," he teased.

"What pen?" I'd forgotten about my made-up excuse.

"The pen you borrowed last night. I think you were going to leave it in my laundry hamper." He got a big kick out of himself and stared at me until the light bulb went on.

"Funny, Ryan. You just can't let anything drop, can you?"

"Not if I can embarrass you," he said. "You're just too cute when your adorable cheeks flush."

Chapter 37

Discarded Sighs

I wasn't about to enter my house parading around in Ryan's clothes. The imaginations of my parents would travel to places they didn't need to explore.

On the other hand, perhaps it's time to show them you're not their good girl?

Wearing the dirtied sweats and T-shirt from our afternoon at Pismo Beach, I quickly ran a brush through my hair and turned out the light. When I walked into Ryan's bedroom and looked at his bed, I felt a sensual shiver go through my body.

What if he was *my boyfriend? Would I spend nights here on a regular basis? Would he expect me to? Would each time we saw each other result in sex? Was it expected to be that way?*

I grabbed his comforter, squeezed it in my hands, then smoothed it and walked into the kitchen. Still on edge from our earlier conversation, I wanted to talk more about the actions of his past.

And then . . . the passive me returned.

My love for Ryan was exploding and I didn't want to rock the boat while he was on the road. I held back—for a little while.

Careful not to challenge anyone you love—they'll leave you.

"You're beautiful in the morning. I guess you know that." Ryan watched me as I stood waiting for my cup of coffee.

Poor guy, he's losing his eyesight. I wonder how many years he has left in baseball.

"In my dirty clothes?" At first I laughed. When I saw his serious look, however, I didn't want to dismiss his compliment. "I don't ever look good to myself. Thank you."

"Guess I'm good for you in some ways," he smiled. "A little cream, right?"

"You're good for me in a lot of ways even though I don't let on," I acknowledged. "You're already too confident. Yes, a little cream is perfect. Where are your suitcases?"

"I've already sent them ahead." He stirred my coffee and capped the mugs for both of us. We left his apartment hand in hand. As we stepped into the elevator we began our descent back to the real world.

I exhaled slowly as I letting go of our trauma. I could almost see my breath rise into the air. I wondered how many sighs from other women might be circling above me from a night of pleasure with Ryan. I knew they were hovering. Invisible lips and eyes waited for a promise to be fulfilled after they were seduced. Perhaps they thought the man standing next to me wanted more of them. Maybe they even left their panties in his bed so they could remind him of the gift they'd shared. I closed my eyes and shook my head, trying to brush away the irrational thoughts.

Come on, Nick, stay in the moment and don't create another

310

wall around your heart.

It was an unpleasant daydream.

Ryan pulled me close and he kissed me as if that would still my fears. It wasn't nearly enough.

Will anything ever be enough to calm my anxiety?

"Where are you, Nicky?"

"I'm here."

"No, you're somewhere else. Tell me."

"I'm wondering how many other women have come out of your apartment bathed in seduction and promises. Was your arm around her in this elevator as she hoped for more of your attention?" I rubbed the lid of my coffee mug with my thumb. "Then they land in the lobby and that's when you lower the boom?"

"Come on." He dismissed me too casually.

"Sorry, it's what I was thinking." He couldn't reassure me enough. "You asked."

He could've told me I was the only one a million times, and still, I wouldn't have trusted him.

I *knew* I'd be abandoned. I couldn't open up as easily the way the women from his past had—I was certain of it.

No matter how many times my father had promised to stop drinking, he hadn't. He reassured us he'd be home for our birthdays, school events and would be sober on holidays.

He wasn't.

His promises . . . broken.

Each new day we knew that *this* time, *this* birthday or *this* Christmas, we'd be a happy family, open presents, laugh, talk about our day, and have a great dinner together.

Those dreams seldom came true.

Believing promises, especially from someone who said he loved me, was almost impossible.

Dad left us waiting for him to come home. It would get so late that we'd turn out the lights and go to bed, hoping he hadn't killed anyone including himself.

"Nicky, I've never made promises to any woman. I've never misrepresented my intentions, tricked her, or played with her emotions. You must know by now that some women, like at the Waterfront—"

"At the Waterfront where they try to sit on your lap and let you peek down their shirt, at the Embarcadero Hotel Lounge where they remind you of a new striptease dance, at the railings where they flaunt their breasts to you . . . it's even rumored you've picked up women that meet you in the tunnels where no one can see. Oh, let's not forget the T-shirt girls that smile as they dance and jiggle on top of the dugout for you . . ."

"They," he cleared his throat. "They have no expectations except sex and it's been mutual. I've made it clear to the few that have wanted more it was a dead end. Do you believe me?"

"I believe you're being honest with me. I also know they must have thought the world of you. You're lovely to be with. I would suggest you *have* to say it loud and no holes bared, *there is no possibility with me.* Women need to hear a man's thoughts in black and white. Don't soft shoe it. Something tells me you still have plenty of hangers on wondering when they'll hear from you again."

"I've always been right out there with what I wanted." He squeezed my hand. "I've never minced my words."

I believe you think you spoke clearly, but you hypnotized them.

"I don't have any reason not to believe you. All the things you've done, the people you know, the women you've been with—I'm afraid someone will jump up to bite."

He put his arms on my shoulders and let his hands fall loosely over my back.

"We control our relationship. How we react and communicate will determine our outcome. Sweetheart, of all the people I've ever met, you're the most intimidating. With anyone else, I never gave a shit how things turned out. I didn't care how they felt or what they thought—"

"But you said—"

"If you let me finish," Ryan interrupted. "I wasn't interested in talking about feelings—theirs or mine. I just wanted what I wanted. I guess I was kind of selfish that way."

"*Kind* of?" I raised my eyebrows.

"Boy you *are* sarcastic." He pulled back.

I looked away.

"Please try not to let your mind create stories where there aren't any."

"I'll try." I put my arms around his waist, carefully balancing my coffee. I turned my head to the side so I could lay my cheek against his chest.

"Ryan?"

"Yes, honey?"

"Why do you still have all those women's clothes?"

I can't let this go and you're not getting off that easy. I imagine everyone has let you off the hook because of your sexy laugh, muscular body and handsome face.

"I don't know."

I knew he'd answered seriously. I hoped he'd finally searched himself, perhaps even looking through his past, examining why he expected them to accept *his* ending.

"That's no answer," I persisted. "Why?"

See how it feels being pushed?

"Habit, a ritual, lack of a father . . ." Ryan pushed every

313

button in the elevator so we'd stop at all floors, giving us the chance to finish our conversation—if we could.

"Ever since high school, I played baseball. After the game was over I'd either go out with the guys or a girl. When I was older, it was a woman at the ballpark. As I became known, women came up to me socially, outside of baseball. That routine became a night at a club and having sex. It was just something to do."

"You counted pussy?" I repeated my sister's concern.

"No, that wasn't it." His mouth thinned into a line. "It was connecting and at the same time staying detached. My only focus was baseball. I didn't want to take a chance on complicating my life with relationships getting in the way of my goals."

And yet you're expecting me to do that for you.

"I'd had enough of being serious after my dad died. Playing adult games was a way I could stay numb and in my fantasy world of controlling everything. I lived fast and furious for years just to stay away from the sadness of my dad's death," he continued. "I had no parents at my games, no one to tell me how proud they were and no one to set boundaries. So I drank for a few years and partied a lot with women to get fulfillment in other ways. When the clothes were left, I thought—"

"They could be discarded, because you'd already discarded the woman who wore them. It happened before they even left your apartment," I completed his thought with my own. "Instead of calling them so they'd understand there wasn't a possibility for anything further with you, they piled up like trophies."

314

Chapter 38

Boxes

"*N*ever thought about it like that." He shrugged his shoulders.

"Oh, come on, Ryan," I complained. "You're intuitive with people. I wouldn't be with you if you were a typical jock."

"Those clothes mean nothing," he argued. "Jeanne takes care of it as part of her routine."

"And . . . you understand how bad that sounds?" I poked. "You had so many it was part of her routine?"

"I didn't mean—"

"So you say," I interrupted. "*Hey Jeanne, those clothes are stacking up. Time to get them out of here.*"

"She takes care of it," he repeated.

"Yuck. I wonder what she thinks as she gathers them. Crap, I wonder what she thinks about *you* collection them."

"She does her job," he said too casually for me to let it go.

"She does it to appease you and *keep her* job you mean. Internally, I'll bet she's disgusted that she has to take care of the remnants of your sex." I turned away.

"Maybe," he sighed. "If she's so disgusted with me, I wonder why she's been with me for three years."

"Heaven only knows." I clicked my tongue.

"I know you were *quite the angel* in school," he mocked. "You never did *anything* you knew you shouldn't have just to fit in?"

I hadn't done much, but I had smoked a couple of cigarettes, a few hits of marijuana and played hooky a few times, so I wouldn't be made fun of when all my friends did it.

"Your point?" I paused and then said pointedly, "I cleaned up my own messes."

"You don't think I did that?" His stare drilled into me.

"Yes," I stammered, regretting my sarcasm. "Except for some women's clothes."

"I needed to fit in," he sighed. "It was a way to feel normal. In the locker room—women, pussy, sex—those are the things men talk about. It's not only cool in my world; it's normal."

"What?" I challenged. "It's normal to make women objects?"

"You and your friends don't talk about sex?" He raised an eyebrow.

"Touché." I couldn't argue that defense.

"I don't mean to offend you. I'm only trying to help you understand by talking openly. I see you start to turn off and it makes me hesitate being honest about everything because of your severe reactions."

That's a bold statement. I have to give him props for that. Gutsy move, Mr. Tilton.

"Are there so many women, you can't even remember who the clothes belong to?" I asked timidly.

"It's not like that." He slipped his arm around my shoulder.

"What's it like?" I turned to face him once again.

"I didn't *see* women, or what they wore. I don't remember anything about them. I saw a body, a wink, and a smile—that's it. I never saw the whole person."

"You said to that boy in the theater, you're good with names."

"Yes, with people I want or care to remember." He closed his eyes and reopened them. "I didn't care about their personalities or who they were or what they did."

"And Jesse?"

"Jesse was comfortable because we had a history. She was a friend of sorts. I didn't have to *put on* with her—"

"Except when—"

He put his thumb on my lips.

"Except when we were in public. Yes, Nicky."

"How many phone numbers do you have for booty calls?"

"I never kept anyone's number," he answered quickly. "Am I making sense?"

"None of this makes sense," I shook my head. "If nothing about them stood out to you, what attracted you to them? You make it sound like they all were robots."

"Uh . . ." he hesitated.

"Never mind." I covered my eyes with one hand. "I hear what you're trying to tell me. Why didn't they have *your* number?"

"I never gave it to them."

"Why not?" I shoved my hands in the pockets of my sweatpants.

"I didn't want to hear from them again," he admitted.

"Once and done?" I eyed him cautiously. "How many times?"

"Don't ask me a question you really don't want answered."

"Too many to remember," I sighed. "That's what I thought."

"They knew what they had with me—I was an uninterested athlete looking for sex and an escort for the evening if I needed one. You know, Ms. Woman, you're making me out to be a sex starved jerk, but ninety-nine out of a hundred times I didn't have to try. Women came up to *me*. They're not bashful."

"No, I guess not."

"I'm just a fantasy for them," Ryan suggested. "There wasn't a real connection for either of us—the woman or me. And if they really wanted their clothes, they could have gone to the front desk or flagged me down at the ballpark. They never did."

"Because they thought you'd call them back," I pushed.

"No. It was mutual. Only sex."

"Did you find their panties tucked in your sheets?"

Oh, damn. Why did I ask that?

"No."

"Because your housekeeper did." My jaw stiffened. "I bet she has some stories."

"I don't know how to reassure you. I've tried to explain it the best way I know how," he said quietly. "It was the past and unimportant."

"You threw them away and boxed them up."

"Would you rather I say that I was hoping to reunite with them?" His voice carried notes of sadness. "You want to hear how I hoped two or three each day would call me and I could have my pick of them or enjoy all of them at once?"

"*Would* it be a lie?" I shot another bullet at him.

"Please don't do that to me." He closed his eyes.

"I'm sorry." *I know I have to stop throwing my arrows.*

"Don't continue to apologize if you don't mean it." His expression turned to a frown.

"I mean it," I held his wrist. "It's all the years of bad habits

318

from dealing with my family. All we do is attack each other through sarcasm. I'm trying to become more aware of it but it's a gut reaction. I'm sorry."

"You make what I did sound awful. It was only sex. It wasn't a sin and no one was hurt."

"You sure about that?" I asked. "You just said—"

"Yes, I'm sure. They may have *wanted* more, but they knew."

"Knew what?" I countered.

"I didn't want anything but sex," he repeated.

"How do you *know*?" I asked. "You weren't interested in talking, so what makes you so certain you were never with a woman who thought you wanted more? Tabitha came to the table and talked about a whole summer of hanging with you and your friends. That's more than casual, Ryan. And what about that one in ten who *you* approached?"

He didn't answer.

"I guess it's my problem," I continued.

"No, it's our problem. If you're not happy then obviously I'm not. I'm doing my best to make your comfortable."

"I'll think about what you said. Can you at least get rid of those clothes in your closet?"

"I've already called Jeanne. She's taking them to Goodwill."

"When did you call?"

"You were in the bathroom. When I get back, they'll be gone. I'm sorry I didn't think of it before now. I just don't relate to sex and women the way you do."

"Thanks." I gave his waist a squeeze to bring myself out of the negative frame of mind into which I'd drifted.

I want to wrap my arms around your world, but can I?

"How could I know that I'd find someone so sweet, who possesses an innocence I never knew was possible?"

"I don't think it's a good thing," I said shyly.

"Yes it is," he argued.

"Like I said, I know it's my problem," I repeated. "I'll work harder to understand you."

What I didn't have the heart to tell him was that no matter how I tried, I didn't think I'd ever be comfortable. Sex without love wasn't healthy to me. Everything about it was confusing. How could he be with women who had been part of his life and not feel *anything*?

As I looked into his eyes, I wondered if I saw a new fear creep inside of them. Was every fear I had, also buried inside of Ryan and even reflected from my own eyes?

Would it really be possible to trust each other?

Deep down, I knew we wouldn't make it because of my fears.

Deep down, I knew we wouldn't make it because of *his* fears.

Deep down, I knew we wouldn't make it because of the women who'd never stop coming.

Deep down, I knew I needed the life experiences he had or I'd never be able to handle dating him.

Deep down, I knew I couldn't open up enough to give him what he wanted.

I *wanted* to be ready for love.

I *wanted* to love him.

Instead, the closer we became, the more frightened I was.

"I appreciate your effort to understand," Ryan's voice rippled the quiet. "I want to understand you, too. It's not that easy, is it?"

"No," I agreed. "I know I'm not easy. That's why—"

"Yes, I know, Nicky. I'm better off with a woman my age, in the spotlight, and by God she needs to be a model and have lived a little. Can we give that one a rest?"

"Okay."

"My sweet woman." His sigh seemed to be one of exhaustion as he pulled me close. "I miss you so much already."

"Won't it be a relief to get away from me?" I laughed nervously.

"Honey, you know I'd stay up all night if you needed to keep talking with you," he kissed my forehead. "You'll stay with me this time, won't you? Emotionally, I mean? Promise me you'll return my call when I leave a message."

Before I could answer, he took possession of my lips. The elevator doors finally opened at the lobby level. He didn't stop. Several residents waited for us to finish so they could step in. He just smiled as he pulled away from me.

"You're a troublemaker," I played with him.

"Uh-huh. I hope to make *plenty* of trouble for you." His wicked tail whipped the air so quietly; I was the only one to feel its sting.

Chapter 39

"Ryan's" Game

*R*yan's Mustang waited at curbside.

We said hello to Lark, the morning valet, and then rode to my house in silence. A million thoughts rushed through my mind. Probably Ryan's as well.

Mom and Dad were sitting at the kitchen table when we walked in my house. It was early enough that my father hadn't started drinking yet—or if he had, the few "nips" he'd taken from his bottle hadn't been enough to heavily medicate him.

"Good morning, sir," Ryan shook my father's hand. "Mrs. Young. How are you?"

"Fine, Ryan, thanks. What's on tap today for you two?" Mom asked after she marked her book.

"I'm going to Ryan's game today." I was excited and could hardly contain myself. "I'm going upstairs to change real quick. We went dune buggy riding at Pismo Beach last night! It was so much fun but I'm all sandy. Have you guys ever been?"

"*Ryan's* game?" Dad ignored the story I was ready to share. Mom sat like a bystander, hitchhiking alongside some dysfunctional road. "I thought it was the *Goliaths'* game."

I looked at Ryan.

What did I tell you? I should've just come home in your shorts and T-shirt from last night. I would have gotten the same reaction.

"Ha-*ha*, Dad." I tried to joke away his remarks. "Be right back." I kissed Ryan's cheek. "Don't crucify him!" I shouted to both of my parents as I ran upstairs.

"Hey." I quietly opened Jenise's bedroom door. She was on her phone. From the conversation, I knew it was with Sean. "How did you do from the other night?"

"Good," she covered her phone. "Talk to you later."

I went into my room and changed into a clean pair of sweats, a fresh T-shirt, grabbed my backpack, our jackets, and headed downstairs. Per my usual practice, I stayed back to observe Ryan with my parents. They seemed to be at ease.

"I'm ready," I said after quietly observing all of them a few minutes. I gave each of my parents a hug, trying to ease their fears and taking care of them in ways I didn't understand—and in ways they didn't understand.

"Jerry called. Did you get back to him?" Dad made his comment purposefully to watch Ryan's reaction.

"Not yet." I turned to my boyfriend. He didn't flinch.

Just stop it, Dad. You have a moment of clarity because you haven't started drinking yet and you throw your sarcasm to a boy I'm trying to have a relationship with?

"You're doing something with Jerry tonight, then?" Mom asked, tightening the noose around my neck.

Neither of you have been present when I've had to make

difficult choices so why bother now? My friends were never good enough and now my boyfriend isn't either. Just leave me alone.

"I don't know if I'll do anything at all tonight, Mom. I'm pretty tired so . . . see you guys later."

God, I just said I was tired and here I am going to watch a baseball game. Do I make sense to anyone?

Ryan said goodbye to them and wrapped his comforting arm around my shoulder. He opened the car door for me—a courtesy I was still getting used to.

"More relaxed now?" he asked as we pulled away.

"Yeah. Thanks for driving me home. Do I look any different?" I joked about my change of clothes—a pair of sweats and a T-shirt.

"You're a riot," Ryan laughed. "You look great, as usual."

"That's my line to *you*," I giggled. "Thanks for saying that. So you caught all the sarcasm? That's the challenge I'm working to overcome. It's how we communicate. Believe me when I tell you I'm sorry. I do mean it and I'm not being flippant. Please be patient as I try and overcome this crap with my family."

"I will."

"I'm so frustrated my parents asked about Jerry in front of you. I'm sorry. They did that on purpose."

"Yeah," he nodded. "I know they did. Maybe it's the only way they can show their concern."

"It might seem like that," I looked out the window. "If you only knew."

"Tell me, then," he requested. "Make me understand."

"Before I started seeing you there was never a word of advice for me. And I mean about boys or anything else going on. As long as I didn't speak up, they assumed I was all right. If I *did* speak up, oh damn. The wicked sarcasm or rage I'd get . . . not right away. Only when Dad got drunk or Mom got mad.

They'd let their feelings simmer for days. It made the poison so much stronger.

"Every little detail they didn't like came flying out as horrible anger or cruel sarcasm. And let me tell you, the way sarcasm comes out in my family? It's not the funny kind. It's mean, mean, and mean. The only purpose is to cut you into pieces so you'll know your place is in the shadows. They don't want anything they do to be questioned. Well . . . you know what?"

"What, baby?" His hand massaged the nape of my neck.

"I'm done keeping my mouth shut. I wish Dad would keep his opinions to himself. Suddenly, he has something to say about a boy I'm dating? Does he really think that after all these years of being absent from my life he has any right? And even more ridiculous, he thinks I'd actually listen to him? Even though . . . " I trailed off. " . . . I do listen."

"Still," Ryan linked his fingers in mine. "I'd love to have my father around so I could argue with him." He squeezed my hand and then let go to tighten his grip on the steering wheel.

Idiot! You're complaining and he lost his father!

"Oh, God. I'm sorry." I rubbed his arm. "That was insensitive of me. I'm sorry I said that. Here's your jacket," I took it out from underneath mine.

"I thought you were leaving it by your front door for me," he winked and then flashed his little boy smile.

"Yeah. I said that but never did," I admitted. "When I thought it over I understood it was wrong."

"Nicky, there are only a few weeks left this summer before you start college."

"Yeah. I was looking forward to it and now all I want is for time to slow down."

"If you want to meet me on our road trip I'll take care of

everything—plane tickets, hotel room, food . . . bring Jenise if that makes you feel more comfortable. Time is running out and I'd love to show you and your sister around."

"I want to." I fiddled with the door lock.

"What?" he encouraged. "Tell me what's on your mind."

"We might alienate my parents," I answered cautiously. "I know it's weird to hear a woman say that. And I just talked about saying what I want, but . . . you know, maybe . . ."

"Keep going."

"No, I agreed I'd drop my someone more appropriate line. The thing is, even though I know you're better off, you know, I can't say it because we agreed, but, even though you would be, I don't want you have someone better. It's just, if we're going to work, I don't want my parents to root against us. I want them to love the man I . . . the man I have feelings for."

"You have *feelings* for me?" he asked with his shit-ass grin.

"Yes. Don't tease me. I'm trying."

"You're right. We want your parents in our corner. It's not a downer. You're very grounded like that."

"Grounded or not, you may not like me once you get to know me. You've got this vision in your head of who I am, but I don't know if I'll be a good girlfriend since I've never been one before. And being exclusive at my age is a lot to expect. I can close down and lock the door pretty quickly. I've been known to cut people off without giving them a fair chance because I'm afraid of being left alone. It's a contradiction. I get that it is. I do it before they can do it to me."

"I've already been cut off and came back for more," he reminded.

"I'm sorry for doing that and—geez. How many times have I apologized today?" I squeezed his thigh, feeling badly about how

I'd treated him. "It seems that's all we do is apologize to each other. I have some growing up to do when it comes to being with you—obviously. I'm working on it."

He pulled over.

Put the car in park.

Turned to face me.

"Nicky, you have a good heart and I do, too. I get your fears. Believe me, I do. Work on your apologies or don't, I'm afraid you're stuck with me."

"Well, that'll be a tough call of duty. How will I ever stand it?"

"That's your problem." A smile softened his statement. "I'm not going anywhere. I'll work hard to make you feel secure." He ran his hand down my arm. "I'm waiting for the day you rush into my arms and say out loud, unafraid, you love me."

"It's coming." I brushed his cheek with the back of my hand. "You make me feel so secure. In many ways it feels like we've been together for months and months."

"I hope you want me in your life in every way."

"I already want that, Ryan."

He brought my hand to his mouth and kissed it. As if having renewed enthusiasm, he pulled away from the curb and continued on to the ballpark.

"I reserved a seat for you near the dugout. It's on the right and at the railing. I know you don't like sitting there but I need to be near you today. Maybe Alex or Tara will be there."

I hope not. They have their suspicions, but I haven't told them I've fallen in love yet. I don't want them to see me.

We pulled into the players' lot. We got out of the car as Kevin passed us.

"Ooh, Nicky," Kevin scolded.

"What did I do now?" I was afraid to hear the answer.

"Did you come straight from Ryan's place?"

"Yes. Uh, no, no, we didn't. We came from my place, but . . ."

"Which is it, Nick?"

"It's not like that, Kevin." I caught on.

"No? What's it like? You happened to come to the ballpark together because you went home last night? Tell me, Nick."

"Dude," Ryan scolded. "Shut up."

Kevin walked away waving his finger back and forth at us like we'd been naughty.

Well, we were naughty, but he doesn't need to know. I wonder if Ryan would tell Kevin about our night? Do these guys gossip?

"I can't decide about him," I pondered out loud. "He was so nice the other night. Now I don't know. Just like Henry."

"Kevin's teasing." Ryan's response was firm and self-assured. "I'll talk to him inside. Here's your ticket. Would you like an escort, Ms. Young? I can walk you to your seat."

"Yuck. No," I shook my head. "I don't want to see a bunch of guys in the dugout doing their disgusting stuff. Hey, Ryan?"

He turned.

Waited for me to say what was on my mind.

"I care deeply for you." I stopped short of saying the words I knew he wanted to hear from me. "I'm asking you to have some patience. Can you?"

"I will." He paused and then added, "I do."

"I'm sure you'll get weary of all my insecurities, but I'm going to give things a go with just you. If you do get tired of battling, please be honest and tell me. Just . . ."

"What, Nicky?" A boyish smile teased me.

"Please don't sleep around on me," I begged. "If you want someone else I'll bow out immediately. Don't use me while you're seeing her, too. I'll understand if you don't want someone like me who wants a career and doesn't have the confidence of a more mature woman. It's . . . please don't put me in your clothes box. I don't want us to end up there."

He looked down to the ground and then in my eyes again.

"Believe me when I say I didn't think about those clothes and how you might interpret them," he pleaded his case. "I'm sorry to have been so callous. I didn't mean anything by it. I love that you're sensitive. Give me time to adjust." He closed the trunk of his car. "I've never been with anyone, man or woman, who analyzes and twists everything around and looks at it from so many angles. If I tell you something, believe me I'm not playing any games."

"I do."

"There is no way in hell you're in the clothes box or a sigh in an elevator. I know exactly what drew me to you. I remember every item of clothing you've worn, the way you walk, lift your chin, the way you style your hair . . . especially the look in your eyes. When it comes to being with you, I *see* you. I've *always* seen you. I notice and want you in every way. Remember, I fell in love with you while you were wearing your sweats, baby."

Holy God. He's like . . . ooh he's lovely.

"This is new for *both* of us." I tugged on his jacket, pretending to take it back. "Am I the most difficult person you know?"

"Just about," he tugged back. "You're hesitant and desperate to hold on to the things that make you feel safe—I get it. I've had more practice to get a hold of those things that haunt me. I know we're meant to be. Would you let me give you a big, luscious kiss in front of everyone? A kiss so hard and deep that makes my heart pound with the dreams I have for us?"

"I don't want to put the cheer team in danger." I placed my hand on his chest.

"Kiss me." He took me into his arms. "Throw it all up in the air and let's see where the pieces fall. Take a chance."

"It's not just me who would be penalized if the wrong person saw us. I could get my teammates in trouble and lose our letters of recommendation." I kept hugging him. "I will soon."

"Mm-hmm . . . soon." His voice drifted off.

Our hands held on as long as they could.

Reluctantly, painfully, the last of our fingertips let go.

I didn't turn around to watch him walk inside the clubhouse.

Instead, I walked out of the player's lot, dreading our goodbye.

Chapter 40

Split In Two

*T*oo early for the ballpark to open to the public and only a

little after ten, I decided to order an omelet from the Java House. I sat at the pier across from the bay gate and also caught up in my journal. I heard James yell my name. I knew that meant at least an hour had passed. I waved, packed my notebook away and went to talk with him.

"I thought this was a day off for you, young lady," James said, searching the bags of the first few fans waiting in line.

"Can't get enough of my favorite baseball team. Guess what?" I waved my ticket in the air. "I've got my own ticket."

"That's a switch. I'm so tired of hookin' you up," he teased. "Hey, what was up with your girl, Colleen, the other night? The way she grabbed the plaque—you should've had that. You the team's captain."

"I don't know what her issue was," I shrugged my shoulders.

"Maybe she needed an ego boost. Once in a while we all lose our confidence. At the time it bothered me. Now it's no big deal."

"Ready to come in? Or you spendin' time by the bay?" he nodded to the pier where I'd been sitting.

"I'll come in. Thanks Jimmy." I laughed at my nickname, thanked him, and walked inside. After grabbing a bottle of water, I settled in my seat and quickly began to write in my journal. Once again, I immersed myself into a world of description and metaphor while I tried to figure out my next move.

When I finally looked up the ballpark was crowded.

Both teams were off the field and in their respective clubhouses making final preparations for the game.

Two women sat to the left of me.

They were dressed to impress.

"How's it goin'?" One of the lovelies asked when I made eye contact with her. She had a big smile and even bigger breasts. The shirt she wore didn't hide that there wasn't any bra holding her blessings from spilling over.

Oh damn, these railings . . . and here I am sitting among women I've judged, in the life of one of the men I've categorized negatively for the way he handled his past. Maybe I have more in common with them than I'm willing to admit.

"I'm great. You?" I retorted.

"Peaches, sweetie." She tossed her hair. "Are you the daughter of somebody important?"

"Just a fan whose friend had an extra ticket." I smiled, thinking about my luscious man.

"Some *friend.*" It was as if her whole body shook in all the right places whenever she spoke. "You can't get tickets for these seats anywhere—they're expensive."

"Are you related to anyone on the team?" I closed my journal.

"I know several of the ballplayers," she replied with a wink.

"Who?" Immediately I was sorry I had asked.

Didn't you learn from the other night when you kept probing Dana for more?

I felt like closing my eyes and covering my ears so I didn't hear her. I *really* didn't want to know—but on the other hand, I *really* did.

"Well . . ." she paused.

When will I learn to shut-up?

"Austin, Henry, Willie—"

"Willie's her favorite," the other informed.

"He's sweeeeet," she giggled. "I've been with a few of them."

"*Been* with?" I asked.

"You know what I mean," she snorted. "You're not *that* young."

Please don't name Ryan.

"God, there's nothing like a jock to . . ." She laughed seductively and took out a compact to reapply her lipstick.

"So I've heard," I shrugged my shoulders.

Oh shit . . . please just stop talking now before I hear things.

"I can't seem to stay away. Their long legs, big bodies, experience . . . it's all so," she licked her lips. "You know what I mean. I'm addicted." Her hands were expressive.

"Okay." I looked away hoping she'd stop.

"Now, I see that look in your eye. You're thinking I'm a helpless groupie who can't control herself. Don't judge me 'til you try one."

"Believe me, I'm not judging you." It was easy to reflect on my own choices. I tried to tune her out. It didn't take long for me to fall into my habit of detaching so I could protect myself. I smiled at her moving lips, but didn't hear the words.

Lowering my gaze once more to the books that had been my

anchor growing up, I continued with my journal writing. I listened without wanting to and watched them wave to some of the ballplayers without wanting to see.

Several visits from the men I knew on the team—Matt, Darrell, and Kevin—brought unwanted attention my way. When Ryan came to the railing, I thought the women next to me might lose their cookies.

"Writing something hot for me?" He grabbed the railing with both of his big hands.

"It *is* hot! And accurate!" I was sure his blue eyes made me blush. "Look! I got my scorecard! I'm ready to mark down all the strikeouts you'll get in the ninth."

"My girlfriend keeping score. Cool."

"Thanks for asking me to come today, Ryan. I'm glad I said yes. I just love baseball."

"It's great knowing you're right here." The attraction buzzed between us. "I love that you're just a touch away. All I have to do is look back to see your green eyes and lovely smile . . . it's beyond what I can express right now."

"You're out of words?" I mocked.

"You do that to me." His voice was flavored with a soft rasp. "You know what?"

"What?" I smiled that he'd picked up one of my phrases.

"When I'm away," he leaned close, "I'll think about you and the way you taste every day." He put his finger in his mouth, mimicking our sweet night together.

"Oh . . . damn." I was sure my entire body heated.

What am I supposed to say?

He laughed and then went back into the dugout, leaving my body twisting in delicious turmoil.

"OMG, do you know the whole team?" One of the women

asked that sat next to me.

"I cheer with my friends here on Fridays and Saturdays."

"Oh, *that's* what it is." She looked at her friends and they nodded their heads. "We wondered. You're cute, but you don't exactly . . ." she trailed off.

"What about Ryan Tilton?" The second woman scooted forward. "He's single and we haven't seen him with a regular girl. You obviously have an in with him. Can you hook up a sistah?"

"Coincidentally . . ." I fumbled, afraid of the gorgeous, mature women around me; the same ones I knew should be with Ryan. ". . . He's—" *Force the words. Women need to be told directly. Don't let them wonder—you just told Ryan the same thing—so say it.* "He's my boyfriend."

"Sure he is." The woman and her friends went into mock hysterics.

"In your dreams," another woman added. "You and your sweatshirt and sneakers. You're a good bull shitter, though. Who knows? In a few years you might have access to a nice buffet."

My Evil Twin poked at me, relentlessly insisting that I speak up.

Don't go down that easy. Show them a woman in sweats can have a boyfriend like Ryan.

I battled my feelings. On the one hand I didn't want to prove anything. Nor did I want to use Ryan to validate my fragile ego. On the other, I'd hid all my life in shadows, allowing the unfair acts and statements from others to pass by without a challenge.

That had to stop.

Now.

When the game was about to begin Ryan looked around to check on me. I motioned at him to come over.

"Would you do me a favor and tell these ladies to my left who I am to you? They want an introduction and a hookup. They don't believe I'm your girlfriend."

I saw his surprise and then his smile bloomed.

"This is my woman," he answered without taking his eyes off of me. "Speaking strictly for myself, if you're trying to connect with one of us, count me out."

They whispered. Perhaps embarrassed, they walked up the stairs. Or maybe it was only to rethink their strategy.

"Thank you." I put my hand on his. "They didn't believe me. I had to prove to them—I don't know, maybe to myself—sometimes their judgments can be wrong, that's all."

"Why?" He looked up through his eyelashes.

"I wanted them to know you're mine," I said bashfully.

"You're welcome." Satisfaction seemed to cover his face. "Whenever you want to use me, ask." He walked back to the dugout and stood against the railing in the line of manly men.

I wondered if I'd just used Ryan the same way I'd used Jerry? I had used each person for my own purpose—an end to a means. Had I used James? What about Ethan?

Are you really *using anyone? Aren't you finally asking for what you need?*

"I've been watching your team for over a year now." Cathy, one of the usherettes standing nearby, introduced herself. "The fans really enjoy it. You're all very good."

"Thank you, Cathy. It was such a whim. But you know? There was a part of me that planned it for years. I'm so glad the Goliaths accepted my proposal. Stunned, really."

"I think Mr. Tilton is, too," she grinned.

"Oh, um . . . what do you—"

"I heard what he said to you," she whispered. "I think you're more than friends."

I could feel a rush of emotion.

My body was barely able to contain it.

"Your eyes just lit up. You're sweet for each other!"

Her positive remark made me feel good. There was no sex talk, nothing about *going for it,* or how hot he was. It was a simple statement about how she'd noticed the way Ryan and I had interacted with each other. I closed my journal after writing down the things she'd said and started watching the game.

As usual, when I didn't want something to end, it flew by.

The ninth inning was upon me.

Ryan came in to pitch.

By the time he was done, he'd chalked up another save and the Goliaths won the game. The boys of baseball congratulated each other with their high-fives, fist pumps and butt bumping routine.

I hung on to the last sounds and smells of the stadium, hoping that if I lingered, Ryan wouldn't leave. I pretended this was just another game. Afterward we would go out together.

But that wasn't going to happen.

Most of the fans in my section had vacated their seats. Ryan stepped out and up to the railing. He was already in street clothes.

I was emotional at the thought of him leaving for ten days.

My eyes welled up immediately.

"Oh, Nicky." He laced my fingers with his. "Won't you come on this trip with me? Just for a few games? We're going to Milwaukee, Atlanta, and Denver." His eyes begged me to give in. "Hey, if you want to come to Denver, we can visit the farm where I took that photo you like so much of the little boy and his rabbits. Wouldn't that be fun?"

"I do love that photo." He let me bring our hands to my chest. "Of course I'm fond of the photographer who took it, too." I sniffled. "I'm dying to give you a big smooch goodbye."

"Me, too. I'd better go." He let go of me. "We're taking off for the airport as soon as everyone is ready and I don't want them waiting on me. I'll, uh . . ." He put his head down.

"Miss me?" I finished his thought.

"You know I will." His smile was wide and beautiful and his eyes seemed full of dreams.

"I'll miss you, too." My voice trailed off. I had to look away. Tears spilled down my cheeks. "Don't forget to text or call me."

"I'm crossing my fingers, hoping to see you and your sister in a few days. I'd love to kiss you on the lips right now." He gave me a kiss on the cheek. "Bye, sweet Nicky."

"Bye, my Ryan," I watched him disappear into the dugout and then got up to leave. Several fans that were season ticket holders wanted to talk about the cheer team. I couldn't say no. It was my obligation and I was happy to do it.

As I was talking, something began to gnaw in my gut.

I had to leave the ballpark.

I made my move.

"I'm rooting for you two." Cathy stood next to me and put her hand on my shoulder.

"Thank you."

Something had turned.

For the first time in my life I seemed to breath.

My beating heart sped up.

My body shifted into drive.

"I'm rooting for us, too," I admitted out loud.

An overwhelming feeling collared me. It seemed to pull me out of the stadium.

"Get out now." A whisper softly blew in my ear. Perhaps it was my Evil Twin, or perhaps it was intuition. I knew I had to follow it.

My insides raced.

My mind whirred and circled.

My chest tightened.

I had to hurry.

I had to get out.

Ryan.

I threw my backpack over my shoulder. Ran halfway up the stairs, stopping only to grab my beeping cell phone.

A text from Jerry: *I'm back. At M gate. Where are you?*

Oh, crap, no!

My entire body thudded.

My heart, my mind, my whole body gave in to the desperate moment—I had to get to the man who had brought me to life. I quickly decided to ignore my childhood friend but then, knew I had to answer. He might walk around the entire stadium, only to find me in Ryan's arms.

"Hey gorgeous!" Jerry's voice danced with excitement. "I'm back early! I called your house and your mom said you were at the ballpark. I couldn't wait to surprise you. Where are you?"

Mom! How could you tell him? I have to tell Ryan I want to come on his road trip! He needs to know I love him!

"I'm, uh—" I stumbled, wanting only to rush in the player's lot and shout my love to the man who held me in his soul.

"I'll meet you," he pushed. "Tell me where."

No! I need to hug my love goodbye!

"I haven't left the ballpark; I'm taking care of some stuff in management's offices and I'll be a while yet."

"Should I come to the Bay Gate and wait?" His voice was heightened. He was obviously excited.

"No!" I shouted my response. "I'll meet you at the gift shop."

"Everything okay?"

"I'll be there shortly." I hung up before he could ask another question. Now, all I could think about was getting to Ryan.

Emotions that would no longer be silenced flooded through me.

The joy of love rose up from deep in my heart demanding release. I finally admitted *I want a relationship!*

I felt open and exposed in a way I had never imagined possible. I was ready to allow myself a chance to enjoy the raw beauty I knew I could have, surrendering to the feelings that burned inside me. Hundreds of love letters circled in my head and around my heart.

The euphoria I felt for my new boyfriend pulsed in every vein.

Filled every thought.

Every wish.

Just as suddenly as the bliss filled me, panic took its place.

He's leaving! No more kisses, bright, blue eyes, or wry smiles.

Once again, my Evil Twin tugged at my body.

Go and claim your man! Plant your feet and grab this moment! Refuse to live the same life your father chose and your mother accepted.

Could I actually embrace him in front of his teammates, the public, and his fans? Would I run again, afraid of another situation that was too complex to handle, overanalyze and let fear fill me?

If our new relationship was going to work, I knew I had to believe and trust Ryan wholeheartedly. I needed to give in to him as he had given in to me.

The refrain that had begun so quietly several weeks earlier now rang out: *"Trust this, trust him, trust yourself."*

I had to get to Ryan to embrace him. Kiss him. Hug him. Yes, I had to tell him, out loud and without fear—*I LOVE YOU!*

My walk increased in speed.

Turned into a run.

As I came to the players' lot, I saw the team's equipment, luggage, garment bags, and other belongings being loaded on to the bus. Most of the staff, players, and coaches were already inside. Busy hands checked lists on clipboards and called out various orders to assistants.

Every sound at the stadium called, *Ryan.*

Every person that walked by whispered: *Ryan.*

The parking lot echoed: "*Ryan is leaving! Go to him!*"

When I was almost to the gate, I turned to see Ryan waving.

There's still time!

His expression was filled with joy, waiting to see what I was going to do.

Fumbling for my gate pass, I walked toward the security guard, ready to present it, ready to reveal everything to him . . . my love.

Then—I stopped as if I'd run into a wall.

A large hole in the ground had just opened.

I was close to falling inside of it.

Jerry.

Running.

Toward me.

Sure and certain I was coming for *him.*

He looked happy and ready to share all the things we talked about before he had left to play summer baseball. As far as he was concerned, our future lay ahead of us, ready to be explored.

A rip tore right down the middle of my mind and continued through my entire body, making me two women.

One was about to meet a young man, a lifelong friend; his goals matched my own. We stood ready to share new experiences in life and sex—together. We were entering college— together. With Jerry, I was safe. I'd have control of our relationship. We shared a past and had a solid foundation. We knew about our darkness and loved each other in spite of it. I

343

could reveal myself to him and he wouldn't leave or judge me.

Wouldn't we be perfect for each other?

Wasn't that what I craved?

After years of the drama and anger that filled my household I'd only wanted evenness. Leveled consistency. Jerry was part of that.

The other woman had fallen in love with a successful, soon to be twenty-six-year-old man—a professional baseball player. He'd already gone to college and accomplished many of his goals.

Ryan had achieved social standing. Was experienced with sex. Seemed ready for a commitment. He stood ready to embrace all the things that would make his life more complete.

I'd claimed him as my boyfriend.

Would I be the only one experiencing new things in our relationship? Wouldn't being with him mean sacrifice and giving up part of what I wanted from my college experience?

He would discover my darkness.

Wouldn't he run like hell?

We were unknown and mysterious to each other.

Beautiful.

Intriguing.

Frightening.

Magnificent.

I felt a completely different life was possible with Ryan.

But was it? *Really?*

Was I only kidding myself?

Could I escape the prison in which generations of my family had been held captive?

My mind spun so fast, I could barely move.

Jerry closed in.

Ryan waved.

Jerry yelled. His arms opened for the hug he expected. There was so much hope in his eyes. The world awaited us.

It was in that moment an answer unexpectedly flashed.

Finally, it all made sense.

What had I been thinking?

It was simple.

I knew what I had to do.

The gates were opening.

Finally, I would be free from my shadows.

My heart beat hard as if one thousand drums pounded inside my chest.

I walked fast.

Jogged.

Broke into a run.

Moved through the crowd, dodging and avoiding children, parents, friends, desperate to get to him.

The grin on Jerry's face was incredibly welcoming.

Who I wanted was so clear. The one I'd always wanted.

He was the one who could open everything and help me see a life I hadn't envisioned before him. He would meet my needs and help me feel secure.

He truly understood who I really was.

He is the one . . . the one . . . the one.

To be continued...

Would you take a moment to leave a review to allow others the insight of your opinion and they may find my book? I'd REALLY, REALLY appreciate it:

Amazon: bit.ly/JaggedHeart

Goodreads: bit.ly/GoodreadsJaggedHeart

Next, the final book in Part I of Broken Bottles:

AMAZING HEART

Special Offer for Readers of Jagged Heart:

For live chats, advance chapters, exclusive announcements, pre-publication dates of future books, and free giveaways, visit:

Website: www.PamelaTaeuffer.com

Newsletter: www.PamelaTaeuffer.com/newsletter

Blog: www.pamelataeuffer.com/dare-to-be-vulnerable

E-mail: PamelaTaeuffer@gmail.com

Facebook: www.facebook.com/BrokenBottlesSeries

Twitter: @PamelaTaeuffer

Pinterest: www.pinterest.com/ptaeuffer/broken-bottles

Resources

Books

Dirty Words, Ellen Sussman
How to Please a Woman In & Out of Bed, Daylee Deanna Schwartz
It Will Never Happen to Me, Claudia Black, PhD
Sexy Words for Writers, Stefanie Olsen
The Emotion Thesaurus, Angela Ackerman and Becca Puglisi
Thinking Like A Romance Writer, Dahlia Evans
The Bald-Headed Hermit & The Artichoke, A.D. Peterkin
The Complete Idiot's Guide to Amazing Sex, Sari Lockner, Ph.D.
The Romance Writer's Phrase Book, Jean Kent and Candace Shelton

Organizations/Web sites

www.AdultChildren.org: Adult Children of Alcoholics
www.al-anon.org: Strength for Friends & Families of Problem Drinkers
ncadd.org: Helping Family Members of Friends
www.thecounselingcenter.org: Ten Ways Families Can Help
www.adultchildren.org: Alcohol & Drug Abuse Affects Everyone in the Family
www.AdultChildrenofDysfunctionalFamilies.com
www.sexualityresources.com Information on rape
www.crimescene.com What to expect reporting rape
www.pandys.org: Pandora's Project
The Joyful Heart Foundation provides information of all sorts, writers, actors, programs, news releases . . . on sexual assault and domestic violence: www.joyfulheartfoundation.org

Acknowledgements

*A*s with any life project, there are many people who influenced my journey. From friends who exist only in my memories, to people who have crossed my path in sweet or dramatic ways, I hold all of you to my heart, even if you're not mentioned below.

For my beautiful sister, whose life ended much too early—I understand you more now than I ever did.

For my father, I wish I had the maturity back then to have understood. I couldn't have stopped you, but I would've spoken differently. You gave me so many twisted gifts, and I thank you in spite of everything.

Claude, my husband, and Aaron, my son, I love you guys so much that sometimes I think I'm sick because the hurt is so deep and the joy is so mountainous.

Louise—I couldn't have done this without you.

My sweet girlfriends from childhood—Colleen, Patty, Lorraine, Kathie, Marilyn

TS Babes—(Santo, Spanky, Uno, GG, Wiseone, BL, Nine, Catnip xxoo) you know who you are, thanks for so much fun during my research.

My editors, Catharine Bramkamp, Robbi Sommers Bryant, and Crissi Langwell, you are awesome and have gone above and beyond!

Mom, you still have problems saying I love you. I get it now.

About the Author

PAMELA TAEUFFER, BIOGRAPHY

My passion is writing books that tell a story and family saga of leaving old fears behind through a love story. My first series, Broken Bottles, details those fears of growing up in a family battling alcoholism. Along with the struggle and pain of a parent's rage, I hope to reveal strength, intelligence, and survival. The challenge is to love intimately in all relationships. For children of trauma, it can take years to let another person come close. When they do? It's like rainbows cover their heart.

You'll read how my characters slowly become vulnerable, reach for the intimacy that has eluded them all of their life, and how they let go of their fears. They struggle and risk everything to trust others—and themselves. My stories are about daring to take the baby steps that let them really come alive and in every way, experience and give love.

MAKING MONEY TO CREATE: The property management and vacation rental company I run with my husband and son in Sonoma County, California allows me to have my creative life. I love where I live and work, and wouldn't trade being born and raised in San Francisco. My father introduced me to baseball when I was six. I've rung a cable car bell, driven a streetcar and saw the old rock legends like Jimmy Hendrix, The Doors, and Jefferson Airplane.

WHAT I'VE DONE/AM DOING – IT'S A JOURNEY OF DREAMS: Broken Bottles is a four part series. Three books, *Shadow Heart*, *Fire Heart,* and *Jagged Heart* are ready. Soon to follow is *Amazing Heart.* I'm honored to have three poems in an anthology called *The Beats Go On,* a story in *Sisters Born, Sisters Found,* and a story in the anthology, *Untold Stories.* I have released the first book in a series for introverts called, *The Introverts Guide to the Galaxy: Attending Conferences.*

My dream? To create beautifully decorate and custom journals with gorgeous paper that accompany with each book series: *The Introvert's Journal, A Family Saga Journal, My Body's Journal,* and *Trauma: You Can't Stop Me Journal.* Journaling was a lifesaver for me. I was in shock. You may be in shock. Don't let that keep your heart frozen!

Also Available by
Pamela Taeuffer

Shadow Heart

What if you were afraid to even turn the doorknob to your front door because of the family dysfunction that waited inside: rage, mental and physical abuse, the fear of sharing love, or waiting for the embrace of your mother. What would it take to bring you out of the shadows, breaking out of the numbness you've used to protect your heart? Could you take a risk that might change everything? A sexy, professional baseball player wants my mind, body and heart. All my life I've controlled who's gotten close. Risk means terror. This is the slow, intimate reveal of how I learned to trust myself, let go of my fears and transitioned into joy.

Fire Heart

My heart is on fire. For the first time in my life I am awake and the desires I've pushed down are smoldering. The shadows of my youth dare me to step away from them. I've just come of age and there is one thing I know—I want to live differently

357

than my parents—an alcoholic father and co-dependent mother. I know I need to forgive them. I must learn to trust myself and take a risk. That means being vulnerable and letting another close. But when we did that in our house, rage and abandonment followed. I have to open my heart and learn to trust myself so I can trust another. I dream of letting go of old fears, daring to be loved, and transitioning into joy.

Amazing Heart

It's amazing, but I am filled with the desire to open my heart and love another, a new person, out of the comfort zone of my childhood, not a relative, not family and breaking through every chain of dysfunction I'd bound myself with. Amazing is how I feel, that I seem to have the love of someone who will accept me for who I am, a bundle of insecurities and fears, wrapped inside my body of round curves that I tend to cover in jeans and sweatshirts. Having someone who seems to want me in spite of all my demons—it feels as if I'm set free! I walk with a light around me: bright, open, shutting out the darkness of my youth—the alcoholism of my father, his rage, his violence, my mom's codependence and support of his addiction—I know I can risk everything now. The freedom to ask for what I want; dare I dream of feeling safe enough, trusting myself enough to share my thoughts, wishes, fears . . . dare I actually hope in another person? Won't his promises fall apart? Am I really free? Can I dare to really, really be alive and through being vulnerable, open to deep, sensual intimacy?